Murder Among the Dead

A Redmond and Haze Mystery

Book 12

By Irina Shapiro

Copyright

Table of Contents

Prologue

The silence was almost eerie, even the birds preferring to keep away from the neglected graveyard. Both ancient and more recent tombstones lined the narrow paths, some inscriptions still sharp, others nearly obliterated by time. The sky had darkened, and rain seemed imminent, but the crisp air held the promise of a bracing walk.

Reverend Brompton ambled along the overgrown path, enjoying the solitude that so often eluded him in his line of work. The burial ground was no longer in use, so there was little chance of being disturbed, although the occasional trespasser did cross his path. Some people were as drawn to graveyards as others were to public houses or dens of ill repute. They found some strange sensual pleasure in being surrounded by the dead, and some actually believed that the veil between the worlds could be drawn aside long enough to speak to the departed. The reverend thought this was utter poppycock and would say as much to anyone who asked, but thankfully, none of his parishioners were foolish enough to seek such heathen pursuits.

The reverend's footsteps inevitably turned toward Ezekiel. It was distinctly unministerial to name a headstone, but the Reverend Brompton thought the marble angel truly beautiful and the meaning of the name, "God is Strong," undeniably appropriate to its purpose. As he drew closer, he saw her. She rested on the marble slab at Ezekiel's feet, her skirts spread out around her, her fair hair framing her pale face, and her hands folded on her breast as if she were praying. The woman's gaze was turned up to the sky, but Ezekiel's shadow fell upon her face, making her features difficult to make out.

Outraged by such blatant disrespect for the dead, the Reverend Brompton hastened toward the woman, about to chastise her in the strongest of terms for her transgression when he realized that she hadn't moved the entire time he'd had her in his sights. His footsteps slowing of their own accord, the reverend drew in a shaky breath as he realized the beautiful young woman gazing up at Ezekiel with such adoration was actually quite dead.

Chapter 1

Saturday, March 6, 1869

The rain was relentless, an icy deluge that pounded the gravestones and soaked into the thirsty earth. Only the funeral of a loved one would bring anyone to a burial ground on a day like today, but there was no funeral, only death. Lord Jason Redmond stood very still, his gaze fixed on the young woman laid out on a marble slab. Her hands were folded on her chest as if in prayer, her eyes open, the unseeing gaze fixed on the human-sized angel that loomed above her, its wings folded, its head bowed. Rainwater ran down the angel's marble cheeks and dripped onto the woman's face, as if the angel were weeping at the senseless loss. No wound was visible, and the water that sluiced off the slab and into the ground at Jason's feet bore no traces of blood, but there was no doubt that the young woman had been murdered.

As a surgeon and a veteran of the American Civil War, Jason had seen death in all its forms, but it still held the power to shock him, especially when the victim was someone he had known. Rebecca Grainger had been Jason's goddaughter's nursemaid and the woman Inspector Daniel Haze had believed might snatch him from the bottomless chasm of melancholy his wife's sudden death had plunged him into nearly a year ago.

Only a short while ago, Daniel and Rebecca had taken the first tentative steps toward becoming a family, but things had changed after Daniel was brutally attacked while investigating a murder. His fragile relationship with Rebecca had fractured, the lady turning cold once she understood the danger and uncertainty of being a policeman's wife. After weeks of nursing Daniel through his recovery, Rebecca gave her notice. A few more days and she would have married another man and set off on a voyage to her husband's ranch in Argentina. Instead of preparing for her upcoming wedding, she lay dead on the cold stone, the only witness to her death the indifferent angel that would keep its secrets long after they were all dead and gone.

Jason tore his gaze from Rebecca's sightless stare to check on the rain-drenched constables who were combing the graveyard for Charlotte. Inspector Haze's small daughter had been with her nursemaid at the time of the attack, presumably on their way home. The policemen had expected to find Charlotte right away, hiding behind one of the ancient stones, frightened, confused, and chilled to the bone in her sodden coat and hat, but with every passing minute, the possibility of finding the child became more remote. Charlotte was nowhere to be found.

The constables periodically called out her name, urging her to show herself, but if Charlotte was within hearing distance, she would have made her presence known—especially since her father had yelled himself hoarse searching the graveyard for her. He now stood stock-still beneath an ancient yew, his eyes wide with terror behind his fogged spectacles as he grappled with the tragedy that had struck so unexpectedly on a peaceful afternoon.

Leaving Rebecca's remains to the police photographer, who had just set up his tripod and was complaining bitterly about the rain, Jason strode over to join Daniel beneath the yew. Daniel barely seemed to register Jason's presence. His shoulders were hunched, his hands balled into fists, and his head tucked into his muffler. The tweed of his coat was drenched, and rainwater dripped from the brim of his bowler hat, but Daniel didn't seem to notice, his gaze fixed on the tall helmets of the constables as they moved between the weathered headstones.

"Daniel," Jason began, but Daniel shook his head, as if to dispel his stupor.

"She's not here, Jason," he said quietly. "She's not here. What if she's dead?" Daniel's voice broke on the final word, and he finally turned to Jason, his face bone white.

"No, Daniel," Jason retorted vehemently. "If Charlotte were dead, she'd be here. Whoever has done this would have no reason to take her away." Jason couldn't bring himself to refer to Charlotte as a body and resolutely spoke of her in the present tense, even though he couldn't be sure of anything. "Charlotte was either taken or she's hiding."

"She's not hiding," Daniel replied woodenly. "If she were, we would have located her by now."

"Daniel, you must pull yourself together," Jason said, his tone brooking no argument. "If you are not up to the task of investigating what happened, then Superintendent Ransome will assign another detective to the case, and then you will have no say in the investigation. You must put your personal feelings aside if you hope to find Charlotte."

"I don't know that I can, Jason," Daniel replied, his voice barely above a whisper. "I've been standing here for a quarter of an hour, and I can't seem to find the strength to move or the presence of mind to formulate a plan. My thoughts are fragmented, and my heart is shattered."

Daniel's gaze slid toward the body of Rebecca Grainger, his eyes misting with tears of shock and grief. Mr. Gillespie had finished and was packing away his tripod and camera, and two constables stood at the ready, a canvas stretcher held between them. They would transport Rebecca's remains to the waiting police wagon and convey them to the mortuary at Scotland Yard.

"Buck up, cowboy," Jason said, knowing the odd expression would force Daniel to focus on him. Daniel found most of Jason's American sayings baffling, but this one was sure to top the list.

"What?" Daniel echoed, staring at Jason in obvious incomprehension.

"It's a call to rally," Jason explained. "We must interview the vicar who found the body right away, while the details are still fresh in his mind. Then I will perform the autopsy. We need to establish the cause of death."

"Jason, I don't think I can formulate a coherent question, much less hunt for clues or draw possible connections. I am numb with shock."

Jason nodded. "Leave it to me. Come, Daniel. Let's get you inside. You're soaked through."

"Really? I haven't noticed," Daniel said as he reluctantly left his spot under the tree and followed Jason toward the porch of St. John's Wood Church.

Chapter 2

Jason was glad to get out of the rain, but the interior of the church, although dry, was no warmer than the outside, nor was it brighter. No candles were lit so early in the day, and the light that filtered through the high windows did little to dispel the gloom that nearly swallowed the nave. Their footsteps echoed on the flagstone floor as they strode toward the hunched, black-clad figure in a front pew.

The Reverend Brompton was a thickset man of about sixty-five with a ruddy complexion and thinning white hair. His dark eyes peered out from pockets of wrinkled flesh, and his jowls rested on his stiff clerical collar. He turned toward Jason and Daniel as they approached, his expression transforming to one of hope.

"Did you find the child?" he asked.

Jason shook his head. "Not yet. May we ask you a few questions, Reverend?"

"Of course. Anything I can do to help."

Daniel sank into the pew across from the vicar and bowed his head. Jason thought he might be praying for Charlotte's safe return and had no wish to disturb him, so he sat down next to the reverend to ensure he didn't tower over the man as he addressed him.

"Please, tell me precisely what happened this afternoon," Jason invited.

"I stepped out at eleven. I like to take a walk before luncheon, you see, just to clear my head and cast my thoughts over the week's sermon. I always keep to the same schedule. I'm a creature of habit," the vicar said. "I take my midday meal precisely at twelve at the chophouse in Wellington Road. They do an excellent oyster stew. And the roast beef is always most tender," he blathered on. "It wasn't raining when I set off, but the sky had already turned dark. I didn't think I'd be able to stay out there for long and hoped I'd get at least a half hour in."

"The body," Jason prompted.

"Ah, yes. Do forgive me. Finding that young woman was something of a shock. I see the dearly departed all the time in my line of work, but I hadn't expected to find her there. She looked so peaceful, as if she were praying. At first, I thought it was a prank, you see," he said, looking to Jason for understanding. "Some strange new ritual perhaps to commune with the dead. There are all these spiritualists about these days, aren't there? They have no respect for the Lord or the teachings of the Bible and seem to think it's perfectly acceptable to try to summon the dead. It's disgraceful," the Reverend Brompton said more forcefully. "I do not condone these practices and say so from the pulpit."

"The young woman," Jason prompted again.

"Ah, yes. I'm sorry. I digress," the reverend said contritely. "I walked toward her, in something of a huff, I might add. I was going to tell her that the burial ground was closed, and she was trespassing. Besides, she'd catch her death lying there, on that cold marble slab." The vicar seemed to realize the absurdity of what he was saying and hurried to finish. "It was then that I realized she wasn't moving."

"Did you see anyone when you stepped outside?"

The vicar shook his head. "I'm afraid I didn't."

"And you saw no sign of the child?" Jason pressed.

"I'm afraid not. When I realized the young woman was dead, I immediately went to summon a constable. It took some considerable time to locate one."

"What did you do then, Reverend?"

"I came back here to wait for reinforcements. I gave my account to Constable Napier of Scotland Yard when he arrived. It was the constable who told me about the missing child."

"Had you ever seen the victim before?"

The reverend considered the question. "She wasn't a member of my congregation, but I have seen her in the street. I believe she lived nearby."

"Yes, she did," Jason confirmed.

The vicar looked at Jason, his gaze pleading. "May I go now? I'm rather hungry, you see. I don't normally take a large breakfast as it gives me terrible indigestion, and it's well past one o'clock."

"Yes, of course," Jason replied as courteously as he could. "Thank you for your assistance, Reverend."

"Damn fool," Daniel hissed as they left the church. "All he cares about is his bloated belly. I reckon he can afford to miss a meal or two."

Jason didn't think a reply was warranted. His mind was on Rebecca Grainger and the final moments of her life. He had yet to perform an autopsy, but there were certain things he had been able to ascertain just by looking at Rebecca's remains. She had not been shot or stabbed, and her clothes didn't appear to have been disturbed, but he had noticed that the skin of her throat, which was partially hidden by the high collar of her gown, was reddened, and the white of the left eye was tinged red as a result of a broken blood vessel. Jason had not looked inside Rebecca's mouth, but her lips had been slightly parted, the tongue visible and unnaturally swollen. All initial signs pointed to strangulation, which would mean that Rebecca had faced her killer and had known she was about to die.

She must have been terrified and had perhaps begged for her life and that of Charlotte. Had she warned Charlotte to run and hide, or had the child listened to her instincts and tried to get away? Had she succeeded and was even now hiding somewhere, waiting until she felt it was safe to come out? Or was there a darker explanation for her continued absence? Normally, Jason would share his thoughts with Daniel, eager to test his theory, but given Daniel's relationship to the victim, it was wiser to keep his counsel for the time being. There was one logical step, however, that Jason could propose that would help divert Daniel's attention from his fears and allow him to focus on finding Charlotte, as well as Rebecca's killer.

"We should speak to Rebecca's fiancé," Jason said. "Will you question him on your own, or would you prefer that I accompany you after I complete the postmortem?"

Daniel stared at Jason for a moment, as if he didn't quite comprehend what Jason was asking of him, but then his gaze sharpened, and an expression of determination replaced one of helplessness. "By the time you've completed the postmortem, the scoundrel might have fled."

"I agree it would be unwise to wait," Jason said, pleased by the reaction his suggestion had elicited. "Do you think Mr. Stanley could be responsible?"

"I don't know," Daniel replied tersely. "I've never met the man."

"Now would be a good time to make his acquaintance," Jason said, wondering if Daniel was in the right frame of mind to question a suspect and if perhaps it would be prudent to send someone else. "Perhaps you should ask Sergeant Meadows to accompany you. He's still in the burial ground."

If Daniel had realized that Jason had assumed unauthorized command, he didn't bother to comment. He seemed grateful to have been given an important task. "Yes. I will," he said with a nod. "I can use the support, to be honest."

"Sergeant Meadows is a competent policeman," Jason said.

"He is," Daniel agreed. "I'll see you back at the Yard."

14

"We will find her, Daniel," Jason said softly, reaching out to touch Daniel's arm in a gesture of support. "We will get Charlotte back."

"You don't know that, Jason," Daniel replied, and his eyes misted with tears. "It may already be too late."

"No. I refuse to believe that," Jason said stubbornly. "Until we know for certain, we keep looking."

"Thank you. If not for you—"

Daniel didn't bother to finish the sentence before turning on his heel and heading down the path, Jason following closely behind. The rain had stopped, but the sky was still a menacing gray, the clouds low and dense. Having summoned Sergeant Meadows, Daniel walked off without a word of farewell, leaving Jason to return to the carriage that would take him to Scotland Yard. Jason dreaded the task ahead, but he owed it to Daniel to be the one to perform the postmortem and treat Rebecca's remains with the respect they deserved before she was laid to rest.

Chapter 3

Daniel huddled deeper into his damp coat and strode purposefully away from the church, Sergeant Meadows at his heels. The police wagon had already departed, removing the mortal remains of the woman Daniel had cared deeply about, possibly even loved, and leaving behind two constables to continue the search for Charlotte. Daniel's chest was constricted with agitation, the pressure like iron bands encircling his ribcage. His breath came in short gasps, and his stomach threatened to turn itself inside out, but he refused to give in to physical discomfort. His every thought was for the wellbeing of his little girl, and although he wished he could remain and join in the search, as an experienced detective, he realized that his purpose would be best served elsewhere.

Daniel spotted an empty hansom heading toward the cab stand on Wellington Road and hailed the driver. As soon as Sergeant Meadows settled in beside him, Daniel called out, "Charing Cross Hotel. And be quick about it. We're about police business."

"As ye say, guv," the driver replied in a gruff tone, seeming utterly unimpressed with Daniel's declaration.

The length of the journey depended on the volume of Saturday afternoon traffic rather than the driver's personal commitment to complying with the request. If a delivery wagon or an omnibus happened to obstruct his path, there wasn't much he could do about it, and all three of them knew it. Daniel sighed irritably and settled back against the cracked leather seat, staring balefully at the street beyond the cab.

The traffic became heavier as they neared Charing Cross. Hackneys, sleek private carriages, and delivery wagons jostled for space, and the level of noise seemed to escalate with every passing minute, the vendors and newsboys screaming themselves hoarse as they hawked their wares to the travelers streaming in and out of the station. Daniel tried to block out the cacophony and focus on the questions he intended to ask, but all he could see was Charlotte's sweet face, her large dark eyes pleading with him to find her, and soon.

Removing his spectacles, Daniel rubbed his eyes and pinched the bridge of his nose, but the headache that had been building since Sergeant Meadows arrived on his doorstep with the dreadful news that Rebecca's body had been discovered finally exploded, blurring his vision, and forcing him to grit his teeth.

Ignoring the pain, Daniel cleaned his glasses thoroughly, then alighted from the cab when it finally drew up before the hotel. The Charing Cross Hotel, one of the hotels recently constructed to provide affordable lodging near Charing Cross station, had been built in the Franco-Italian style and harbored aspirations of grandeur not entirely in concert with its location, but if not a desirable address, at least it had convenience to recommend it. On any other day, Daniel might have taken a moment to appreciate the ornate architecture and learn something of the many luxuries offered by this modern establishment, but today, he hardly noticed his surroundings.

He strode past the uniformed doorman, heading directly for the reception desk, which was manned by two somber-looking young men. They were both helping newly arrived guests, who seemed to have an inordinate number of questions that prevented Daniel from gaining access to one of the clerks. A large clock mounted on the wall behind the desk cruelly reminded Daniel just how much time had passed since he'd last seen Charlotte, when she had stood in the foyer as Rebecca buttoned her coat and tied the ribbons of her hat beneath her chin, then smiled and waved to Daniel, calling cheerfully, "See you later, Papa."

At last, the matronly woman who'd been hogging the clerk's attention had moved away, and Daniel approached the desk.

"What room is Leon Stanley in?" he demanded.

"Is Mr. Stanley expecting you, sir?" the clerk asked, his gaze sliding anxiously toward Sergeant Meadows, who was in uniform but had removed his helmet upon entering the foyer.

Daniel whipped out his warrant card, and the clerk immediately held up a placating hand, not wishing to draw any more attention to the presence of the police.

"Four hundred fifteen, Inspector. That's on the fourth floor. Is something amiss?" he asked.

"We need to speak to him urgently," Daniel replied, but his attention was no longer on the young man behind the desk. Daniel pushed past an adolescent bellboy struggling with two large cases and hurried toward the stairs, taking the steps two at a time, Sergeant Meadows behind him, his helmet under his arm.

The two men mounted the stairs to the fourth floor and paused before approaching Leon Stanley's room. The corridor was quiet, only one maidservant cleaning a chamber that looked to have been recently vacated. She paid them no mind and went about her duties, leaving the door ajar so that anyone who passed by would notice her economical industry.

At room 415, Daniel knocked and listened intently. He wasn't at all sure what he would do if Leon Stanley weren't in. There was movement inside the room, and then footsteps approached the door, and it opened.

"Mr. Stanley?" Daniel inquired before asking to come inside.

"Yes. And you are?" he asked, his attention turning to Sergeant Meadows.

"Inspector Haze and Sergeant Meadows of Scotland Yard."

"You're Rebecca's employer," Leon Stanley said, his brow creasing with confusion. "Why are you here?"

"May we come in, Mr. Stanley? This is not a conversation to be held in the corridor," Daniel replied, and stepped forward.

Leon Stanley had no choice but to step back, allowing the two men to enter. Sergeant Meadows shut the door behind them, while Daniel took a moment to study Leon Stanley in the light streaming through the window. The man was around forty, possibly a few years younger, with neatly oiled auburn hair, dark blue eyes, and a carefully brushed moustache. He wore well-cut black trousers, a crisp white shirt, and a waistcoat of dark blue and silver silk with a matching puff tie. His shoes were polished to a shine, and a coat made of black broadcloth lay slung over a chair, as if the man had taken it off upon entering the room.

"Do sit down, gentlemen." Leon Stanley indicated the two chairs that stood on either side of a small round table.

Daniel unbuttoned his coat as he sat down, then took off his hat and settled it on his thigh, while Sergeant Meadows remained standing.

"Please, take a seat, Mr. Stanley," Daniel said, his gaze never leaving the man's face.

Although Leon Stanley was clearly surprised by the unannounced visit and was probably more than irritated by the unwelcome intrusion, he did not seem frightened nor behave in a way that would speak to his guilt. He sat down across from Daniel and laid his hands on the table, interlacing his fingers.

"Inspector Haze, I cannot account for your presence here. The only thing that comes to mind is that something has happened to Rebecca. Please, won't you allay my fears?" Leon Stanley's gaze was so anxious that Daniel actually felt pity for the man.

"Mr. Stanley, I'm terribly sorry to tell you that Rebecca's body was found in St. John's Wood burial ground this morning. We have reason to believe she was murdered."

"What? Are you certain it's her?"

"I'm certain. I saw her myself. I'm very sorry," Daniel said again.

Leon Stanley erupted out of his seat, nearly knocking Sergeant Meadows sideways, and began to pace the room. After prowling for a few moments, he stopped before the window and stared out at the bleak afternoon. "No," he moaned miserably. "No." Daniel realized he was crying.

When he finally turned, Leon Stanley looked as if he had aged several years. His shoulders were stooped, and his mouth quivered as he tried to hold back the tears that glistened on his cheeks. "Why? Who would do such a thing? Rebecca was…" His voice trailed off as he fumbled for his handkerchief and dabbed at his eyes. "She was an angel," he whispered. "She was my angel."

As much as Daniel wanted to disbelieve the show of grief, his instinct told him it was genuine, and Leon Stanley had had no idea what had happened to his beloved.

"Mr. Stanley, Rebecca and Charlotte were out for a walk when—" Daniel was about to say that Rebecca had been accosted and dragged into the burial ground, but he didn't know that was the way it had happened and chose to keep to the facts. "Rebecca was with Charlotte," he said, his voice hoarse with feeling. "We don't know what occurred."

"Oh, I'm so sorry. I pray Charlotte was not harmed."

"We haven't been able to locate her."

"I don't understand," Leon Stanley said, and sank onto the bed so heavily, the mattress springs groaned in protest. "I just don't understand. Rebecca and I were to be married next week. We were—" He buried his face in his hands, and his shoulders heaved with sobs. "I—I'm sorry," he muttered. "I'm just…"

He went silent, unable to finish. Daniel sat still, giving the man a few moments to compose himself.

"Mr. Stanley," Daniel said at last. "I need to ask you a few questions. Time is of the essence."

"Yes, of course," Stanley said as he wiped his eyes and blew his nose, seemingly ready to talk. "Forgive me. I'm in shock. Anything I can do to help, just ask." He wiped his eyes again and fixed his gaze on Daniel.

"Is there anyone you know of who might have wanted to harm Rebecca Grainger?"

"Aside from you?"

"Why would I wish to hurt Miss Grainger?" Daniel asked, stunned by the accusation.

"Rebecca led me to believe that you had feelings for her and were deeply upset by her decision to marry me," Leon Stanley replied. Daniel saw no malice in his gaze, only earnestness.

"Miss Grainger and I had a complicated relationship, Mr. Stanley, but that hardly suggests that I wished to harm her."

Leon Stanley turned to Sergeant Meadows, and Daniel noticed a change in his demeanor. He still looked bereft, his eyes reddened from crying, but his shoulders were drawn back and his chin now jutted forward, his expression more aggressive. "Is it appropriate for a detective who was involved with the victim to be investigating the crime, Sergeant?" he demanded.

"There are no rules against it," Sergeant Meadows replied.

Daniel had no idea if that were the case, since he'd never come up against such a situation before, but he had no intention of surrendering this case without a fight. "Mr. Stanley, I ask again. Was there anyone who might have wished to hurt Rebecca?"

"I don't know. She never really talked about her life," Stanley said. "I got the impression the past few years had not been happy ones."

"Rebecca told me you were a friend of her father's," Daniel tried again.

"Yes, I knew Rebecca's father some years ago, before I left England for good."

"In what capacity did you know him?"

Leon Stanley looked distinctly uncomfortable. "How much do you know of Rebecca's family, Inspector Haze?"

"Clearly not enough," Daniel replied.

"Rebecca's father was a fence."

Daniel felt as if he'd just taken a punch to the gut. Rebecca had told him that her father was a shopkeeper, but she had neglected to mention that he'd fenced stolen goods.

"I was led to believe he died some years ago, leaving Rebecca to fend for herself," Daniel said.

Leon Stanley nodded. "Yes, he died when Rebecca was seventeen. Stabbed in the gut over a silver snuffbox at his shop in Seven Dials."

"Oddly, she had never mentioned her father's criminal past," Daniel said angrily.

His innards were twisting into a knot, his heart rate accelerating by the moment. He had entrusted his child to a woman he had believed to be of good character, and now he was discovering that he hadn't known anything of Rebecca Grainger's true nature.

"We don't choose our parents, Inspector, any more than we choose our social class when we're born, but Rebecca was a good woman," Leon Stanley said quietly, as if reading Daniel's mind. "She was honorable, and kind, and I won't hear a bad word said against her. She did everything in her power to elevate herself from the gutter into which she'd been tossed by her father."

"Forgive me," Daniel muttered. "I did not mean to impugn her character."

"Rebecca didn't deserve the upbringing she had, but Edgar Levinson got what was coming to him."

"Levinson?"

"Grainger was the name Rebecca took when she went into service," Leon Stanley replied rather smugly. Despite his grief, he seemed to derive satisfaction from how little Daniel actually knew of the woman he thought he'd loved.

"And how is it that you came to be acquainted with a fence, Mr. Stanley?" Daniel asked.

If he had hoped to frighten Leon Stanley with the possibility of an arrest, the threat was lost on the man. Stanley shrugged. "We'd had some dealings in the past, but I left that life behind a long time ago. I'm proud of the man I have become, and Rebecca would not have spared me a second glance if I were engaged in anything even remotely unethical."

"And would you have told her if you were?" Daniel asked.

Leon Stanley met Daniel's gaze squarely. "I would. I was completely honest with her. I'm thirty-eight years old, Inspector. What I want…wanted," Leon Stanley amended, "was a good woman by my side and a chance at a family. That's why I had traveled to England, to find a wife. There are many beautiful women in Argentina, but they're not the sort of companion an Englishman wants to take to wife. They're all Papist, for one thing, and I wanted my wife to share my beliefs."

"How did you find Rebecca?" Daniel asked.

"How do you mean?"

"Well, if she had changed her name when she went into service, how did you know where to look for her? Had you kept in contact all these years?"

"No. Rebecca wanted nothing more to do with that sort of life after her father was murdered. They didn't just kill the man, they eviscerated him and then sacked his shop. Took everything of value and destroyed the rest. Rebecca was left with nothing."

"How did she survive? It's not an easy thing to find a position as a nursemaid without a character." Of course, one could always forge a character reference and hope that the prospective employers never bothered to check with one's previous employer. Rebecca's references had been impeccable, but were they pure fiction?

Leon Stanley looked uncomfortable, as if he were betraying a confidence, but his desire to bring Rebecca's killer to justice seemed to prevail. "I called on her grandfather," Stanley said.

"Her grandfather? Rebecca told me she had no living kin," Daniel replied, trying in vain to suppress his anger.

Leon Stanley smiled wryly. "She didn't pull the name Grainger out of thin air, Inspector. It was her mother's name. There was bad blood between Rebecca's mother and her family, I reckon on account of her having married so far beneath her station, but Rebecca did have a living grandfather, and it was to him that she'd turned in her desperation."

"And did he welcome her, this grandfather?"

Leon Stanley shook his head. "He did at first, but in the end, they fell out. Rebecca's grandfather wouldn't receive me, but I was able to learn where to find Rebecca. The housekeeper told me."

"And does the grandfather have a name?" Daniel inquired.

"Abel Grainger. Lives in Brook Street."

"Brook Street, you say?"

Brook Street was a desirable address, its affluence reflected in rising real estate value. If Abel Grainger lived there, he had to be relatively well off. Surely he could have supported his granddaughter instead of allowing her to go into service, but there was clearly more to the story.

"Nineteen, Brook Street. It'll break his heart to learn what has happened to Rebecca," Leon Stanley said. "But he deserves to know."

"Mr. Grainger will be informed." *And thoroughly questioned*, Daniel added silently. "Surely, given Rebecca's past associations, there must have been someone who'd held a grudge against her, or her father," Daniel tried again.

"I don't believe so. Rebecca earned her living honestly and devoted herself to the children in her charge. She loved Charlotte, Inspector. She told me so on more than one occasion," Leon Stanley said. "And she loved me," he added in a whisper, as if he still couldn't believe that what had happened was real and permanent.

"And what about you, Mr. Stanley?" Daniel pressed. "Might someone have wished to retaliate against you?"

Leon Stanley looked momentarily stunned but then nodded in understanding. "Inspector Haze, this is the first time I've been back to England in nearly seven years. Whatever debts I once had were settled long ago, and if they weren't, I could now easily afford to repay them. No one would have any reason to hurt Rebecca to get to me, nor would they bother with taking her charge. What use is a little girl to them? My past associates have children aplenty."

The man sighed deeply, his gaze straying to the leaden sky beyond the window. "I know you need to ask your questions, Inspector, and I have answered them to the best of my ability, but may I now be left in peace to grieve the life I have so suddenly lost?"

Daniel nodded. He felt compassion for the man despite the resentment that had been bubbling away in him since Rebecca had informed him that she would be marrying the man.

"Please accept my condolences, Mr. Stanley," Daniel said, rising to his feet. He didn't think Leon Stanley had anything more to tell them. "I will ask you not to leave London until the case is closed."

"May I bury her, Inspector Haze?" Leon Stanley asked. He was clearly broken by Rebecca's death and was groping for something to hold on to, even if it was the organizing of a funeral.

"I expect we'll be able to release the body in a few days, Mr. Stanley, at which point you can proceed with a funeral. If Mr. Grainger has no objection. Since you were not married, he's legally her next of kin."

Stanley nodded. "I'm sure we can come to some arrangement. Please, keep me apprised of any developments."

"I will," Daniel promised, even though he wasn't at all sure he ever wanted to see the man again.

"Where to, sir?" Sergeant Meadows asked once they had descended the stairs and were back in the reception area.

Daniel glanced at the clock. "You may return to the Yard, Sergeant. There's something I must do."

"Are you sure you'll be all right, sir?" Sergeant Meadows asked, eyeing him with concern.

"Yes," Daniel promised. "I will see you there in about an hour."

"Very well, sir." Sergeant Meadows donned his helmet and departed, leaving Daniel in the crowded foyer.

"Do you need a cab, sir?" the doorman asked when Daniel stepped outside.

"Yes, I do."

The doorman lifted his hand, and a hansom pulled away from the line waiting just down the street and stopped at the door.

"Where to?" the driver asked.

Daniel almost gave the cabbie his home address in the hope that Charlotte would be there when he returned, sitting in her chair in the kitchen while Grace went about preparing dinner, but Charlotte would not be at home. Daniel knew that, just as he knew that this case would not be solved quickly.

"Nineteen, Brook Street," he said instead and slumped against the seat. He felt as if every ounce of strength had been sapped from his body, and he wanted nothing more than to curl into a ball and howl until his fear and grief abated, but this was only the beginning, and he couldn't give in to weakness. He'd howl later. Right now, he had Rebecca's grandfather to interview, and he wanted to speak to Mr. Grainger on his own.

Chapter 4

Daniel's assumption that Abel Grainger was a man of means proved correct. The house in Brook Street was decorated in a somewhat outdated fashion, but the ponderous pieces of furniture were of good quality and the carpets so thick, Daniel's feet sank into the wool when he stepped on them. The pale green silk-upholstered walls were covered in oil paintings of various sizes, and in some cases, the ornate gilt frames overpowered the subjects within with their heavy-handed ostentatiousness. The dark green velvet curtains were partially drawn, keeping out most of the daylight, but a warm fire burned in the grate and the gas lamps were lit against the gloom.

Abel Grainger, when he finally entered the room, was not at all what Daniel had expected. He had imagined a frail, elderly man, but Abel Grainger couldn't have been more than sixty. He was tall, broad-shouldered, and imposing. His dark hair was liberally threaded with gray, but it made him look distinguished rather than aged. Bright blue eyes, so similar to his granddaughter's, fixed Daniel with an inquisitive stare.

"Inspector, to what do I owe the pleasure?" Abel Grainger asked once he had settled in an armchair of ivory damask with a pattern of scrolled leaves picked out in gold thread.

"Mr. Grainger, I'm very sorry to tell you that your granddaughter, Rebecca is… has…" Daniel found he couldn't bring himself to utter the words.

"Speak up, man," Abel Grainger snapped. "She has what?"

"She's dead, sir. We believe she was murdered."

The transformation in Abel was drastic and immediate. It was as if all the air had been let out of a hot air balloon, leaving behind a heap of pooled cotton and rope. His gaze was bewildered, and his hands quavered as he grabbed the armrests to steady himself.

"Are you quite sure it's my Becky?" he rasped.

Daniel nodded. "Rebecca was in my employ. She looked after my daughter, Charlotte, who was taken from the scene of the crime," Daniel replied, his voice nearly as hoarse as the older man's. "Please, sir, if I am to find my child, I need your help."

"And I will give it," Abel Grainger said, but Daniel could see the effort it cost him not to cast Daniel out so that he could grieve in private. "But first, tell me how Becky died."

"We believe she was strangled but won't know for certain until the postmortem is complete."

"Postmortem?" Abel Grainger exclaimed, his eyes flashing with anger. "Surely one must obtain permission from the family before carving up a young woman like a side of beef."

"We would naturally have asked for your permission, Mr. Grainger, but Rebecca told me she had no living kin."

"Did she now? I suppose she truly saw it that way."

Abel Grainger looked toward the window, his gaze clouded with the pain of his loss. Daniel wished he could offer him a few moments to gather himself, but he simply couldn't wait. Charlotte was out there, frightened and alone, and no one's loss or grief could come before his own purpose.

"What happened to drive Rebecca away?" he asked, forcing Abel Grainger to turn back to him.

The older man sighed and nodded absentmindedly when a maidservant arrived with a tray bearing a coffee pot, a jug of cream, a bowl of sugar cubes, and a plate of raisin cake. Daniel didn't think he could eat, but the smell of coffee and cake told him different. He hadn't eaten anything since breakfast, and the emotional toll of seeing Rebecca's body had left him depleted. Daniel gladly accepted a cup of coffee from the maidservant and acquiesced to a slice of cake, which was still warm from the oven.

Abel Grainger refused the cake but asked for coffee with cream and two sugars. He took a sip, leaned back against the chair, and closed his eyes, as if waiting for the beverage to pump strength into his veins. Daniel took a sip of his own coffee and broke off a bite-size piece of the cake, all the while watching Abel Grainger intently. His grief appeared to be genuine, and Daniel couldn't help but wonder why Rebecca chose to reject this man's love and support.

At last, Abel Grainger opened his eyes, set down his cup, and faced Daniel. "Everything that happened is my fault, Inspector Haze," he said, his voice low and laced with guilt.

"How is it your fault, Mr. Grainger?" Daniel asked, leaning forward in his eagerness to learn the answer and praying it would lead him to Charlotte.

"I'm a collector of Roman artifacts. Ancient Rome has always been a passion of mine, and I let it be known that should an item of value become available, I would be willing to purchase it, regardless of its provenance."

"You mean you bought stolen goods," Daniel said, his compassion for the man quickly evaporating.

"At times, yes." Abel Grainger exhaled deeply, as if bringing up the memories from somewhere deep within his chest and resurrecting events that had happened long ago.

"Please, go on," Daniel prompted.

"A young man by the name of Edgar Levinson called on me one day. He was in possession of a ring that was clearly Roman. Carnelian set in gold with a depiction of an antelope on the stone. It might have belonged to a Roman noblewoman in its day, and it really was a thing of beauty," Abel Grainger said with a doleful smile. "There were a few other items as well, several coins and a badly damaged torque necklace, but it was the ring I was really interested in. It was in excellent condition, hardly a scratch on it. I was so excited, I asked my daughter to join us. Nellie had a keen eye and often advised me on my acquisitions."

Abel Grainger sighed again and gripped the armrests. They seemed to anchor him to the present.

"I had no reason to suspect that Nellie and Edgar ever saw each other again, but a few months later, she told me she was with child and she and Edgar planned to be married. I know now that I should have reacted differently, should have welcomed Edgar into the family so as not to lose my only child, but I was livid and allowed my pride to get the better of me."

Abel angrily swiped at a tear that had snaked down his cheek. "Nellie wrote to me when Rebecca was born and begged me to reconcile, but I ignored her letter and threw it on the fire. She died in childbirth five years later, the infant with her, and left my only grandchild to be raised by that unscrupulous man. I went to see him then. Tried to reason with him. I told Edgar I would raise Rebecca. She'd want for nothing, but he refused. She was his daughter, and he would bring her up as he saw fit. Edgar was angry on Nellie's behalf and wasn't willing to give me a chance to make amends. I begged him to at least allow me to see Rebecca from time to time, but he refused me in that as well."

"But Rebecca came to you when her father died?"

Abel Grainger looked taken aback by the question. "She did eventually come, but it was several years after Edgar died."

"Where was she in the interim?"

Abel shook his head. "I couldn't tell you, Inspector. Rebecca refused to answer any questions, and I didn't want to push too hard. I knew it wasn't easy for her, not when all she'd ever heard about me was what a rapscallion I had been to her mother. I welcomed her and swore I wouldn't make the same mistake twice. I thought Rebecca was grateful to have a comfortable home and the prospect of something better, but she was too much her mother's daughter in the end."

"She left?"

Abel Grainger nodded. "After the life she'd led, she felt trapped and bored. She had no interest in painting watercolors or playing the pianoforte. Nor did she wish to marry. She refused to attend the social gatherings we were invited to or to entertain the gentlemen I invited to dine in the hope that one of them would win her over. In the end, she found herself unable to stay."

"Where did she go?"

"She had decided to seek employment. We argued bitterly. She had all this." Abel Grainger made an expansive gesture. "I would have respected her wishes, but she said she had no wish to remain under my roof and needed to make her own way." The older man's eyes misted again. "She said I was stifling her."

"How was she able to obtain a position without a character?" Daniel asked.

"I expect she forged the first one," Abel Grainger replied. "She was no stranger to skullduggery."

"What of the rest? Were they legitimate?"

The older man shrugged. "I should think so, but I couldn't swear to it."

"Did you remain in contact once Rebecca found employment?" Daniel asked.

"She came to visit from time to time but refused to speak of the future or give up her ill-conceived quest for independence. If I so much as made a comment about her living situation, she would leave, so we discussed banal subjects over tea until it was time for her to depart."

"Did you know Rebecca was to be married?"

"Was she?" Abel Grainger asked, his eyes widening in surprise. "I hadn't seen her in some time. I didn't even know where she was employed. She didn't want me turning up at the door."

"But your housekeeper knew. She told Rebecca's intended where to find her."

Abel Grainger nodded. "Mrs. Linnet is a good woman. Kind," he added. "I think Rebecca longed for a mother figure and turned to Mrs. Linnet when she needed someone to confide in. I'm surprised to learn that Mrs. Linnet had divulged Rebecca's whereabouts, but I suppose she must have had her reasons."

"I'd like to speak to Mrs. Linnet, if I may," Daniel said.

"Of course," Abel Grainger said. His eyes were filled with a burning intensity as he met Daniel's gaze. "Inspector Haze, promise me you'll find my granddaughter's murderer. I want my face to be the last thing he sees in this world, just as his face was the last thing my precious Becky saw when he took her life."

"I will do everything in my power to find Rebecca's killer," Daniel replied.

"Thank you. And I hope your daughter will be returned to you safely."

Abel Grainger pushed to his feet and walked to the door, his shoulders stooped with grief. "Mrs. Linnet," he called. "You're wanted in the drawing room, madam."

Chapter 5

Mrs. Linnet was about the same age as her employer, but that was where the similarity ended. She was short and plump with kind pale-blue eyes, fine lines that crisscrossed her aging skin, and a friendly manner. She wore a gown of black bombazine and a starched white lace cap over the tightly bound hair that was more gray than the rich brown it must have been when she was a younger woman.

"How can I help you, good sir?" Mrs. Linnet asked once she settled in the wingchair her employer had vacated a few moments ago.

Daniel explained the reason for his visit and sat, watching helplessly as Mrs. Linnet wept. It took her some time to calm down, but once she did, her face assumed an expression of steely determination.

"What do you need to know, Inspector?" she asked.

"Everything," Daniel replied, and meant it. Mrs. Linnet knew considerably more than he did, and anything she told him might help.

Mrs. Linnet sighed and nodded. "Well, then, I suppose I had best start with Miss Nellie. Like Rebecca, Nellie lost her mother at a young age. I always thought Mr. Grainger should have married again. A child, especially a girl, needs a mother. But Mr. Grainger never seemed to take an interest in anyone. Nellie was his world. He spoiled her and gave in to her whims," she said accusingly. "No governess lasted more than a few months. Nellie made sure of that. But for all his tender regard, Mr. Grainger never really understood the girl. He treated her like one of his prized artifacts, something beautiful to possess and occasionally show off. He never really tried to decipher what was going on in that head of hers."

"And did Edgar Levinson understand her?" Daniel asked.

"Edgar was a youthful act of rebellion, Inspector Haze. He was a handsome young man, clever, ambitious, and more than a little dangerous. Much more exciting than the vapid dandies Nellie met at the society soirées her papa took her to. She used to poke fun at them most cruelly. Said they were ridiculous and affected and had not a shred of masculinity between them. Edgar Levinson had masculinity to spare, Inspector, but I don't think she ever really thought of what would happen if she got caught out."

"Would Mr. Grainger have come around to the match had Edgar courted Nellie in a more traditional way?"

Mrs. Linnet shook her head. "He never would. Mr. Grainger's own father made his money in trade, and he could respect a man who earned his living as an honest merchant, but Edgar Levinson was a criminal by trade and a Jew by birth, two things Mr. Grainger could not abide in a prospective suitor. There was never going to be a happy future for those two."

"And Rebecca?" Daniel asked, trying to envision what Rebecca's childhood must have been like with a man who had operated on the fringes of society, both professionally and socially.

"Rebecca was her parents' daughter, Inspector Haze," Mrs. Linnet said. "Willful, clever, and stubborn as the proverbial mule. You'd think Mr. Grainger would have learned his lesson with Nellie, but when Rebecca came along, he tried even harder to make her into a young lady he could be proud of. He imagined he could marry her off to a man of his choosing. Well, Rebecca was having none of that, I can tell you. She came to her grandfather in her hour of need, but she had no wish to be molded or passed from one controlling man to another. She wanted to make her own choices, even if those choices led to hardship. So Rebecca decided to become independent of her grandfather."

"And did she intend to remain a nursemaid?" Daniel said. What he was hearing about Rebecca did not square with the things she'd told him about herself, but he was only now coming to realize how little he knew of the woman who'd lived under his roof.

Mrs. Linnet smiled sadly, her eyes misting again. "She did tell me about you, Inspector. She was beside herself when you were injured in the line of duty. The possibility of losing you scared her witless. Rebecca had seen her father, and others before him, die a violent death. She couldn't bear the thought of her husband suffering the same fate. Criminal and policeman are two sides of the same coin, aren't they, Inspector?"

"Well, not quite, but I take your point," Daniel said, inwardly bristling at the unfair comparison. "Did you advise Rebecca not to become involved with me?" he asked, not caring if his bitterness plainly showed on his face.

"I told her that no one knows how one's life might turn out. You might marry an outwardly pious man only to find that he's mired in sin, as I did. I ended up destitute and alone, questioning everything I thought I knew and wondering what the Almighty had in store for me when he allowed me to be so cruelly deceived. At least your inspector is a man of principles, I told her. A man who wants to make the world a safer place for us all."

"I wasn't able to make it a safer place for Rebecca," Daniel said softly.

"Maybe not, but you tried and will continue to try, and that's what counts."

"And Mr. Stanley? What made you help him?"

"Mr. Stanley called when Mr. Grainger was out one day. I did think that was no accident. It was me he wished to see. He asked after Rebecca and begged me to pass a letter to her. I wouldn't tell him where she worked, but I sent her a note, asking her to come around since she had mentioned Mr. Stanley to me in the past. I thought she'd like to see the gentleman again."

"And how did Rebecca react when you gave her the letter?"

"She was pleased. She said Mr. Stanley had been kind to her and she had nothing but fond recollections of him. She said she'd write to him care of the hotel."

"Do you think she loved him, Mrs. Linnet?" Daniel asked, his voice breaking with grief.

"I think she wanted a peaceful life, Inspector, away from here and all the unhappy memories of the past. Mr. Stanley could have given her that, although I do think she might have come to regret her decision to settle in a foreign land, and I told her as much. What would an Englishwoman do in Argentina, and on a ranch of all places? Rebecca was hardly a farm girl."

"And what did Rebecca say?"

"She said she wanted to get as far from London as possible. She longed for sunshine, warmth, and open spaces, not the sooty fog of the city or the bone-deep chill of an English winter. She wanted to raise her children in safety and love. She won't be having any children now," Mrs. Linnet said, a sob tearing from her very soul. It was obvious she'd loved Rebecca and had been the closest thing to a mother Rebecca had had after losing her one remaining parent.

"No, she won't," Daniel agreed. "Can you think of anyone who might have wanted to harm her, Mrs. Linnet?"

"I'm sorry, Inspector, but I can't. Rebecca kept herself to herself, happy to have a position where she didn't have to rely on her grandfather for approval or financial support. Many a young lady would have gladly allowed herself to be guided by her male kin as long as she had a place of safety, but not Rebecca. She didn't care to be controlled. That's why she felt so strongly about you, Inspector. She recognized a kindred spirit, a man who needed to be true to himself in order to find purpose in his existence."

Mrs. Linnet looked at Daniel, her eyes brimming again. "Oh, I do hope you find your little daughter. Rebecca was so fond of the motherless little mite. She hated the thought of leaving her. And you," she added sorrowfully.

Daniel swallowed back the lump that had formed in his throat and threatened to choke him. He had a job to do, and he couldn't afford to give in to his emotions.

"Mrs. Linnet, Rebecca did not come to her grandfather immediately after her father died. Did she tell you where she had been in the intervening years?"

"With friends. That's all she would say. She had no wish to speak of that time, but it was clear to me it had been difficult. Is there anything else I can help you with, Inspector?" Mrs. Linnet asked, as if sensing that the interview was coming to a close.

Encouraged by her sympathetic manner, Daniel said, "Would you have any headache powder, Mrs. Linnet?" His headache had worsened, the pounding in his temples echoing the beating of his heart.

"Of course, Inspector. I'll be back before you know it."

She was, and Daniel mixed the powder into the glass of water that Mrs. Linnet brought and gulped it down, hoping the pain would cease before long. His day was nowhere near finished.

"Thank you, Mrs. Linnet. You've been most helpful," Daniel said sincerely.

"You will let us know if you discover anything, won't you, Inspector?" Mrs. Linnet asked. "I know it won't bring her back, but I'd sleep easier knowing that the rogue who hurt our dear girl got his just deserts."

Daniel nodded and took his leave. Once back in the street, he had a choice to make. He could head over to Scotland Yard and wait for Jason to finish the postmortem, or he could follow the next lead. He had no concrete plan, but the thought of wasting even a minute of precious time waiting around while he could be doing something to find Charlotte sent him hurrying toward the nearest cab stand. He needed to go home.

Chapter 6

Daniel let himself into the house. It was completely silent, as if no one lived there anymore, all traces of his family erased in a matter of hours. When he didn't see the maidservant downstairs, he rushed to the upper floor, taking the stairs two at a time. He found Grace huddled on Charlotte's bed in the nursery, her eyes swollen from crying and her apron grubby with snot. She looked at Daniel, her face momentarily lighting with hope, but Daniel shook his head, then left her and hurried to his study.

When Sarah had been alive, the desk positioned between the two windows overlooking the street had been neat and tidy, the bills, correspondence, writing implements, and household accounts all in their proper places. Daniel couldn't be bothered with organizing the contents and usually just shoved things randomly into the drawers. He rummaged through the desk until he found what he was looking for. It was a cream-colored envelope that contained the character references Rebecca had presented to him when she'd come to apply for the position of nursemaid to Charlotte last year.

Daniel yanked the pages out of the envelope and spread them on the desk. He ignored the one with the earliest date, assuming it was fraudulent, and turned his attention to the latter two. The first was from Mrs. Porter of Earl's Court, the second from Mrs. Norris of Uxbridge Road. The references were detailed and complimentary, written in a neat hand and concisely presented, but the handwriting was not the same, Daniel noted, and the wording was different enough to suggest that the missives had indeed been written by two separate people.

What a fool I was, Daniel berated himself savagely as he refolded the pages and stuffed them back into the envelope. He should have contacted Rebecca's previous employers to verify her claims, but cretin that he was, he'd trusted his gut instead and had hired her on the spot. In his defense, he'd been so bewildered by Sarah's death and desperate for someone to offer Charlotte the care and tenderness she needed. He'd made up his mind as soon as he saw the gentle expression in Rebecca's eyes and the dimples in her cheeks when she'd smiled at Charlotte and the child smiled back.

It was a bit late to check Rebecca's references, but if her past employers could tell him anything that might give him greater insight into the woman he had trusted, then he would do so now. Daniel glanced at the carriage clock on the parlor mantel as he hurried toward the front door. It had gone three, so Jason would be finishing the postmortem soon. The two families where Rebecca had worked lived within walking distance of each other. Daniel could call on them both, then arrive at Scotland Yard in time to hear the results of the postmortem and report to Superintendent Ransome.

Not bothering to look for an unoccupied hansom, Daniel hastened toward Earl's Court. Upon finding the correct address, he gave himself a moment to catch his breath, then used the knocker to announce his presence. The door was answered by a woman in her twenties with neatly coiffed dark hair and a starched apron and cap.

"Yes, sir?" she asked with a touch of irritation, most likely assuming that he was collecting subscriptions or endeavoring to sell some service.

"Inspector Haze of Scotland Yard to see Mrs. Porter," Daniel announced loftily.

The maidservant looked abashed. "Mrs. Porter?"

"Yes. Did I not state that clearly enough?"

"You did, sir, but there's no Mrs. Porter living at this address."

"Whose residence is this?" Daniel asked.

"Professor Roberts."

"And how long has Professor Roberts resided at this address?"

"Three years now. The Porters did live here, but they've moved away, sir."

"Where to?" Daniel demanded, his impatience making him unnecessarily brusque.

"Singapore. Mr. Porter was a civil servant, or so Professor Roberts was given to understand. Transferred overseas, he was."

"I see. And I don't suppose your employer has a forwarding address?"

"Not to my knowledge, sir."

"Is the professor at home?"

"No, sir. He's giving a series of lectures in Edinburgh."

"Of course," Daniel muttered under his breath. "Thank you for your help, miss."

"Not at all, sir."

Daniel left Earl's Court and walked briskly to Uxbridge Road. Normally, he would have paid greater attention to his surroundings and would have arrived at several conclusions about the family before he so much as knocked on the door, but today all his attention was focused on speaking to Rebecca's past employers. Their domestic circumstances were secondary.

A woman of middle years answered the door when Daniel knocked. She wore a gown of unrelieved black and a black lace cap, but Daniel did not think she was the housekeeper since there was nothing subservient in either her expression or her posture.

"Inspector Haze of Scotland Yard to see Mrs. Norris," Daniel said.

The woman's expression betrayed her doubt, so Daniel held up his warrant card to assure her that he was indeed with the police.

"I'm sorry you've had a wasted journey, Inspector, but the Norrises no longer reside at this address," the woman said.

"And you are?" Daniel demanded.

"Mrs. Garson."

"Is Mr. Garson at home?"

"Mr. Garson passed two months ago," she replied, the first hint of emotion showing in her dark eyes.

"Please accept my condolences, Mrs. Garson," Daniel said, softening his tone. "Would you happen to know where the Norrises have decamped to?"

"Canada, I believe."

"Canada," Daniel repeated, nearly choking with disbelief. "How convenient."

"Convenient for whom, Inspector?" Mrs. Garson asked, looking at him as if he'd taken leave of his senses.

"Convenient for the person who has—had lied to me."

"Well, I'm sorry you were deceived, but if there's nothing else…"

"I'm sorry to have troubled you, Mrs. Garson," Daniel said, and watched the door shut in his face.

Thus disappointed on both counts, Daniel swallowed his distaste for traveling beneath ground and hurried toward the nearest underground railway station, wishing only to get to Scotland Yard and confer with Jason.

Chapter 7

As a rule, Daniel avoided the mortuary even more stringently than he eschewed the underground railroad, but today, he headed directly to the basement and knocked on the door before entering. He averted his gaze from the woman who'd been gloriously alive only that morning but now lay naked on the granite slab, a Y-shaped seam marring the alabaster skin of her stomach and chest. The smell of raw meat and bodily fluids nauseated Daniel, so he focused all his attention on Jason, who was scrubbing his hands with carbolic soap.

Jason dried his hands, removed the apron and linen cap he wore while working, and reached for his coat. Seeing Daniel's horrified expression as his gaze strayed toward the body, Jason hastily pulled a linen sheet over the corpse, although the attempt at modesty was more for Daniel's sake than Rebecca's. Rebecca no longer had such worldly cares.

"Well?" Daniel demanded.

"Let's speak in Ransome's office," Jason replied. His gaze softened as he looked at Daniel. "Any news?"

Daniel shook his head, unable to speak the words. Charlotte had been missing for roughly four hours now. She would be hungry, and it was time for her afternoon nap. He couldn't bear to think of how frightened she must be or wonder where she was at that precise moment. It would tear him to shreds and he wouldn't be able to function.

"Come," Jason said, and gently pushed Daniel through the door.

Superintendent Ransome was in his office, seated behind his nearly bare and highly polished desk. He was a tightly wound person at the best of times, but today he was practically pulsating with tension, the points of his waxed moustache quivering in his agitation.

"What's the cause of death?" he barked as soon as the two men entered his office and settled in the guest chairs.

"Miss Grainger died of asphyxiation. The bruising on her neck indicates that whoever killed her had large hands, so most likely a man. The victim was still in possession of her reticule and betrothal ring, which would suggest that the motive wasn't robbery."

"How long would it have taken her to die?" Daniel choked out.

"Not long, but she would have been fully aware of what was happening," Jason said apologetically. "Strangulation is a very personal method of murder. The murderer's and the victim's faces are inches apart, their gazes locked for the duration of the struggle."

"Was the victim violated before she was killed? There are some men who enjoy strangling their partner while they're in the throes, so to speak. Could this be rape gone wrong?" Ransome inquired.

"There's no evidence of recent sexual intercourse," Jason replied.

"So you believe she was targeted, but not sexually, Lord Redmond?"

"All I can offer you at this stage is speculation, Superintendent," Jason said. "The only definite answers are those of a scientific nature and those that pertain to the postmortem."

Daniel was grateful that Jason wasn't one to embark on a quarter hour of baffling medical jargon before getting to the point. He usually outlined the salient points, which was all Daniel could manage just then.

"I discovered a tumor that measures approximately three centimeters in the left breast and several sizeable growths in the womb. I have taken samples and will study them under the microscope once I return to the hospital."

"What for?" Ransome asked. "Are these findings relevant to her death?"

"They are not, but if the growths are malignant, the victim might have had limited time, Superintendent."

"Do you believe Miss Grainger had cancer?" Ransome asked, watching Jason with narrowed eyes.

"That's very likely."

"Would she have recovered had she lived to receive treatment?" Daniel asked, wondering if Rebecca had known something was amiss or had felt no discomfort and wouldn't have realized she was ill until it was too late.

"I can't answer your question without undertaking further study of the samples," Jason replied patiently. "But the only treatment for cancer is surgery, and there's no guarantee that it would be successful, given the location of the tumors or the fact that Miss Grainger was about to sail for Argentina."

"Don't bother," Ransome said. "If the tumors have nothing to do with the victim's death, then they're irrelevant to the investigation. We must focus only on the pertinent facts."

"As you wish," Jason replied and turned to Daniel. "Inspector Haze, would you prefer to know if there was a malignancy?"

Daniel shook his head. He wanted to remember Rebecca as he had known her, not imagine her wasting away from an illness that was devouring her from within.

"How long would she have had if it was cancer?" Daniel asked.

"I really couldn't say," Jason replied. "But I should think it would be months rather than years."

Daniel nodded. "I think Rebecca would have preferred a quick death."

"Well, she certainly got that," Ransome cut in. "Do you mind if we return to the investigation now, Haze? We have a crime to solve."

"Of course, sir."

"Right. Since nothing was taken and no one seems to have witnessed an altercation or heard cries for help at the time of the murder, we must assume this was no random attack. I would venture to suggest that we're dealing with someone Rebecca Grainger knew and possibly trusted."

Daniel had to agree with Ransome's assessment. Strangulation was brutal, prolonged, and extremely personal. The individual who had killed Rebecca had looked her in the face, watched her struggle for breath, had savored her fear. He had watched the life drain out of her body, her gaze going from sheer terror to the sightless stare of death. If robbery wasn't the motive, then Rebecca had been chosen, the murder intentional, if not necessarily premeditated.

And Charlotte. Daniel couldn't bear to think of what she had witnessed and might be enduring even now. If she was still alive.

Ransome turned to Jason. "Lord Redmond, can you tell from your examination if Miss Grainger was murdered at the burial ground or killed elsewhere, her body dumped on the grave after the fact?"

"Given that there are no other wounds and Miss Grainger's clothes and shoes are not soiled or torn as they would be if the body was dragged, I would hazard to guess that the murder took place where the body was found or very near there. Of course, the killer could have lifted Miss Grainger into his arms and carried her over to the grave where he left her. The body was carefully laid out on the slab, her hands folded, as if in prayer. This suggests that the killer felt some regard for the victim."

"Or took pleasure in his handiwork, and remorse never figured into the laying out of the victim," Ransome interjected, his fingers twirling the end of his moustache.

Jason inclined his head in agreement.

"But given your assessment of the injuries and the state of the victim's garments, my lord, I think it's safe to assume that Miss Grainger was either forced to accompany her killer or had met him at the burial ground of her own accord. If it was someone she knew and trusted, she might have felt safe in his company."

"That's a plausible scenario," Jason agreed.

Daniel knew he should participate in the conversation, but his thoughts kept straying to Charlotte, her face floating before his eyes, her mouth opening in a cry of terror.

"Haze," Ransome said. "Haze," he called again when Daniel failed to respond.

"Yes, sir?"

"Is it possible that Charlotte had run off and Miss Grainger had followed her into the burial ground?"

"I have never known Charlotte to run away from Reb—Miss Grainger," Daniel amended.

"But say she did. Perhaps she saw a pretty bird or a stray puppy," Ransome mused.

"And someone Miss Grainger knew just happened to lie in wait, murder in their heart?" Daniel retorted, angry that Charlotte was being blamed for Rebecca's death.

"What if the person was not someone Miss Grainger knew but a lunatic who'd taken refuge in the burial ground and found himself face to face with a woman who might scream and reveal his whereabouts?" Ransome turned toward the open door and bellowed, "Sergeant Meadows. In my office please."

Sergeant Meadows appeared a few moments later, his face tense. "Sir?"

"Do we know of any escaped lunatics in the area? Check with the other divisions if they've had any reports."

"Yes, sir."

Ransome turned back to Jason as soon as Sergeant Meadows was gone. "Was the victim a virgin?" Ransome asked, clearly having returned to his previous train of thought and the supposition that the attack was somehow sexually motivated.

"I don't believe so," Jason replied.

"Perhaps she was killed by a jilted lover," Ransome mused, and his gaze slid toward Daniel. "Where were you this morning, Haze?"

"Are you suggesting I strangled her?" Daniel demanded, anger surging in his breast.

Ransome fixed Daniel with a reproachful stare. "It would be remiss of me not to ask, given your past relationship with the victim and her imminent marriage to another man, as well you know, Haze. Where were you? Just answer the question."

Daniel wasn't sure how Ransome had got wind of his feelings for Rebecca, but he could hardly fault the superintendent for asking. He would do the same if the situation were reversed since the man who'd been rejected in favor of another would be an obvious suspect, as he clearly was.

"I was at home, sir," Daniel replied, his voice firm, his gaze fixed on Ransome. He had nothing to hide.

"Can anyone vouch for you?"

"My maidservant, Grace Bainbridge, can confirm my whereabouts."

"The whole time?" Ransome asked.

Daniel was about to reply in the affirmative, then remembered that Grace had gone to the butcher to buy some chops for their dinner, and admitted as much to Ransome.

"What time was that?"

"Around ten."

"So you could have left the house and returned before your maidservant got back."

Daniel felt like a dormant volcano that had just come to life, burning lava surging upward and threatening to erupt all over his loathsome superior, turning him to ash.

"Are you suggesting that I followed Rebecca to the burial ground, strangled her with my bare hands as my daughter looked on, and then disposed of my child in order to divert suspicion from myself?" he roared, too furious to moderate his tone.

"I'm suggesting no such thing, Haze, but I must be able to conclusively rule you out as a suspect. Had it been any other man in your shoes, I'd have charged him with murder by now."

Daniel opened his mouth to reply, then shut it. In his own way, Ransome was trying to help him since Daniel's relationship with Rebecca and her decision to marry Leon Stanley would inevitably be questioned by the commissioner if the case dragged on. Ransome needed to be sure.

"You went to see Miss Grainger's betrothed. What did he have to say for himself?" Ransome asked, seeming satisfied by Daniel's reaction to his questions.

"He appeared genuinely distressed, sir," Daniel replied, still furious but glad the conversation had moved away from his possible role in Rebecca's death. "He wasn't able to shed any light."

"And your little girl?" Ransome asked, gently this time.

"There's no word, sir."

"I'm sorry, Haze. I really am. I will keep Charlotte in my prayers."

Daniel wasn't sure what surprised him more, Ransome's pity or the suggestion that he prayed, but he nodded his thanks.

"If the child was taken with a view to demanding a ransom, then we will hear from her kidnappers shortly. If not, she will not be easy to find, assuming she's still alive," Ransome said, bursting Daniel's bubble of gratitude and simultaneously stabbing him through the heart.

"Why would someone want to use Charlotte to demand a ransom?" Daniel asked, his voice catching.

"Perhaps someone holds a grudge against you, Haze. Or perhaps they were after Miss Grainger and your daughter simply got in the way. They might use her to their advantage or simply dispose of her."

"If Charlotte Haze wasn't part of the plan, the killer could have simply left her where he had found her," Jason pointed out.

"Charlotte is how old?" Ransome asked, turning to Daniel again.

"She's nearly three," Daniel said.

"A child who's nearly three, especially an intelligent child, can describe what she saw and answer simple questions. Perhaps whoever did this didn't want to take the risk of being identified."

"In which case, they'd most likely kill her," Daniel concluded for him as bitter bile rose in his gorge and he prayed he wouldn't be sick.

"Daniel, there's no evidence at this time that Charlotte is dead," Jason said gently, his eyes conveying sympathy and asking Daniel to have patience with his superior.

"I will allocate every available constable to the search for the child and will ask for help from the other divisions," Ransome said. It was evident from his gruff tone that he realized the pain he'd caused with his speculation as to Charlotte's chances, but his expression remained stony, his mind on the case. "Do you have a photograph of Charlotte?"

"Not a recent one," Daniel replied. The only photo he had was the one they'd taken shortly before Sarah had topped herself, when Charlotte was nearly two.

"Any likeness will be helpful. I will show it to the searchers." Ransome's expression grew even more pitiless. "Haze, I will ask you to step away from this case. I don't believe you capable of murder, but you're too involved and cannot remain objective, not when your feelings are so thoroughly engaged. In fact, I will go so far as to recommend that you do not enter the building until this case is resolved."

"Sir, please—"

Ransome held up his hand. "I give you my word that you will be kept abreast of any developments."

"Who will you assign?" Daniel asked.

An hour ago, he hadn't thought he could feel more hopeless, but the thought of waiting in his silent house for word of Charlotte was more than he could bear. And what if Ransome assigned someone Daniel didn't think was up to the task?

Ransome turned his dark gaze on Jason. "Lord Redmond, I believe you are the only person Inspector Haze will trust to handle this case in the way he sees fit, so I respectfully ask if you would be willing to accept a temporary commission."

"Yes!" Jason exclaimed before Ransome had even finished the sentence. "I will."

"You will be issued with a temporary warrant card and put on the payroll. I know you don't wish to be paid for your services and ask that your surgeon's fee be donated to charity, but I cannot make use of you unless you are a paid detective."

"I realize that," Jason replied. "And I will agree to whatever terms you set forth in order to help Inspector Haze. Charlotte is my goddaughter. I will do whatever it takes to find her."

"That's what I'm counting on. If you will excuse me, gentlemen, I have another appointment," Ransome said as he pushed to his feet. "Haze, consider yourself on leave until the case is solved. Lord Redmond, feel free to request whatever resources you see fit. Sergeant Meadows will see to it. Good luck," he added.

"Thank you, sir," Jason replied.

"Thank you, sir," Daniel muttered under his breath.

Angry to find himself on enforced leave, Daniel was nevertheless grateful to Superintendent Ransome for putting Jason on the case. There was no one in the world Daniel trusted more, and Ransome, for all his outward brusqueness, had taken that into account, knowing that his choice was the only way Daniel could remain involved.

Chapter 8

Dusk had settled on the city, the clear sky a lovely shade of purple, with stars twinkling through the plumes of smoke belched out by a forest of chimneys silhouetted against the heavens. Daniel paused on the bottom step, suddenly unsure what to do. He wasn't officially on the case but had no reason to hurry home. Charlotte wouldn't be there, and the realization was more painful than any physical wound.

Sensing his despair, Jason laid a hand on Daniel's shoulder. "Come, Daniel. Let's get you something to eat."

"I don't think I can—" Daniel began to protest, but Jason refused to listen.

"I know you feel terrified, angry, and helpless, but you must look after yourself. Besides, since I'm now investigating the case, I need to ask you a few questions, and I'd prefer to do that over a hot meal rather than on a street corner."

"You want to ask me questions?" Daniel repeated. "But I wasn't there when it happened."

"No, you weren't," Jason agreed, "but that doesn't mean you don't know anything."

Some part of Daniel's brain acknowledged the truth of this, but his mind simply refused to work, his fear and grief blocking every rational thought. He followed Jason to a nearby public house and allowed himself to be steered toward a leather banquette in the corner, where they would be free to converse in private. Jason ordered a bottle of Scotch and plates of roast beef with boiled potatoes and peas. Daniel didn't care what he ate. At this point, it was simply the fuel that would get him through until tomorrow. Jason poured them each a healthy measure of whisky and waited for Daniel to raise his glass.

"Are we drinking to something?" Daniel asked, sounding angrier than he'd intended to.

"We're drinking to dull our fear," Jason replied. "That's as good a reason as any."

Daniel nodded and tossed back the whisky. It burned its way down his gullet, and he felt a warm glow in his belly despite the unshakable chill that had settled in his extremities as soon as Sergeant Meadows had appeared on his doorstep that afternoon. Daniel found that he was hungry and tucked into the roast beef, relishing the normalcy of sharing a meal with Jason. Jason gave him a few minutes to eat, then pulled out a small notebook and pencil.

"What do you wish to ask me?" Daniel asked.

"I need you to tell me everything you know about Rebecca Grainger, no matter how insignificant."

"I now know that she has a maternal grandfather who lives in Brook Street. Her father, Edgar Levinson, was a well-known fence who was murdered over a snuffbox. And I can't verify any of her references since her past employers have conveniently left the country. How's that for a start?"

Jason looked momentarily taken aback, but then gave Daniel a wry smile. "It's more than you knew about her yesterday, so I'd say that's a fine start, all things considered."

"Is it?" Daniel asked sourly.

"It is. As things stand now, we have three possible scenarios. First, Rebecca was attacked by a random madman when she wandered or was lured into the burial ground. Second, Rebecca's murder and Charlotte's abduction were premeditated and used as a means to send a message to you. Third, Rebecca was always the intended victim and the murder had nothing to do with either you or Charlotte, who was simply at the wrong place at the wrong time."

"So, where is she, then?" Daniel demanded angrily, furious with the cavalier way Jason had referred to his beloved child.

"Daniel, if I am to solve this case, I need to remain objective, and I can't do that if you glare at me that way. I love Charlotte, and my heart breaks for you, but I need to think of her as a piece of the puzzle in order to reason effectively."

Daniel nodded. "I'm sorry, Jason. I know you care. I am not able to think clearly just now."

"Which is why Ransome has assigned the case to me. Please allow me to proceed as I see fit."

"Go on," Daniel replied grudgingly.

"Are you sure you're okay with me thinking out loud?"

"I am *okay* with it," Daniel replied, smiling ruefully at the nonsensical term he just couldn't seem to get used to.

"All right, then. I will not discount the possibility of a random attack, but until I know more about possible suspects, I must concentrate on Rebecca herself. If someone had intended to murder Rebecca to retaliate against you, it would make sense for them to come better prepared. Rebecca was strangled, which implies that this was a spur-of-the-moment act likely brought on by a fit of anger or fear."

"If this act was meant to send a message, then perhaps Charlotte was the intended target all along," Daniel argued. "Perhaps Rebecca had tried to intervene and paid for that decision with her life."

"That's a very valid point," Jason said, and jotted something down in his notebook. "However, if it was Charlotte that the perpetrator was after, I expect we'll be hearing from him shortly. A message only has meaning when it's understood. In the meantime, we must focus on Rebecca."

"All this time I believed that Rebecca was a vulnerable young woman who had no one to turn to in London, but she had visited her grandfather, had maintained close ties with the housekeeper, Mrs. Linnet, and had reconnected with Leon Stanley, whom she'd known in her past life as the daughter of a fence. What else didn't I know about her?"

Daniel stared down at his half-eaten meal, afraid that if he didn't get hold of himself, he would dissolve into tears. It was as if he'd been broken apart, his vital organs exposed to the elements, his body struggling valiantly to keep functioning in the face of increasing adversity. The only thing he knew for certain was that he knew nothing.

"Rebecca had her secrets, but I don't think she ever meant to hurt you, Daniel. She was simply protecting her interests."

"By lying to me outright?"

"By concealing the facts she thought might prevent her from moving forward. Perhaps she thought you would dismiss her if you found out about her past. Would you have?" Jason asked.

That was not a question Daniel had been expecting, but he took time to consider it carefully. Would he have dismissed Rebecca if he'd found out her father had been a career criminal who was killed in a violent altercation over stolen goods?

"I think if I had found this out in the beginning, I would have dismissed her without a character," Daniel admitted.

"But once you became fond of her, your judgment became compromised," Jason said.

"Yes."

"And that's precisely what she was betting on," Jason replied, a bit too smugly. "She wormed her way into your home and into your heart and made a place for herself there in case she wished to stay."

"But then something better came along, and she decided to move to Argentina," Daniel said bitterly.

"Daniel, for what it's worth, I think Rebecca genuinely cared about you, but having grown up among the criminal element, she understood better than most what marriage to a policeman would entail."

Daniel nodded warily. Rebecca had said as much when he'd confronted her about her abrupt change of heart, but now her words took on a deeper meaning. She had been speaking from experience, her brush with violence having reinforced her need for security.

"We'll never know exactly what was in her heart unless she left a written record," Jason said. "Did she keep a journal?"

"I don't know. It never occurred to me to go through her things, but I will as soon as I get home. If I find anything, I will bring it with me tomorrow."

"Bring it where?" Jason asked, his brows knitting as he considered Daniel over the rim of his glass.

"If you think you're investigating this murder on your own, you're very much mistaken," Daniel said forcefully. "I might not be officially on the case, but I will be with you every step of the way, whether you want me there or not. And I would ask that you keep my involvement from Ransome for the time being. I don't have the wherewithal to contend with his barbs just now."

Daniel was already regretting his outburst and hoped he hadn't offended his friend. He'd made Jason the butt of his anger when the person he truly wanted to punish was himself. This was his fault, the result of his carelessness and failure to do due diligence when he'd hired Rebecca. He could hardly blame Jason, who was doing his best to help.

"Forgive me," Daniel said. "I didn't mean—"

"There's nothing to forgive," Jason replied. "I don't care what Ransome said. I don't answer to him. I answer to my conscience, and to my sense of loyalty, and I wouldn't ask you to stay away, not when Charlotte is still out there."

"I will do everything in my power to remain objective," Daniel promised. "You have my word."

"Daniel, few people could remain objective in the face of such tragedy. You are a father before you're a policeman, and even if you hadn't been fond of Rebecca, she was still a young woman who lived under your roof and was a companion to you since Sarah died. All I ask is that you don't make any rash decisions."

Daniel nodded in acquiescence. "I will not do anything without conferring with you first."

"All right, then, Inspector," Jason said with grim determination. "Let's concentrate on what we know. How did Leon Stanley know Edgar Levinson?"

"It would seem he had dealings with the man. I can only assume they were of the unsavory kind."

"How old was Rebecca when her father died?"

"I believe she was seventeen," Daniel replied.

"If we are to entertain the possibility that she was murdered by someone from her past, why would they wait all this time to come for her?" Jason asked.

"Perhaps they'd only just found her again. She had changed her name from Levinson to Grainger and gone into service. She wouldn't be easy to track down in a city of millions."

"But Leon Stanley managed to find her."

"He left a letter with Mrs. Linnet. It was Rebecca who contacted him via the hotel," Daniel corrected Jason.

"But he knew to approach Mrs. Linnet, and by extension, he must have known about Rebecca's grandfather. It is possible that others did as well."

"I suppose so, but as you have pointed out, it's been years since Edgar Levinson was murdered. Why wreak vengeance on Rebecca today?"

"Let us suppose that the murder had nothing to do with the past and everything to do with the present. Who would have cause to retaliate against you, Daniel?"

"I've sent a fair number of individuals to both prison and the gallows," Daniel replied. "Part of my job, I'm afraid."

"But does anyone specific spring to mind?"

"The only person I can think of is Tristan Carmichael. As you're well aware, our paths have crossed more than once, in both Brentwood and London, and both times I suspected him of murder. I interfered with his business dealings and gave him ample reason to believe I might do so again. Tristan Carmichael has an army of thugs ready to do his bidding. He could have easily sent someone to follow Rebecca, but, by the same logic, he could have just as easily dispatched someone to deal with me directly. Why harm an innocent woman and child?"

"Because to hurt those you love would inflict a deeper wound," Jason replied. "Perhaps murder was never part of the plan."

"Then what was?"

Jason shook his head. "Impossible to say. Rebecca bore no defensive wounds, so there doesn't appear to have been a struggle. The attack must have been unexpected, and if she had fought back at that stage, then the killer would bear the wounds, most likely on his hands and wrists."

"And because there are no defensive wounds, we come back to the supposition that it was someone Rebecca knew," Daniel said. "Had the man approached her in the street and tried to drag her off into the burial ground, she would have resisted, and someone would have witnessed the commotion. And had it been one of Carmichael's men, I expect he would have been better prepared and most likely not on his own."

"The method of the attack doesn't bring Tristan Carmichael to mind. Despite his criminal activities, or maybe because of them, Tristan Carmichael operates by a certain code. I can't see him killing an innocent young woman and snatching a small child just to get at the policeman who had dared to do his job, especially when he has a wife, sisters, and several nieces and nephews and wouldn't wish to make them a target for retaliation. No, Daniel, there's something else at play here."

"Yes, but what? Or who? Where do we begin, Jason?" Daniel asked desperately. "How do we find Charlotte?"

"We begin by getting you home. You're exhausted and need to rest."

"Do you honestly think I will be able to sleep?"

"You will if you take a few drops of laudanum, and I suggest that you do, because tomorrow, we begin our investigation in earnest, and I expect you to be alert. I will come for you at eight. Make sure you eat a hearty breakfast. It will be a long day," Jason warned.

"Thank you, Jason," Daniel said with feeling. "Knowing that you're on my side makes me feel a little less terrified."

"I'm always on your side, Daniel. Now, are you ready to go?"

"As ready as I'll ever be," Daniel said, and pushed wearily to his feet.

Chapter 9

Having delivered Daniel to St. John's Wood and watched him walk dejectedly to his front door, Jason considered his next steps. He longed to go home, to see for himself that his family was safe and to hold his baby girl in his arms, the solid weight of her reassuring him that she wasn't in any danger. But unlike the cases he and Daniel usually investigated, where the victim was already gone and it was just a matter of piecing together the motive behind their death, Charlotte was still out there, and every moment counted if they had any hope of finding her alive.

There wasn't much more Jason could do tonight, but there was one person he could speak to, and he couldn't permit himself to go home until he'd had a conversation with Tristan Carmichael. It was entirely possible that Carmichael wouldn't be at home. He had many concerns in London, ranging from opium dens and gaming hells to both upmarket and seedy brothels. He and his father, Lance Carmichael, who was still overseeing operations in their native Essex, had steadily moved in on the established London gangs, carving out a place for themselves in the literal sense of the word. Their takeover had been brutal and swift.

"Where to, sir?" Joe asked when Jason had failed to give him a directive.

"Forty Upper Brook Street," Jason replied, and settled in for the ride.

It was rather a coincidence that Rebecca's grandfather lived a stone's throw from the man who might have had her killed, but Jason swiftly admonished himself not to jump to baseless conclusions. It was all too easy to form a theory and then try to twist the facts to fit the solution he'd already embraced. He would remain objective and take the information at face value rather than try to manipulate the result.

Jason was relieved to note that the ground floor windows of Tristan Carmichael's elegant home were brightly lit, the heavy velvet curtains not yet drawn against the gathering darkness of the spring night.

"I won't be long, Joe," Jason said as he shut the carriage door behind him.

"Take as long as ye need, my lord. I ain't complaining," Joe said in his usual gruff tone.

The door was opened by Carmichael's butler, Simcoe, who'd seen Jason recently enough to recognize him immediately.

"Lord Redmond to see Mr. Carmichael," Jason informed the man.

"I'll see if he's at home, your lordship."

"I know he's at home, and I must speak to him urgently," Jason replied.

Simcoe looked set to argue, so Jason simply pushed past him and walked toward the drawing room, from which he heard the low timbre of masculine voices. He pushed the door open and strode in, his intention to take the occupants by surprise. The drawing room, tastefully decorated in celadon green and pink, was an oasis of tranquility and comfort. A merry fire blazed in the marble-topped fireplace, and a decanter of what appeared to be brandy sat on a low table between the two men. A generously heaped platter of fruit and cheese filled the room with a sweetly pungent aroma.

Tristan Carmichael looked up in some surprise as his companion, who, although well dressed, couldn't be mistaken for anything other than a foot soldier in Carmichael's army, grabbed for the pistol he wore in a leather holster just beneath his heart.

"Ah, Lord Redmond," Tristan Carmichael drawled, his generous lips stretching into a sardonic smile. "What an unexpected pleasure to see you again. And so soon."

He didn't bother to disguise his sarcasm, but neither did he seem particularly alarmed. As far as Tristan Carmichael was concerned, Jason wielded no authority and was in no position to harm him.

"Morey, give us a moment, will you?" Tristan Carmichael said to the armed man. "In fact, I'll speak to you tomorrow. Our business is concluded for tonight."

"Are you sure you don't want me to remain, Mr. Carmichael?" the man asked, still eyeing Jason with barely disguised hostility.

"No need. Lord Redmond is an honorable gentleman. He would never disrespect a man in his own home. Would you, your lordship?" Tristan Carmichael asked, smiling at Jason in a way that made Jason want to wipe the smirk off his face.

"I only require a few moments of your time, Mr. Carmichael," Jason replied in as civil a tone as he could muster given Carmichael's derisive manner.

"See, what did I tell you?" Tristan Carmichael said to Morey. "Off you go, Roger. I'm perfectly safe."

Roger Morey gave Jason a look of pure malice but obeyed his employer's request and made for the door, where Simcoe handed him his things and saw him out. Once Jason heard the front door close, he advanced further into the room, coming to stand before Tristan Carmichael.

"Well, don't stand there like a tree," Carmichael said irritably. "You'll give me a crick in the neck if I have to look up at you. Sit down, your lordship. Brandy? A bunch of grapes?" he asked solicitously.

Jason accepted the offer of a seat but refused the refreshments. This wasn't a social call, nor was he in the mood to make polite chitchat over expensive fruit. He settled in the chair vacated by Morey and studied his host. As on previous occasions, he was amazed at the cherubic beauty of the man. With his golden curls, wide blue eyes, and pouty lips all carefully arranged on a face with enviable bone structure, Tristan Carmichael looked like one of Michelangelo's angels or one of Caravaggio's exquisite young models. There was not a hint of coarseness in the man who made his living from bottomless addiction to opium and men's baser desires.

"How can I be of service, my lord?" Tristan Carmichael asked, watching Jason with those dark blue eyes.

Jason had one chance to catch him off guard, so the first thing he said had to be utterly unexpected. If Tristan Carmichael was involved in Rebecca Grainger's murder, his reaction would instantly give him away, even if it was only a momentary slip.

"Why take the child?" Jason asked as he nailed Tristan Carmichael with a probing gaze.

"What child?"

Jason was in no doubt that the man before him was a master of duplicity, but his confusion seemed genuine as he studied Jason with a furrowed brow.

"What child?" he asked again.

"Charlotte Haze."

Carmichael lifted his shoulders in the universal gesture of incomprehension. "Who's Charlotte Haze?"

"Daniel Haze's daughter," Jason replied.

"And what would I want with her?"

"Charlotte's nursemaid, Rebecca Grainger, was found strangled this morning at St. John's Wood burial ground. Charlotte was with her at the time. She hasn't been seen since."

Tristan Carmichael looked genuinely nonplussed. "And what would make you think I had anything to do with that?"

"You might wish to send a message to any policeman who dared to investigate your less-than-legal activities."

Tristan Carmichael sighed and shook his golden head in sheer disbelief. "First of all, I don't kill innocent women and children. And second, if I were to resort to murdering nursemaids to teach nosy policemen a lesson, London would be littered with corpses. I know you find this difficult to believe, being such an exalted personage yourself, but there is such a thing as a code of honor, even among thieves. I won't hesitate to teach some thug a much-needed lesson, but I will not harm his family or take his children."

"Because you live by this agreed-upon code of honor or because you're afraid they'll harm your family in turn?" Jason asked.

"Both. What will happen if we start slaughtering each other's women and children? Where will it end? Contrary to what you think, I'm not a monster. I am a businessman who provides a supply for an already existing demand. If a man craves a woman or can't get through the week without relying on an opium pipe, he will find those needs met by someone else if I'm not there to take care of them. I don't force anyone to do anything. I simply provide a reasonably priced alternative to the services that are already readily available."

"You make it sound so noble," Jason replied, irritated by the man's placid demeanor. Tristan Carmichael was not even remotely intimidated by the law or its rather brutal punishment of those who dared to break it.

"As a gesture of goodwill, Lord Redmond, I will do my utmost to help you find the child. How old is she?"

"Nearly three."

"Goodness me, what a tender age. My own son is nearly that old."

"Your son?" Last Jason had heard, Tristan Carmichael had only just married. As on a previous occasion, there was no sign of Mrs. Carmichael. Tristan seemed to permanently keep her at their home in Brentwood, where she would not only stay out of his way but remain under the watchful eye of her father-in-law. This was clearly no love match, but the woman must have brought something to the bargain or Carmichael would have never married her.

"Born on the wrong side of the blanket, I'm afraid, but that doesn't mean I love him any less. I look after my own."

"Very admirable of you," Jason replied. "Now, how can you help me?"

"I'll get the word out. If anyone has heard of anyone taking a little girl, I will be sure to let you know."

"You can send a message to me at Scotland Yard," Jason said, pushing to his feet.

"I can do better than that. I can send a message directly to your home," Tristan Carmichael said. "I'm sure your charming wife will pass it on to you should you happen to be out."

Carmichael was the picture of amiability, but Jason felt a frisson of fear at his words. He was being told in no uncertain terms that Carmichael knew where he lived and that he wouldn't hesitate to retaliate should Jason do anything to jeopardize either the Carmichael criminal network or the men themselves. This was a warning that Jason intended to heed. He wasn't fool enough to endanger his family, nor did he believe that Tristan Carmichael would never harm women and children should a clear message need to be sent.

"Thank you for your kind offer, Mr. Carmichael. I'll see myself out."

"Sure you don't want that drink? To toast our new partnership?" Tristan asked, smiling guilelessly.

"We do not have a partnership, Mr. Carmichael. More of an uneasy truce."

"Call it what you wish, but I'd rather have you as a friend than a foe, my lord. I might have need of your services one day," Tristan Carmichael said in parting, making Jason wonder what he meant.

Chapter 10

By the time Jason returned to his own townhouse in Kensington, it was nearly seven thirty. He took the stairs two at a time, hoping to catch Lily before she fell asleep. The door to the nursery was closed, but Jason pushed it open gently, relieved to find Katie seated in the rocking chair she favored when reading Lily a bedtime story.

Lily, who'd be turning one next week, was wide awake, her cherubic mouth stretching into a wide smile when she saw her father.

"Jason, it's past her bedtime," Katherine reminded him sternly.

"I need to hold her, Katie. For just a moment," Jason said, and reached into the cot to lift out his daughter.

Lily instantly wrapped her chubby arms around Jason's neck and pressed her head to his cheek, her heart beating against his chest with reassuring steadiness. He held her close and kissed the top of her capped head. She smelled of the lemon verbena soap Katherine preferred and her own wonderful childish scent.

"Dada," Lily muttered contentedly as she snuggled in closer.

"Oh, my precious darling," Jason murmured. "I don't know what I would do if anything ever happened to you."

"Jason, what on earth—" Katherine whispered urgently.

She was an astute woman who understood only too well that something momentous and terrible must have happened to cause Jason to behave in this manner, and her fear showed in her bespectacled gaze.

At last, Jason let go of a protesting Lily and set her down, tucking the eiderdown quilt around her shoulders. "Sleep well, my darling," he said, and kissed her velvety cheek.

Lily looked mutinous and let it be known that she had no intention of going to sleep, but her parents sat quietly side by side until tiredness took over and she finally gave in to peaceful slumber. Tiptoeing from the room, Jason and Katherine made their way down to the drawing room.

"Have you eaten?" Katherine asked. "I had a nursery supper with Lily since I had no idea what time you'd be back."

"I'm not hungry, but I could sure use a drink. Join me?"

"Well, maybe just a small sherry," Katherine replied. Her gaze told Jason that she knew she'd need it. "Jason, what happened today?" she asked once they were seated in front of the fire, glasses in hand.

Most men of Jason's generation and social class, particularly British men, would not have told her the truth, choosing to protect her sensibilities and peace of mind, but Jason was not a typical man of his generation, nor was he British. And he didn't believe women needed to be coddled or protected from the truth, especially when that truth pertained to someone they cared about so deeply.

"Katie, Rebecca Grainger was found dead this afternoon, her body laid out on a stone slab in the St. John's Wood burial ground."

Katherine's hand flew to her breast. "Dear God," she exclaimed. "The poor woman. And Daniel..." Her voice trailed off as realization dawned. "Oh, no," Katherine moaned. "No!"

"I'm afraid so. Charlotte was with her at the time and hasn't been seen since."

Katherine clamped her hand over her mouth to keep from crying out and shook her head violently, her eyes huge with shock.

"Katie, we don't know that Charlotte is dead. All we know is that she appears to have been taken."

Katherine sucked in a shuddering breath and lowered her hand. "Taken by whom?"

"We don't know."

Draining her sherry, Katherine set the glass on the occasional table and fixed Jason with her direct stare. "Do you believe she's still alive, Jason?"

"Believe is a strong word, but I pray that she is and will do everything in my power to find her."

Alive or dead, Jason added mentally, and Katherine nodded because she read the truth in his eyes.

"Oh, Jason, please find her alive. That little girl—" Tears spilled down her cheeks. "That family has been decimated by the death of Felix and then Sarah's—" She didn't finish the sentence, but they both knew what she was going to say. Suicide. Katherine dabbed at her eyes. "Daniel will never recover if—"

"I know," Jason interjected. He couldn't stand to hear the words spoken out loud, not by his wife. It was necessary to consider all the possibilities during an investigation, but he couldn't bear to speak of Charlotte's possible death with Katie while their own little girl slept upstairs, tiny and vulnerable, and so easily destroyed if someone put their mind to it.

"Does Daniel have any leads?" Katherine asked.

Jason shook his head. "Not yet."

He didn't tell Katherine that Ransome had taken Daniel off the investigation. He had no wish to speak about tomorrow. Tonight, he needed to be with his family, to know that Lily was safe and that Katherine, devastated as she was, was by his side. He also knew that his house was staffed with people who were devoted to him and would do his bidding when he informed them tomorrow that no one, especially Katherine and Lily, was to leave the premises. Katherine wouldn't be too happy with his decision, but until he knew what he was dealing with and whether Rebecca's death was the handiwork of someone who held a grudge against Daniel and by extension Jason, he would keep his family safe.

"I'll be heading out early tomorrow," Jason said instead.

"Will you be taking Joe?" Katherine asked, her mind clearly having moved on to practicalities as it was wont to do.

"Did you need the carriage?"

"I have a meeting with my charity committee in the morning, and then I was going to go to St. Brigid's shelter for fallen women. I'm teaching some of the women to read," Katherine said proudly.

Jason wanted to order Katherine to remain at home, but her charitable works were extremely important to her, and she would be safe if Joe brought her there and back. And Lily would be safe at home if Katherine weren't there to take her out for a walk in the park.

"I'll find my own way," Jason said. "I can manage without a carriage for one day."

Katherine gave him a stern look. "The Easter holidays start on Monday, and I promised Micah you'd be there to collect him after school. Did you forget?"

"I was somewhat preoccupied today," Jason said without rancor.

"Yes, of course. I'm sorry. Don't give it another thought, my dear. Joe will collect Micah, and I will keep Micah occupied while you're investigating this case. I have some diverting activities planned."

"Katie, until we know who took Charlotte, there will be no activities outside this house."

"Are you serious?" Katherine reared. "You mean to keep us prisoner?"

"I mean to keep you safe. I have assisted the police on a dozen cases. If someone has a grudge against Daniel, they might just as easily have one against me and decide to retaliate against those I love."

Katherine looked as if she were about to argue but nodded resolutely instead. "My priority is to keep everyone safe. Lily will not leave this house until the case is solved and Charlotte has been returned to Daniel."

"Thank you, Katie. I will need your support on this."

"It won't be as easy to keep Micah at home," Katherine said.

"Perhaps we won't need to. Let's just see what tomorrow brings."

Katherine stood and held out a hand to Jason. "Let's go to bed."

It was early, but Jason didn't protest. He was emotionally hollowed out after this terrible day, and the only thing that could restore him, even marginally, was the intimacy only Katie could provide.

Chapter 11

Sunday, March 7

The laudanum, which Daniel had finally reached for after several hours of tossing and turning miserably in the dark, did its job and kept him in its grip for most of the night, but there wasn't much it could do about the nightmares. If anything, it probably made them more vivid. Daniel's drugged mind conjured up a procession of horrific images that all culminated in Charlotte's death, and he woke drenched in cold sweat, the memory of her bloated body as it was pulled from the river with hooks used for floaters etched into his brain.

It was still dark out, but Daniel couldn't bear another moment of helpless agony and decided that he'd rather deal with whatever was to come head on. He washed away all traces of his night sweats with the ice-cold water left in the pitcher from yesterday, shaved, then dressed and headed downstairs. He'd expected to find himself alone for another two hours at least but Grace was there, at the kitchen table, her face mottled and puffy from crying and lack of sleep. Their eyes met, and Daniel felt his resolve give way as hot tears slid down his cheeks.

"We'll get her back, Grace," he swore, but he wasn't really speaking to Grace. His doubts gnawed at him like some rapacious monster sucking on the bones of its victim, and he found it hard to keep the faith.

Grace nodded and wiped her eyes with her apron. "Can I make you some breakfast, sir?"

"If you would be so kind," Daniel replied as he collapsed into a chair. "Lord Redmond is collecting me at eight. Superintendent Ransome has assigned him the case."

"Oh, that's good news, sir. He's a clever one is Lord Redmond."

"He is my only hope," Daniel replied.

Grace nodded her understanding. "Shall I bring your breakfast to the dining room, then?"

"I'll just have it here, if you don't mind. I could use the company. Perhaps you'll eat with me?" Daniel suggested shyly.

"I don't think I can eat, Inspector, but I'll take a cup of tea, if it's all the same to you."

"Please," Daniel said.

"Boiled or fried, sir?"

"What?"

"How do you want your eggs? Boiled or fried?"

The thought of eggs in either incarnation made Daniel feel sick to his stomach. "How about some toast and marmalade? I don't think I can do the eggs justice just now."

"Of course, sir."

It took some considerable time for Grace to get the stove going and then to boil the water for tea and make the toasted bread, but Daniel was in no hurry. He sat quietly, his thoughts on the day ahead. When, at last, Grace set down the plate of toast, a crock of butter, and a jar of marmalade before him, Daniel carefully buttered his toast and waited for Grace to join him at the table.

"Grace, I want you to think very carefully before you answer," Daniel said. "Did Rebecca ever share anything of a personal nature with you?"

"Such as, sir?"

"Such as where she had lived before coming to us. Where she grew up. The people she might have kept company with. A friend she held in high regard. It's important, Grace."

Grace took a sip of her tea and considered Daniel's request. "Now that I think of it, she hardly ever spoke about herself. Always changed the subject whenever anything of a personal nature came up, and I didn't want to press her."

"Did you ever suspect she was hiding something?" Daniel asked. He'd gone through Rebecca's room last night but found nothing that would offer a glimpse into Rebecca's personal life. There was no journal and no photographs. Not even a forgotten letter between the pages of a book or a hastily scribbled note.

Grace nodded. "That I did, sir. She was slippery, that one. God rest her soul," Grace added hastily, not wishing to speak ill of the dead.

"Do you think she was capable of violence?" Daniel asked, the question having slipped out before he'd even thought it.

"Do you?" Grace countered.

"I didn't think so, but now…"

"I don't think she had a violent nature, sir, but I do think she was frightened."

"Of whom?"

Grace shook her head. "She never said, and I never asked. Not my place to pry into her private life. But she cared for Charlotte, sir. I know she did. I saw it in her eyes and heard it in her voice. She wouldn't have hurt her for the world."

Daniel nodded, unable to either swallow his toast or produce anything that resembled speech. Only yesterday Charlotte had been there, chattering to Rebecca as she ate her breakfast before they set out for their morning walk. They had both been so present, and so alive. Daniel had heard them laughing as he hunkered down in the parlor with his book and wished they'd give him an hour of uninterrupted peace on his day off. And now the house was as silent as a tomb, and he would give anything in the world to turn back the clock and have them both back.

"You eat your breakfast, Inspector," Grace said. "You'll need your strength today."

And Daniel did, even though with every bite he swallowed, he felt as if he were being force-fed and he'd be sick if he didn't stop.

Chapter 12

Daniel was ready and waiting by the time Jason came to collect him. He had expected Jason to arrive in his brougham, but he was in a hansom driven by a grizzled older man with wooly muttonchop whiskers. He wore a misshapen top hat and a patched overcoat and spat a gob of chewed tobacco into the street as he waited for Daniel to alight.

"Did something happen to your carriage?" Daniel asked once the cab had set off for some unknown destination.

"Joe took Katherine and Lily to church, and then Katherine wanted to visit St. Brigid's. And Micah is coming home for the Easter holidays tomorrow. I was supposed to bring him from school, but Joe will go in my stead. Maybe Micah won't be as disappointed if Joe allows him to take the reins."

Jason glanced at Daniel apologetically, as if suddenly realizing that his domestic arrangements were quite trivial compared to what Daniel was going through. Daniel simply nodded to indicate that he had heard and understood. Normally, he would inquire about Jason's young charge, whom he thought of affectionately, but today, he had no thought to spare for anyone but Charlotte.

"Where are we headed?" he asked instead.

Jason held up the Sunday edition of the *Daily Telegraph*. Daniel read the headline and recoiled in horror.

DANGEROUS INMATE ESCAPES FROM

PINE GROVE ASYLUM FOR THE INSANE

"I've no doubt that Ransome has seen this and will send someone to speak to the director of this establishment, but I would like to interview the man myself," Jason said.

"Where is this Pine Grove Asylum?" Daniel asked.

"It's in Southwark, not too far from Bethlem Hospital."

"Have you been there before?"

"No, it says so in the article."

Daniel shrank deeper into the grubby seat of the hansom. He'd never been to Bethlem, or Bedlam as it was more commonly known, but he had heard of the appalling conditions and inhuman treatment of the inmates. He didn't think places like Bedlam should continue to exist, not without some measure of government intervention to ensure humane conduct toward the patients and an acceptable level of cleanliness. He did, however, believe that some individuals were not only incurably insane but inherently violent and would be better off detained at the newly established ward for the criminally insane, as they were a threat to public safety. The fact that the inmate who'd escaped had not been kept in Bedlam could mean only one thing. He was a scion of a prominent and well-to-do family.

"Does it say who the man is?" Daniel asked.

"He's not identified by name, but we'll find out soon enough."

"And do you suppose this inmate's escape is in some way relevant to Rebecca's murder?" Daniel asked, failing to identify any other reason for this trek to the other side of the river.

"It's too soon to say."

Jason seemed reluctant to speculate, so Daniel unfolded the newspaper and read the article for himself. It was brief and uninformative, the story meant to offer the cheap thrill of fear felt from a distance rather than any real understanding of what had occurred or what the man was truly capable of. The author did not explain how the inmate had broken out or mention whether anyone had been hurt in the process. Likewise, he did not offer any information as to the man's history of violence, saying only that he was extremely dangerous.

The cab crossed Blackfriars Bridge into Southwark. It traveled along Borough High Street before turning onto Kent Street. The Pine Grove Asylum was located in Hunter Street, a discreet redbrick building surrounded by tall wrought-iron paling and hidden from view by thick shrubbery planted along the inner perimeter of the fence. A watchman took his time examining their warrant cards before finally opening the gates to allow the carriage to enter. The hackney drew up before the front door, and the two men climbed out.

"Ye ain't said ye was going to a lunatic asylum," the cabbie grumbled, his accusing gaze fixed on Jason.

Jason pulled a coin out of his pocket and tossed it to the cabbie, who caught it deftly and peered at it to assess its value, his expression instantly transforming to one of disbelief.

"We won't be long," Jason said. "And there's more where that came from."

The man shoved the coin into the pocket of his ratty coat. "Take as long as ye need, good sir. I ain't going nowhere. Not for as long as ye've need of me."

"How much did you give him?" Daniel asked, amazed by the man's abrupt change in attitude.

"A half crown. That should keep him sweet until we're finished here."

"I should think so," Daniel replied, glad Jason could afford to throw his money around. He wouldn't like to find himself stranded here for any length of time. The place gave him the creeps.

They found the front door was locked when they tried it, and there were iron bars on each window, the building an impregnable fortress designed to keep the insane in and the sane out. After knocking for what seemed like a half hour but was probably no more than a few minutes, Jason and Daniel were finally admitted and questioned by a young, burly attendant who made certain they were not armed before escorting them to the office of the director, Dr. Elias Garfield.

The office was spacious and tastefully decorated in shades of dark green and gold with heavy, carved furniture made of dark wood. The man behind the massive desk appeared to be in his mid-to-late thirties and had deep-set brown eyes and longish dark hair gently threaded with silver at the temples. Even when seated, he was obviously tall and solidly built, his biceps straining against the broadcloth of his well-cut coat. Dr. Garfield had a penetrating gaze that seemed to widen with amazement at the sight of them.

"Well, I'll be damned," Dr. Garfield exclaimed, his generous mouth splitting into a wide grin. His accent proclaimed him to be American, a development Daniel found as unexpected as it was welcome. Perhaps he'd prove more helpful than his British counterparts, who tended to close ranks when it came to their livelihood and reputation.

"Captain Jason Redmond as I live and breathe," Dr. Garfield gushed. "Why, I haven't seen you in the flesh since we got our backsides handed to us at Chancellorsville in sixty-three. I did hear that your detachment was at Gettysburg, but it seems our paths never did cross in the melee. How've you been keeping, brother?"

"It's good to see you again, Elias," Jason said, but Daniel thought he could sense Jason's underlying reserve. He wasn't nearly as pleased to see Dr. Garfield as the other man was to see Jason, and if Daniel knew his friend, there was bound to be a good reason for his aloofness.

"Lord Redmond now, is it? Who'd you have to kill to swing that?" Dr. Garfield asked as he gestured for them to sit down.

"I inherited the title and estate after both my grandfather and father passed within months of each other."

"Oh, I am sorry to hear that. But you did make out like a bandit," Dr. Garfield pointed out, his abrasive laugh grating on

Daniel's already frayed nerves. "Did you marry yourself a sweet little debutante? Weren't you engaged to that—oh Lord, what was her name?—Cecilia? Cecily? God, she was a looker. Is she here in London with you?"

"She is not," Jason replied.

"Whatever happened to her? If I'd known you'd called it quits, I'd have married the chit myself."

"She married someone else while I was away," Jason replied patiently. He clearly didn't want to discuss his personal life, but Elias Garfield's exuberance had to be assuaged before Jason would be permitted to ask his own questions.

"I know it's early in the day, but the sun is over the yardarm somewhere," he boomed. "What say you to a drink, boys? I have some very fine whisky, or brandy if you prefer," Dr. Garfield said, his gaze settling on Daniel for the first time. "In this job, you have to keep the liquor cabinet well stocked. And I do."

"Thank you, Elias, but we're both on duty," Jason replied politely, putting paid to the social niceties.

"You're right. It's barely nine o'clock," Dr. Garfield agreed. "Maybe we can meet up for dinner, talk over old times. You're welcome to join us, Inspector Haze. The more the merrier, I always say," he added, but it was obvious he was only being polite. The person he really wished to spend time with was Jason.

"I would really enjoy that, but I am unable to commit to anything until the case is solved," Jason replied.

Elias Garfield shook his head in disbelief. "That's just like you, Jason. Your old man dies, you tumble into the lap of luxury, and what do you do? You offer your services to Scotland Yard rather than lording it up and charming sweet young virgins with your American accent. Lord knows I'd be living the posh life and savoring every day. Shooting grouse in Scotland and riding to hounds, or whatever it is these English bluebloods do to keep the boredom at bay. But then again, I never did suffer from a social conscience like you."

"How did you come to be here, Elias?" Jason asked, deftly bypassing the need to comment.

"That's a story for another time," Elias Garfield replied, his expression turning somber. "So, how can I help you with your case, Jason?"

"Tell me about the inmate that escaped, Elias. What landed him in this place?"

Elias Garfield glanced out the barred window at the gentle spring day outside and sighed heavily before turning back to face his visitors. "I've met many a cruel man, especially during the war years, when men could let their darker desires come out to play without having to account for their savagery, but I've never met anyone like Edward Marsh. Most men know when they've done wrong, even if they feel no remorse, but Edward Marsh is completely devoid of a sense of right and wrong. He has no conscience. In fact, I think he's the closest thing I've ever met to pure evil. My predecessor referred to him as The Demon."

"Who's paying to keep him here? I assume this institution is privately owned and the exorbitant fee is meant to pay not only for lifelong incarceration but for absolute discretion," Jason said.

"You assume correctly. Edward Marsh, which is incidentally not his real name, comes from a very old, very noble family that will spare no expense to keep him locked up. His deeds were hushed up to keep his neck out of the noose and to avoid scandal, but as far as his nearest and dearest are concerned, the sooner he pops his clogs, the better."

"How old is Edward Marsh?" Daniel asked. "And what is his real name?"

"I can't tell you his surname, but his Christian name is Jack. He's twenty-three, and strong as an ox."

"How long has he been an inmate?" Daniel inquired.

"Eight years now."

"And what exactly landed him in a lunatic asylum?" Daniel asked, unable to bear the suspense any longer.

Elias Garfield sat back in his studded leather chair, looking for all the world like he was about to tell an amusing story rather than a tale of madness in a young man. His gaze was fixed on Jason when he spoke.

"Edward started small, torturing animals, and hurting the female servants. Marsh's father naturally turned a blind eye to the misdemeanors of his son and heir. High spirits he called it and sent his son to an exclusive school for boys. He hoped the harsh discipline would set him on the path to righteousness. It didn't," Elias Garfield assured them. "Only a few months into his first term, Edward lured one of the maidservants into the woods behind the school and ravished her. Once he finished, he sliced her belly open with a knife no one knew he had. The victim's tortured screams roused the porter, but, alas, too late to save her. By the time they found the poor creature, Edward had choked the breath from her, and her innards were spilling from her body, the ground soaked with her blood."

"Dear God," Daniel exclaimed, but Jason remained silent. "Was that how he came to be here?"

Dr. Garfield shook his head. "The identity of the culprit was hushed up by the school governors. They couldn't allow the parents of their students to believe that such a thing could happen on their watch. They blamed a halfwit from a nearby village and the poor man went to his death never knowing what it was he was meant to have done. Edward Marsh was taken out of school, and a tutor was engaged not only to teach him but to beat the violence out of him."

"I can only assume the situation grew worse," Jason said, his mouth set in a grim line. He was a firm believer that violence begot violence, even if it was used to teach a lesson or frighten the perpetrator into considering the consequences of his actions.

"A few months after returning from school, Edward Marsh murdered the housekeeper's three-year-old granddaughter. They found her remains laid out on the kitchen table, Marsh looking at her lovingly, his hands and clothes still covered with the child's blood, a knife clutched in his hand. He'd strangled her, then cut her open, much like the maidservant. That same week, he was delivered to Pine Grove by his father with the instruction that he was never to be set free."

Daniel swallowed hard at the mention of the little girl, trying desperately not to give in to his despair in front of Dr. Garfield. He didn't seem like a man given to compassion.

"Are there any female staff here?" Jason asked.

"We employ only male attendants, but there are women who come in to clean once a week. An inmate is taken outside for a walk or to one of the communal areas if he's not dangerous while the charwoman cleans his room, then brought back after she's finished, and the next inmate is taken out. We do our utmost to keep everyone safe."

"Has Edward Marsh ever shown any interest in the women?" Daniel asked.

"He's never been allowed to come near them."

"And the men?" Jason inquired.

"The male attendants are all selected for their size and well trained before they take up their positions."

"So how did Edward Marsh escape, Elias, and what's being done to apprehend him?"

"He strangled the attendant who brought him dinner on Friday evening, then changed into the man's uniform, tucked him up in bed, locked the cell, and walked out, bold as brass. It was dark outside, and the watchman opened the gates without looking very closely, assuming the unfortunate Mr. Loos was leaving for the day."

"I thought the attendants were trained before working with the patients," Jason said.

"The attendants normally work in pairs, but Mr. Loos' partner was taken ill earlier in the day and sent home. Mr. Loos was on his own since there was no one available to take Mr. Pike's place. He should never have turned his back to the inmate, but Edward Marsh had never laid a finger on anyone since the day he was brought to Pine Grove. There was no reason to think he would suddenly attack the man who'd looked after him for months."

"Sounds like he didn't need much of a reason," Daniel said. "The man is mad and clearly more cunning than you ever gave him credit for."

Dr. Garfield nodded. "I make no excuses, Inspector Haze. Edward Marsh took advantage of an oversight and succeeded where another man might have failed. I alerted the police as soon as I was informed of the escape and have given them all the information they might need to apprehend Mr. Marsh and bring him back to us, including the name of his father."

"Which is?" Jason demanded. "I need this information, Elias."

Dr. Garfield nodded. "All right. I suppose it won't do any harm to tell you. Jack's father is the Earl of Leyton."

"Where would Edward Marsh go, in your opinion?" Jason asked.

"I doubt he'd go home, although if I were Marsh's father, I'd be soiling my breeches right about now," Elias Garfield replied. "Most likely he found a hiding place to wait out the manhunt that was sure to follow his escape. Every constable in London is on the lookout for Marsh," Elias Garfield said. "I met with Commissioner

Hawkins in person to impress on him the remorseless nature of the man."

"Might Edward Marsh have strangled a woman in St. John's Wood on Saturday morning?" Daniel asked, his voice hoarse with fear.

"Edward Marsh is capable of anything. In my conversations with him, he relished telling me of his crimes, lovingly reliving every detail. The memory of fear and pain he had caused never failed to arouse him sexually. After our sessions, the attendants would tie his hands behind his back to prevent him from pleasuring himself," Elias Garfield informed them with grim satisfaction. "However, I highly doubt that Marsh murdered your victim."

"Why?" Jason asked.

"Edward Marsh was admitted to Pine Grove as a fifteen-year-old boy, delivered to us straight from the family's ancestral pile in Bury St. Edmunds, Suffolk. His parents wanted to put considerable distance between their home and the institution where their son would spend the rest of his days. Marsh is not familiar with London, nor did he have any money on him when he left, since the attendants don't carry anything on their person while on duty. I can't see that Marsh would have found his way to St. John's Wood or known of a suitable place to corner his prey during the day. His immediate concerns would be food, shelter, and anonymity."

"He was resourceful enough to find a means of escape," Jason pointed out. "I can't imagine that he would find it too difficult to avail himself of the basic necessities."

Elias Garfield inclined his head in agreement. "No, he wouldn't. Not if he was willing to use force."

"Elias, did Marsh ever talk about what he would do if he ever left this place? Did he fantasize about revenge?" Jason asked.

"We never talked about that, since there was little chance of him ever going free."

"And you're certain he wouldn't go home?" Daniel asked.

"I would dearly love to tell you that I can predict what Edward Marsh would or wouldn't do, but I cannot, Inspector. To get into the head of such a monster, one has to be a monster, and I would like to think that I have managed to retain some shred of humanity."

"Why now, Elias?" Jason asked.

"Why now what?" Dr. Garfield asked, clearly confused by the question.

"Why did he mount an escape now? He's been here for the past eight years. Had he ever attempted to escape before?"

"To be frank, I think he was biding his time."

"To what end?"

"Edward Marsh was kept in a private cell that remained locked at all times, but he wasn't permanently restrained. There was no need. If he had been planning an escape, he'd realize that he'd have one chance, and if he failed, his situation would alter. He would no longer remain unfettered, nor would he be permitted to walk in the grounds or spend time with other inmates. He waited for the perfect opportunity, and that opportunity presented itself when Mr. Loos joined our staff a few months ago."

"What was so special about Mr. Loos?" Daniel asked.

"For one, he is of a similar build and coloring to Edward Marsh. I never paid attention to the similarities between the two men until I had a reason to," Elias Garfield admitted ruefully. "Also, I think Edward worked hard to win Mr. Loos' trust."

"By doing what?" Jason asked.

"By talking to him when they walked in the garden, asking after his family, and speaking of missing his own, perhaps allowing Mr. Loos to see his loneliness and distress, emotions he didn't feel but knew how to mimic. Mr. Loos was a sensitive young man. Perhaps he was taken in by Edward's act enough to let his guard down. And he paid for his oversight with his life."

"Was Mr. Loos married?" Jason asked. "Might Edward Marsh have gone to his home?"

"Mr. Loos rented a room in a boarding house. The proprietor has been alerted, and so have the police. As far as we know, Edward Marsh has not gone near Mr. Loos' lodgings. Men hold little appeal for him."

"Do you have a photograph of Edward Marsh?"

Dr. Garfield nodded. He pushed to his feet and walked over to a cabinet from which he extracted a thick file. He pulled out a photograph of a young man and slid it across the desk. The photograph had been taken years ago, probably around the time Edward Marsh was admitted to Pine Grove. He had soft dark eyes that looked imploringly into the camera, neatly brushed dark hair, and a sensitive, almost feminine face that did not in any way reflect the murderous urges within.

"Like the serpent in the garden of Eden," Dr. Garfield said with wary disgust. "All beauty and charm on the outside, but pure evil rippling beneath the skin."

"Has Edward Marsh changed much since this photograph was taken?" Jason asked.

"He performed a series of daily exercises in his cell," Elias Garfield said. "Claimed that physical exertion was good for the body and soul. Marsh is more muscular and wears a beard and moustache. We didn't trust him with a razor, for obvious reasons, but he was given a haircut and a shave once a month. He was kept fettered during those times."

"Do you not think this photograph should be given to the press? The public has a right to know that a dangerous criminal walks among them," Daniel said, watching Dr. Garfield.

Something about the man put Daniel off. Perhaps it was the fact that his attitude was too cavalier for a man who'd allowed a criminally insane inmate to escape and murder one of his staff in the process, but then again, Dr. Garfield was American. Daniel had come to understand from speaking with Jason that there was a difference between the British and Americans not only in the general attitude toward common events but also in the handling of dangerous situations. Dr. Garfield had been a soldier with the Union Army. Perhaps he felt the need to exhibit a certain bravado, especially before a man he'd known years before and seemed to wish to impress and connect with socially.

Elias Garfield appeared irritated by Daniel's remark and didn't bother to hide it, but his annoyance wasn't directed at Daniel when he spoke.

"The governors pride themselves on discretion and owe their support to the families of their patients, namely the people who line their pockets, not to the public as a whole. They will not reveal either the name or the likeness of the inmate to the press voluntarily, since that would violate the promise of confidentiality. The photograph has been shown to the policemen searching for Marsh. That's as far as the governors are willing to go to facilitate his capture. If the information is released to the press by Scotland Yard, then the governors will not be held liable."

"That's not enough," Jason snapped, not bothering to hide his anger.

"No, it isn't, but it's not my decision to make, not if I hope to retain my position," Dr. Garfield replied.

"Do you not fear for your own safety, Dr. Garfield?" Daniel asked, not bothering to hide his dislike for the man.

"I do, which is why I won't be leaving this building until Edward Marsh is apprehended and brought back in chains. Right now, this building is the safest place in London, at least for the next few days."

"Do you believe he will be apprehended?" Daniel asked, surprised by the man's seeming confidence that Edward Marsh would be captured within the coming days.

"Edward Marsh never bothered to deny his crimes, nor did he try to get away before he could be connected to the atrocity. He enjoyed looking at his victims, relishing his handiwork. I don't believe he has the mental faculties to cover his tracks. As soon as he kills again, they will get him."

"He's managed to elude you," Jason said tartly. "And I don't see you making any real effort to find him before he kills again."

Dr. Garfield's smug look slid off his face, his resentment of Jason showing for the first time. "I was never as high-minded as you, Jason, but then again, I didn't have a family like yours to fall back on. Had to make my own way in the world, since my parents couldn't afford to pay for my education. I worked hard to put myself through both university and medical school. I don't think I did too badly for myself in the end. Captured or not, the world will soon forget about Edward Marsh, and I will go on as before, enjoying a comfortable existence at the expense of the feeble-minded and the insane. Now, if you don't mind, I have work to do."

Thus dismissed, Daniel and Jason left the building and headed toward the waiting hansom.

"Where to, gentlemen?" the cabbie asked as he climbed onto his perch behind the conveyance, his good humor still very much in evidence.

"Whitechapel," Jason replied.

"Why are we going to Whitechapel? Do you think Edward Marsh is there, hiding in plain sight?" Daniel asked as he settled next to Jason.

"I think we need to focus our energies on learning more about Rebecca," Jason said. "What are the chances of an inmate escaped from an asylum in Lambeth coming across Rebecca in St. John's Wood?"

"Probably about the same as an American of your acquaintance, whom you haven't seen since some obscure battle in 1863, being in charge of said asylum," Daniel replied.

"Touché," Jason replied with a humorless grin. "However, there's nothing we can do about an escaped inmate. That's the bailiwick of the Metropolitan Police. All we can hope for is that they apprehend Marsh before he claims another innocent victim. In any case, I really don't think he's our man."

"Based on what?" Daniel demanded, his mind cruelly forcing the image of the disemboweled child before his eyes.

"The two times Edward Marsh killed for pleasure, he disemboweled his victims and remained at the crime scene to enjoy his work. I'm inclined to think that individuals of a sadistic nature tend to return to a particular fantasy in order to fulfill their desires."

"That's quite a leap of reasoning, Jason," Daniel said. "If a man is capable of murder, I doubt he cares about the particulars. He'll do it again and again to feed his appetite for death."

"Perhaps," Jason said, but he didn't sound convinced. "In the meantime, we need to discover something of Rebecca's past associations. I still think that she was targeted rather than selected at random, which would rule out Edward Marsh. Since we now know that her father was a fence who was murdered over stolen goods in Seven Dials, there's a very good possibility that he was known to the local police. That would be Division H in Whitechapel, if I'm not mistaken. And if they've never heard of Edgar Levinson, we'll move on to Division F in Covent Garden. Those are the two most likely station houses to have had dealings with Levinson. Anything we can learn about Rebecca's life before her father was murdered might offer up a clue."

"That's a good suggestion, Jason," Daniel said with some relief. He'd been utterly unable to come up with a plan of action, not even so much as a first step, and was more than happy to follow Jason's lead, since he had several viable ideas.

"It's only a good suggestion if it works."

Since they had some time before they'd arrive in Whitechapel, Daniel thought he'd ask Jason about Elias Garfield. "You don't much like Dr. Garfield, do you?" he inquired.

"Was it that obvious?" Jason asked, his brows lifting in surprise. "I thought I was civil to the man."

"Civil, yes. Pleased to see him, no."

Daniel had thought Dr. Garfield's manner toward Jason abrasive but refrained from saying so. Jason might have taken the man's comments as a sign of camaraderie rather than overfamiliarity if their relationship had been a friendly one.

"Dr. Garfield is an excellent surgeon who saved many lives during the war, but I suspect his sudden relocation to London was not entirely of a voluntary nature."

"How do you mean?" Daniel asked.

"It's possible that Elias Garfield fled the United States after the war to avoid a court martial."

"For what crime? You just said he saved multiple lives."

"I never saw it for myself, but there were persistent rumors that Dr. Garfield took anything of value off the dead before they were consigned to mass graves. When confronted by the friends of the deceased, he claimed that he had intended to forward their effects to their loved ones, but as far as anyone knew, he had never actually followed through on that promise."

"And someone made a formal complaint?" Daniel asked.

"I heard something to that effect after I was freed from the Confederate prison, but to be honest, I was in no condition to care. Given that Dr. Garfield is here in London and made it clear that he had no wish to explain the circumstances of his posting, I think it's feasible."

"You obviously believe him capable of what he was accused of," Daniel pointed out.

"There was always something mercenary in his nature," Jason replied. "For some men, money is the greatest motivator."

"And do you suspect that he's somehow abusing his position as director of the Pine Grove Asylum for personal gain?"

"I see no reason to make unsubstantiated accusations, but I hope our dealings with him are at an end."

Daniel didn't pursue the subject any further, but he was surprised by Jason's reaction to Dr. Garfield. Jason was the most open-minded, unbiased man Daniel had ever met, so much so that he often unwittingly made Daniel feel ashamed of his own provincial small-mindedness. Jason would never condemn anyone without factual evidence, but if he suspected Dr. Garfield of wrongdoing, it was probably warranted. Likewise, if Jason didn't believe Edward Marsh was their prime suspect, Daniel was willing to go along with his theory until facts either bore it out or proved them wrong.

Daniel forgot all about Dr. Garfield as the hansom drew to a stop, its path blocked by an awkwardly positioned dray wagon. Several people screamed obscenities at the driver for blocking the road, their insults as creative as they were vicious. Jason appeared too preoccupied with his own thoughts to pay much attention to the particulars, but Daniel thrummed with annoyance, and if he were honest, shame. London was a city of extremes, the stately mansions and shady gardens of the rich sharply juxtaposed by filthy slums and people who lived in conditions better suited to vermin.

Ragged women with pinched faces hurried down the street, empty baskets slung over their arms as they hunted for supplies they could afford on the meager wages of their husbands. Barefoot children dressed in nothing but threadbare shirts and breeches despite the cold weather darted between passersby and wagons, intent on their own survival as they begged for handouts or attempted to pick the pockets of those who looked like they might have a few coins in their purses. Whitechapel wasn't the worst of London, but it came damnably close.

Daniel was relieved when the hansom finally lurched forward and eventually deposited them before the redbrick building that housed Division H and the overworked and underpaid policemen who valiantly fought against a tidal wave of criminality every minute they spent on duty. It was only a few paces to the door, but Daniel was jostled by several men who pushed past him, their unwashed faces tense with grim determination, while Jason blocked a teenage boy's hand as the urchin tried to reach into his pocket. Jason's expression was one of pity rather than anger, and he drew out a sixpence and tossed it to the boy before making his way into the building.

Chapter 13

Division H proved to be a dead end, but the desk sergeant at Division F was an amiable fellow who seemed eager to help, especially when he heard the particulars of the case.

"I've not been here long, gentlemen. Transferred from Division M when my missus and I moved from Southwark, but I reckon I know of someone who might be able to assist you in your inquiries. Give me a moment, if you will."

The sergeant disappeared into the warren of rooms in the back and returned a few minutes later followed by a thickset man who appeared to be in his late forties.

"Inspector Warren," the man said, extending his hand, first to Jason and then to Daniel. "Been at this station since it first opened its doors. How can I help?"

Inspector Warren reminded Daniel of a walrus he'd seen in Charlotte's picture book. His voluminous moustache completely obscured his upper lip, and his wide nose and fleshy cheeks were covered with a spiderweb of broken capillaries. Daniel thought the man might have a fondness for strong drink. The inspector's dark eyes were hooded and shadowed by shaggy eyebrows, his ginger hair liberally silvered. His handshake was firm, his gaze sympathetic and, more important, intelligent.

"Step into my office, gentlemen," he invited. "I don't care to converse in the corridor."

Inspector Warren's office was small and dim, the dark wood furniture and green-painted walls giving it an almost forest-like appearance, except that this forest was shrouded in deep shadow since the window faced the side of the adjacent building and didn't allow in much daylight. Inspector Warren sat behind his desk and invited them to sit, but there was only one other chair, so Jason volunteered to stand. On any other day, Daniel would have argued with him, but despite getting a modicum of sleep and forcing himself to eat his breakfast, he felt as if his legs might give way at any moment.

"Now let me see," Warren said after Jason had explained the reason for their visit. "The name Edgar Levinson does ring a bell, but I need a moment to recollect the details."

"Do you not have a file?" Jason asked.

"Not after seven years. And I wager it was archived or destroyed once the filthy bugger breathed his last. Hold on a moment."

He left the office and returned a few moments later with a fresh-faced young man. The constable looked no older than twenty and was as tall and thin as a reed. A strong gust of wind would probably blow him over, but his inquisitive gaze put Daniel in mind of someone who was quick-witted and not easily misled, despite first impressions.

"This is Constable Harkness. Not the most fearsome fellow, but he has a memory like an elephant," Warren said with a deep laugh.

Constable Harkness did not appear to take offense at being described thus and turned his attention to the two visitors. "I recall Edgar Levinson," he confirmed. "Had the pleasure of arresting him twice in my first year with the service."

Daniel quickly reassessed the young man's age. He had to be older than he appeared if he had been with the service seven years ago. Some of the new recruits were very young, but not as young as thirteen.

"What do you remember about him, Constable Harkness?" Jason asked, smiling at the young man with obvious approval.

"He was composed. And polite," Constable Harkness added. "No foul language or threats of death and dismemberment like most others of his ilk spew when collared. It was all 'Thank you, Constable' and 'If you would be so kind, Constable,'" he said, smiling at the memory. "He was quite dapper in his dress and spoke like a gentleman. A real posh cove," Constable Harkness concluded with a satisfied nod.

"What did you arrest him for?" Jason asked.

"Possession of stolen property, sir, but we had to let him go both times."

"Why was that?"

Constable Harkness's already pink cheeks reddened. "Not enough evidence," he said, clearly still embarrassed by the police's failure to make the charge stick. "We got a tip-off from a trusted source that Mr. Levinson was in possession of valuable items that had been recently nicked, but when we got there, the pieces were nowhere to be found. His shop was always above board."

"What did he sell?" Jason inquired.

"Oh, buttons and bobbins, and other sewing notions. Couldn't conceal stolen jewels among the buttons even if he tried."

"Do you remember the incident that resulted in his death?"

Constable Harkness nodded eagerly. "Some men came into the shop at closing time. It was a winter's day, so it was dark out with few people about on account of the bitter cold. They were after a silver snuffbox. Mr. Levinson swore he'd never seen such a thing, so they called him a liar and knifed him in the stomach."

"How do you know that's what happened?" Jason asked.

"Found his daughter when we got there," Constable Harkness said. "She was frozen with terror, the poor girl, and she was clutching a snuffbox to her breast. That's the bit of silver that got him killed. I reckon the men who were after it thought there was something valuable inside."

"Was there?" Jason asked.

"No. There was nothing inside. I checked."

"What happened to the snuffbox?"

"I gave it back to the girl. It was hers by rights," Constable Harkness said.

"Did you ever find out who killed Edgar Levinson?" Daniel asked.

"To be perfectly frank, gentlemen," Inspector Warren interjected, "we don't often bother with the likes of Edgar Levinson. He got what was coming to him, and not a man here would tell you different. Why, if we investigated every dispute between common thieves, we'd have no time to devote to honest policework. We're short on manpower at the best of times, but now with this lunatic on the loose, we're here on our own, aren't we lad?" he asked, directing the question to Constable Harkness.

"Nearly everyone is out looking for him," Constable Harkness complained, his eyes glittering with excitement. "By order of Commissioner Hawkins."

"Like searching for a needle in a haystack, if you ask me," Inspector Warren grumbled. "Half the men in this part of London could be your escaped inmate. Dark hair, dark eyes, straggly beard, and wearing a dark coat. Can't throw a stone 'round these parts without hitting someone as looks just like it."

"Do you suggest the police simply twiddle their thumbs until this lunatic kills again?" Daniel demanded, the memory of Rebecca's limp body draped across the grave invading his thoughts and causing an unbearable tightness in his chest.

"I do not, Inspector Haze, but there's no sense running around like chickens without heads when we don't even know the fellow's still abroad. Might have gone back to Suffolk or got on a ship bound for foreign parts. Complete waste of manpower is what this is, but then again, the powers-that-be are not the ones out on the streets, risking their lives every single day in the hope of making a difference to folk that see us as their mortal enemy," Inspector Warren said, clearly wounded by Daniel's criticism.

Ignoring Inspector Warren's outburst, Daniel turned to Constable Harkness, who was keeping his opinion on the escaped inmate to himself but would have clearly preferred to be out searching for him rather than manning the nearly empty police station.

"Did you know Edgar Levinson's daughter well, Constable?" Daniel asked.

"A fetching young thing she was," Constable Harkness replied, brightening at the mention of her. "Minded the shop most days."

"What became of her after her father died?" Jason asked.

"Didn't see her again after the night of the murder," Constable Harkness said.

"I expect she wound up in some knocking shop," Inspector Warren said with a self-satisfied nod. "Not qualified to do anything other than whoring."

Jason winced at the man's crude assessment but said nothing, since Rebecca Grainger's name had not come up in conversation thus far and Jason clearly had no intention of discussing the case with Inspector Warren, who hadn't even bothered to inquire why they were asking after Edgar Levinson after all this time.

"Thank you for your time, gentlemen," Jason said, and replaced his top hat on his head, ready to leave.

"Ask Tatty Betty," Constable Harkness blurted out.

"And who is Tatty Betty?" Jason asked, turning back to the young constable.

"She's that old crone that hangs about the Covent Garden market, begging for scraps. Been there for donkeys. Acts the daft sow but knows everything that goes on. Keeps her ear to the ground."

"She'll be at the southeast corner after three," Inspector Warren added grudgingly. "Likes to get to the market just as the vendors start packing up for the day. That's when pickings are best."

"I'm afraid we can't wait that long," Jason replied. "Where does she go in the morning?"

Inspector Warren looked perplexed, but Constable Harkness wasn't similarly afflicted.

"She'll be at the deadhouse," he said, pointing vaguely toward the window. "Goes there every blessed day."

"Why?" Jason and Daniel asked in unison. The deadhouse was not a place anyone would visit willingly, not even a beggar woman.

"The attendant, Mr. Pinter, he's a kind soul. He feels sorry for Betty, so he gives her things," Constable Harkness explained.

"What sort of things?" Daniel asked.

"If a body's not been claimed and is for the pauper's grave, then Mr. Pinter sees nothing wrong with relieving it of its worldly goods."

"So, Mr. Pinter strips the corpses and gives whatever he doesn't want to this Tatty Betty?" Jason clarified.

"That's right. Doesn't cost him anything, but to Betty it's manna from heaven," Constable Harkness said.

"What does she do with her ill-gotten gains?" Daniel asked.

To him, robbing the dead was no different from stealing from the living. Daniel hadn't given much thought to the matter before Sarah's death, but once he'd learned just how many graves were desecrated, not only for the material goods buried with the deceased but for the fresh corpses that were sold for a hefty sum to the medical schools, he'd adopted a grim view of the crime. It was odd that the subject had come up twice in one day.

"Sells her bounty to the rag and bone man. I'd say it was Mr. Pinter's generosity that's kept her alive these last few years," Constable Harkness replied.

"And what does the generous Mr. Pinter get in return?" Jason asked, watching the constable intently as he colored to the roots of his hair.

"A man gets lonely when he's not married, especially when he's stuck minding corpses all day."

"Thank you, Constable. If you'd just point us in the direction of the deadhouse, we'll leave you to your duties," Jason said.

"'Course. I'm headed that way anyhow. I'll show you the way."

Chapter 14

Jason and Daniel followed Constable Harkness to a squat building behind St. Giles-in-the-Fields Church. The ancient church had been rebuilt several times since its inception and was a shining example of modern architecture. But the deadhouse dated back to its earlier, darker days, the low, forbidding structure windowless and built of gray stone. Accustomed as he was to the presence of the deceased, Jason braced himself for the horror they would no doubt encounter within. The recently bereaved often kept their dead at home long enough for decomposition to set in. Once their loved ones lost their value to the resurrection men, they were ready to be buried, their peaceful rest assured. The individuals who were cognizant of the health risks associated with displaying a decaying corpse indoors with the windows closed paid the attendant of the dead house to guard their loved ones until the burial.

In an area surrounding St. Giles, the dead were most likely the dregs of London society: men, women, and children no one cared about, or if they did, they couldn't afford to bury. The bodies of the deceased were collected where they fell and carted off to the nearest deadhouse or brought from the slums, where they had died either of illness or starvation or had been murdered for their meager possessions. The deadhouse would be a cesspit of suppuration, its contents best avoided.

"Cover your nose and mouth when we go in," Jason advised Daniel as they approached.

Daniel pulled out his handkerchief and held it to his face in readiness. When Jason pushed open the damp-swollen door, the stench was eyewatering, the rectangular space occupied by at least a dozen corpses in various stages of decomposition. An eerie blue glow hovered about the bodies, its source the flame-topped metal tubes that protruded from the abdominal cavities of the deceased and burned like candles. One of the more gruesome duties of deadhouse attendants was to release the gasses that accumulated within the bowels and pancreas of the deceased to prevent the corpses from exploding once the pressure could no longer be contained by the decaying organs. Jason had witnessed the process many times but had never had to perform it himself, since the bodies he worked on were mostly fresh.

A man who stood with his back to the door turned abruptly and demanded, "Can I help you?"

"Mr. Pinter?" Jason asked, taking an involuntary step back toward the open door.

"I am."

"Can we have a word?" Jason asked, his voice muffled by the handkerchief he was pressing hard enough against his nose and mouth to suffocate him if he didn't relieve the pressure within the next few minutes.

"Of course."

Jason and Daniel hurried outside and stopped far enough from the deadhouse to be able to breathe freely, but despite the fresh air, Jason could still smell the noxious odor that would probably remain trapped in his nostrils and cling to his clothes for the remainder of the day.

Mr. Pinter, when he finally emerged and yanked down the kerchief tied about the lower half of his face, was of middling height and build, with sparse brown hair, dark eyes, and a short, bushy beard. His clothes were protected by a leather apron, and he wore a pair of leather gloves. He pulled off the gloves and untied the apron, revealing a shabby suit underneath.

"Forgive me. I was just releasing the—" He didn't finish the sentence, clearly deciding they didn't need to know what he'd been doing if they didn't already.

Jason's gaze slid toward the deadhouse, where a dark shadow hovered inside, keeping well out of sight but still within hearing distance of the conversation.

"Mr. Pinter, I'm Dr. Redmond, and this is Inspector Haze of Scotland Yard. We were hoping you might know where to find Betty. We were told she sometimes comes to see you."

"What do you want with Betty?" Mr. Pinter asked suspiciously.

"Only to ask her a few questions about someone she might have known many years ago," Jason said, his explanation deliberately vague.

He kept his eye on the shadow beyond the door and wondered if there was a back door Betty could escape through. Deciding not to risk it, Jason extracted two shillings from his pocket and held the coins between his gloved fingers, a small price to pay if Tatty Betty was able to tell them anything of use.

"I'd be happy to compensate her for her time," he said, raising his voice so that the person within could hear him clearly.

Betty erupted from the deadhouse, her filthy gown and hair reeking of death. "'Ow can I 'elp ye, Doctor?" she asked, her gaze fixed on the coins in Jason's hand.

At first glance, Jason thought Betty to be around seventy. Her hair was mostly gray with a few remaining streaks of dirty brown. Her teeth, of which there were few, were tobacco stained. And her skin was sallow and sagging, the flesh below her chin hanging loosely. On closer inspection, however, Jason realized that Betty was probably no more than forty. Decades of hard living had robbed her of her vitality, and the endless fear that came with living hand-to-mouth had done the rest.

"Do you remember a man called Edgar Levinson?" Jason asked. He wished he could reach for his freshly laundered handkerchief again, since the smell that came off Betty's person was nearly as bad as the stench inside the deadhouse, but he didn't wish to offend the poor woman.

Betty nodded, her surprise at being asked about someone dead these seven years evident. "What 'bout 'im?"

"He had a daughter," Jason said, his gaze never leaving Betty's weathered face.

She nodded. "Rebecca."

"What can you tell me about her?"

"Why ye askin'?" Betty asked, her gaze once again straying to the coins Jason still held.

"Rebecca Grainger, as she was calling herself, was murdered yesterday. And the small child who was in her charge was taken," Jason explained.

"Murdered? 'Ow?" Betty demanded.

"She was strangled."

Moisture gathered in Betty's pale eyes. "She were a good girl, Becky. Sweet and trustin'. 'E loved 'er, Edgar did. She were torn to bits when 'e died."

"What happened to her after her father died, Betty?" Jason pressed.

"Well, seeing as 'ow ye know it were 'er as were murdered, why ye askin'?"

Rather than telling them what she knew, Betty was risking losing the money that Jason had promised her by questioning their motives. She must have felt some regard for Rebecca all those years ago, Jason concluded as he studied the stubborn set of Betty's chin.

"We are trying to establish if there was anyone who might have held a grudge against her. She gave false references when she secured her position, and we don't know of any friends that we can ask," Jason explained patiently. He didn't mention Abel Grainger since he was more interested in the years following Edgar Levinson's death.

"She were a good girl," Betty repeated under her breath.

"Do you want this or not?" Jason asked, his patience finally ebbing away.

Betty nodded, greed winning over loyalty as it so often did. "She were frightened, so she left. But she didn't leave empty-handed."

"We were told nothing of value was found in her father's shop save a silver snuffbox that was still in Rebecca's hand when Edgar Levinson's remains were discovered by the police," Jason said.

"Oh, Edgar, 'e were too clever to get caught red-handed, even in death," Betty said, smiling for the first time and revealing several gaps where teeth should have been. "'E 'id the stolen goods in plain sight, where no daft copper would even think to look."

"And where was that?"

"'Neath 'is daughter's crinolines, for one," Betty replied with an amused chuckle. "Edgar didn't deal in large items. No family silver tea set ever passed through 'is shop. 'Tis the small bits as 'ave the greatest value, 'e said. Rings, watches, earbobs, jeweled snuffboxes, and silver cigarette cases; that's where 'e made 'is coin."

Betty cackled with glee as she recalled something amusing. "Why, I remember this one time, the bluebottles came knockin', and Edgar 'ad a diamond tiara in 'is possession. And a thing of beauty it were too. Never seen the like," she said dreamily. "The way those diamonds sparkled in the sunlight."

"Bluebottles?" Jason asked. He'd heard of a blowfly called by that name but was certain Betty wasn't speaking of insects. There were so many colloquial terms he had yet to learn, especially when dealing with the working classes, if Betty could be referred to as such.

Betty gave him a look that spoke volumes, but Daniel answered in her stead. "It's a derogatory term for a policeman." He turned back to Betty, studying her with renewed interest. "And why did Edgar Levinson trust the likes of you with his secrets?"

Betty's chuckle died in her throat. "Things was a bit different for me then," she replied. "I weren't always the sad wretch ye see before ye. I'm a victim of reduced circumstances, ye might say," she added bitterly, and Jason wondered what had happened to the woman to bring her so low.

"Please, go on," he said. "Where did Edgar hide the tiara?"

"Well, Edgar, 'e looked at Becky meaningful like, and she snatched the thing from its 'iding place in a cabinet and put it 'round 'er thigh, like a garter." Betty cackled with delight. "They turned the place upside down, those bungling clodhoppers. And all the while, Becky just sat there, 'er 'ands in 'er lap, all prim and proper like, the tiara right there beneath 'er skirts. I reckon she saved Edgar's life that day, the clever girl. 'E would 'ave swung for sure 'ad they found it. Belonged to a duchess or some such exalted personage," Betty said. "Fancy owning something like that when some people can't afford a heel of stale bread or a warm fire on a cold night." She sighed heavily, her sadness draped like a mantle over her stooped shoulders.

"Did Edgar Levinson have any friends?" Jason asked. "Or family?"

"Nah. Associates and competitors, but not friends. Edgar's family turned 'im out years before. Wouldn't honor their ways, or so 'e said. I reckon 'e 'ad a 'ankering for sommat a bit more exciting. And 'e found it when 'e married that fancy ladybird. Nellie. Ye wouldn't expect a proper little thing like that to fall for a fraudster like Edgar, but 'e were a good-looking devil in those days. Always turned out as fine as any gentleman of fashion. They was a lovely couple to be'old, devoted, until poor Nellie breathed 'er last. Died in childbed," Betty added. "The babe with 'er. Edgar were a broken man, but 'e 'ad Becky to look after, and 'e did. 'E were a good father to that girl."

"So, who would Rebecca have turned to when her father died?" Jason asked, hoping that Betty would continue to reminisce long enough to offer up a clue. "Might she have asked Leon Stanley for help?"

"Leon Stanley?" Betty asked, gaping at Jason. "Now there's a name I ain't 'eard in years."

"Did you know him?" Daniel asked.

"I did. 'E were an associate of Edgar's for a time, but then 'e left not long after Edgar were murdered. Went abroad, or so I 'eard."

"Rebecca must have been close with someone," Jason said, his exasperation mounting. "A doting father is all well and good, but surely she had at least one friend."

"Sally Malvers," Betty said, giving up the name with obvious reluctance. "They were thick as thieves for a time."

"Did you ever see Rebecca after her father died?" Daniel asked.

Betty shook her head. "I 'ad me own problems, Inspector. I 'ad no time for anyone else's."

"Where can we find Sally Malvers?" Jason asked as he handed over the coins.

Betty snatched them and pushed them deep into the soiled bodice of her gown. Jason was happy enough to help out this desperate woman and could certainly afford to, but he had hoped for something a little more concrete.

"Ye'll find Sally on 'er back or up against the wall most nights," Betty replied nastily. "Last I 'eard, she were working Covent Garden."

If Sally Malvers walked the streets of Covent Garden, she'd likely be easy enough to track down, but women of her profession didn't make an appearance until much later in the day since their best customers were the gentlemen just leaving the theater in Drury Lane or carousing with their friends after a lavish supper.

"I do 'ope ye find whoever done this awful thing to Becky," Betty said. "She deserved better. We all do," she added sadly, and shuffled off.

Chapter 15

It took several hours of asking after Sally Malvers to obtain the location of a tumbledown building in Seven Dials. It seemed that no one had seen Sally in about a fortnight, not a good omen when searching for a woman who made a living from selling her body, Jason concluded as they trudged down the crowded street. The life of a prostitute was brutal, frightening, and often short, since it became more difficult to survive once the girls lost their looks and vitality and their customers went on to seek younger, prettier prey to satisfy their urges. There had been plenty of prostitutes in New York, but not in such numbers, and not as young.

Jason had seen girls as young as eight or nine offering men old enough to be their fathers and grandfathers sexual favors, their dead-eyed stare telling a story all its own. It was heart-wrenching and infuriating, more so because the government that spent millions on armaments, trumped-up political conflicts, and colonial expansion saw no good reason to care for its most vulnerable citizens at home and offer them the education and training needed to find employment that would pay them enough not only to survive but to thrive. Jason could easily afford to give every girl he saw a coin, but a bed for one night or a hot meal wasn't enough to make a difference, nor would his charity alter the general view that fallen women were responsible for their downfall and therefore not worthy of help or redemption. How was a child of eight responsible for her fate when the only thing that stood between her and starvation was the stiff phallus of a depraved man?

Jason was jolted out of his angry thoughts by Daniel, who glanced up at the broken windows and sagging doorway before trying the door. The address had been provided by a young woman in a tawdry yellow gown who'd claimed to be mates with Sally, but like the other women they had asked, she hadn't seen Sally since St. Valentine's Day and hadn't bothered to inquire as to her whereabouts, preoccupied as she was with her own problems.

"Do you think Sally's still alive?" Daniel asked, his gaze full of doubt.

"I hope so."

The door was slightly warped, the black paint peeling to reveal the scarred wood beneath. A darkened stairway led to the upper floor, and the narrow corridor smelled of urine and trash. Two doors flanked the corridor, presumably entrances to separate apartments. Neither was locked or even properly closed. Jason stopped dead when he heard a low moan coming from a room at the back of the apartment on the right. He recognized that timbre. It was the sound of a woman in great pain. He walked through the front room, which was empty but showed signs of multiple occupants in the form of sleeping pallets, a table covered with chipped, unwashed crockery, and a chamber pot that hadn't been emptied. He knocked on a closed door, then pushed it open without waiting for a response.

The back room looked much like the one he'd just passed through but without a table and chairs or remnants of past meals. The single window was covered with a curtain that must have been scarlet at some point but was now the color of dried blood and threadbare enough to let in sufficient light to see by. A young woman fitting the description of Sally her yellow-gowned friend had provided lay curled into a ball on the far side of the room. Her damp fair hair was plastered to her forehead, and her cheeks were flushed and moist with perspiration. She wore a linen shift, and her dirty feet were bare. There were three more pallets in the room, two of them empty, one occupied by a girl who managed to sleep in the face of her roommate's pain. Jason heard Daniel's sharp intake of breath, but all his attention was on the suffering woman.

"Sally Malvers?" Jason asked softly.

"Sorry, gents," the woman replied through gritted teeth. "I'm afraid I can't accommodate ye today, but if ye kick Janice awake, she'll be happy to see to yer needs."

Jason crouched next to Sally, whose skin seemed stretched right over her narrow skull, and her thin arms were wrapped tightly over a heaving belly. Her bony knees were drawn up in an effort to contain her pain, but she was clearly in agony.

"How long have you been in labor, Sally?" Jason asked.

Sally looked up at him, her gaze dull. "Days," she muttered.

"I'm a doctor, and I'm going to deliver this baby."

"I can't pay ye," Sally moaned.

"I don't expect payment. Please, allow me to examine you."

Sally looked dubious, watching from beneath half-lowered lids as Jason removed his coat and hat and handed them to Daniel, then peeled off his leather gloves and tossed them into the upturned hat, but given her profession, she was realistic enough to realize that she had little to lose by allowing Jason to help her.

"Please, lie on your back, Sally," Jason said.

Sally rolled onto her back and allowed Jason to push her arms away from her belly and lay his hands on her stomach. He pressed down in an effort to feel the child within.

"It 'urts," Sally protested.

"I know. I will be gentle, I promise," Jason said as he eased the pressure.

He undid the onyx cufflinks and rolled up the sleeves of his shirt. Sally let out a low, desperate moan and drew up her legs again, an involuntary response to pain. Jason ignored the smell that emanated from her body as he sank to his knees on the soiled mattress. Sally likely hadn't eaten since yesterday, and her roommates hadn't been considerate enough to bring her water to wash. All the usual odors of the human body intermingled with the odors of impending childbirth, but Jason was accustomed to both.

He slid his hand beneath the chemise, and Sally's eyes flew open in shock. She screamed as he pushed his fingers deep inside her and into her cervix. Jason pulled out his hand before the next contraction seized Sally's womb and would injure his wrist as the contracting muscles clamped down on his bones. He had all the information he needed.

"Sally, you're fully dilated, but your baby is coming out feet first. I will need to guide it out."

"I don't care what ye do, just get it out of me," Sally moaned. "I can't bear this pain no more."

"I will work as quickly as I can," Jason replied.

He waited until the next contraction eased and slid his hand back inside, feeling for the feet. It took a few moments before he located a tiny heel and wrapped his fingers around the ankles, then he pulled the child's legs gently toward the opening but had to let go when the next contraction rolled over Sally. Jason took a deep breath and tried again. He had no trouble locating the feet this time and realized that they hadn't moved. Putting his fears for the child aside, Jason focused all his energy on maneuvering the baby through the birth canal. It took a few minutes since he had to stop every time Sally had a contraction, but eventually the baby's skinny legs and hips slid through the opening.

"We're nearly there, Sally," Jason said softly to a panting Sally. "I have to ease out the shoulders and then the head, and then it will all be over. When I tell you to, bear down."

Sally nodded but seemed to lose her ability to speak and had turned inward, all her attention on bringing her child into the world. Jason had intentionally not used any words that would mislead Sally about the outcome. The baby had not so much as twitched, and the rigid legs told their own story. Time seemed to stand still as Jason worked to ease the shoulders and head through the opening without doing damage to Sally. He didn't bring his medical bag and would have no means to sew Sally up should she require stitches.

"Daniel, I'll need something sharp to cut the cord," Jason said over his shoulder, and heard Daniel walk into the other room.

At last, the infant was free of its mother's body. Jason severed the cord with the filthy knife Daniel had found and held the child in his arms. It was a girl, and there was nothing he could do to save her. He couldn't be sure, but he thought she had passed long before he'd arrived. Wrapping the child in a towel he had found on the floor, Jason held it tenderly. "I'm very sorry, Sally, but your daughter is stillborn," he said, watching Sally's face for a reaction. What he saw was relief.

"Best thing for 'er," Sally said. "This 'ere is no life for a girl. The good Lord 'as spared 'er. Wish 'e'd spare me as well." The despair in Sally's voice was unmistakable. "I would dearly love to join 'er."

Jason ignored Sally's words. Her sentiments were coming from a place of grief and hopelessness. He couldn't promise Sally that life would get better or that her next baby would live, because there would always be another pregnancy for a woman in her profession. All he could do was care for her until he was sure she'd be all right on her own.

"Would you like to hold her?" Jason asked.

"No."

Jason wondered how Sally would dispose of the child's remains but didn't ask. Ordinarily, he would have offered to help, but he had to focus on the child that was hopefully still living, and he had already spent two hours he didn't have to assist Sally. He could feel Daniel's gaze boring into his back, urging him to ask Sally the questions that needed asking and get on their way. The day was quickly slipping away.

"Do you have any food?" Jason asked as he set the wrapped remains of the child on the floor beside the pallet, where Sally didn't have to face the sad bundle until she was ready to deal with it.

Sally shook her head.

"Daniel, would you mind?" Jason asked. "Something with meat and a jug of ale."

"Of course," Daniel replied, and left, heading to the nearest tavern while Jason went in search of water to wash his hands and help Sally tidy herself.

Chapter 16

Once Sally was cleaned up and resting comfortably, she turned her pale gaze on Jason.

"Why are ye 'ere, anyway?" she asked. "What did I do to deserve a posh cove like yerself attending on me in my 'our of need?"

"Sally, Inspector Haze and I are with the police. Rebecca Grainger was murdered yesterday, and we were hoping to speak to you about her. You might have known her as Rebecca Levinson," Jason added.

"I ain't seen 'er in years," Sally replied, her surprise at hearing Rebecca's name and what had befallen her evident. Her voice was hoarse.

"But you did know her?"

Sally nodded, and her eyes filled with tears. "She got away. Made a life for 'erself away from this dung 'eap."

"Where did she go, Sally?" Jason realized he couldn't ask too many questions. Sally was depleted and needed to rest, so he had to keep it brief.

Sally let out a deep sigh, as if releasing all the suffering of the past few days. "When 'er da died, she went with Malcolm."

"Malcolm who?"

"Malcolm Briggs. 'E were 'er sweet'eart."

"Where did they go?"

Sally shrugged. "No one knew where Malcolm lived."

"Why?" Jason asked.

"'Cause 'e were wanted by the rozzers, I s'pose."

"So how did she meet him?"

"Mr. Levinson fenced Malcolm's ream swag. Malcolm could 'ave taken 'is takings to a jerry'ouse, but Mr. Levinson could get 'im a better offer, and Malcolm dealt in real posh loot."

Jason wasn't familiar with the slang of the streets, but it wasn't difficult to deduce that Edgar Levinson had acted as a middleman and disposed of the items Malcolm Briggs had stolen.

"He was a common thief?" Jason asked, unexpectedly disappointed in Rebecca for taking up with a criminal.

"'E were *the* thief," Sally said. "Malcolm were a notorious cracksman in 'is day."

"So what happened to him?"

Something must have since Rebecca had turned to her grandfather and then decided to go into service when she could have lived off her beau's ill-gotten gains.

"'E were nabbed. That were 'bout four years ago now. Broke 'is mother's 'eart." Sally was fading fast, so Jason let her rest, watching her pale face as it relaxed in sleep.

When Daniel returned, Jason considered leaving the food and drink next to Sally and simply leaving, but he wasn't at all sure it would still be there when Sally woke. When one was as hungry as these women often were, right and wrong didn't come into it.

"Sally," Jason whispered so as not to startle her out of sleep. "Sally, you must eat."

Sally's eyelids fluttered. "Wha'?" she muttered.

"You must eat in order to get stronger. Inspector Haze brought you a game pie and some ale."

Sally's eyes flew open at the mention of the pie. "Oh, thank ye, sir," she said with feeling, and sat up awkwardly, falling on the food. Daniel had brought two generous slices, and Sally inhaled

117

them both in moments, chasing them with the entire contents of the pitcher.

Jason's chest constricted with pity for this girl. She probably hadn't eaten in days, and her roommates hadn't bothered to look after her. He was amazed that the other girl, Janice, had slept through the commotion without so much as stirring on her pallet.

Suddenly worried, Jason walked over and crouched next to the sleeping girl. She was no older than sixteen or seventeen. Her hair was greasy, and she was so thin, she barely made a dent in the mattress. Jason knew she was gone as soon as he saw her face up close. There were no obvious signs of violence, and Jason didn't have the time to delve into Janice's untimely death. He pulled a soiled sheet over her face and returned to Sally.

"Janice has died," he said softly.

Sally nodded, as if a girl of sixteen passing in the night were the most natural thing in the world.

Saddened to the core of his being, Jason took a five-pound note from his purse and handed it to Sally. Her eyes widened with shock. "Use it wisely, Sally. Use it to get away from this place."

"And where would I go?" Sally asked, looking at him with tear-filled eyes. "What would I do?"

"I don't know, but surely anything is better than this," Jason said.

"Easy for ye to say," Sally replied. She was clutching the note to her breast, as if fearful that he might change his mind and take it away.

"There's a women's shelter. St. Brigid's in Whitechapel," Jason said. "They can help."

"Help me to do what? Recite scripture?" Sally asked derisively, but Jason could see she was considering it.

"Make sure you eat well these next few days. Your body is weakened. You need to get better before you make any decisions about the future."

"Thank ye, Doctor," Sally said, her eyes brimming with tears. "I reckon ye saved my life today."

"I only wish I could have saved your baby," Jason replied, but the look in Sally's eyes told him she'd meant what she'd said earlier. She was glad her baby had been stillborn. It was one less thing to worry about in a life where every day could be her last.

"Thank ye," Sally said again, and Jason knew she wanted them to go.

"Be well, Sally." Jason put on his coat and hat, pulled on his gloves, and followed Daniel from the room.

Chapter 17

"Were you able to learn anything from Sally?" Daniel asked as they left the dilapidated building and stepped out into the gloomy afternoon.

"After her father's death, Rebecca went off with a man called Malcolm Briggs. According to Sally, he was a well-known safe breaker who'd used Edgar Levinson to dispose of stolen goods. About four years ago, around the time Rebecca arrived on her grandfather's doorstep, Malcolm Briggs was arrested."

"Given that Rebecca had decided to seek employment, it stands to reason that Malcolm Briggs never came back to her," Daniel said with obvious satisfaction.

"Are you angry with her?" Jason asked.

"I don't wish to speak ill of the dead, but the more I learn about Rebecca, the more disappointed I am in the woman she has turned out to be. But I have no one to blame but myself," Daniel added bitterly. "I allowed my judgment to become clouded by a pretty face and a kindly manner. So much so that I didn't even bother to check her references."

"Your lapse in judgment was caused by unbearable loss," Jason said gently. "Don't judge yourself so harshly, Daniel."

"There's no excuse," Daniel said angrily. "My idiocy led to Charlotte's abduction." Daniel didn't say the words out loud, but it was obvious what he was thinking. *And possible death.* "Still think we'll find her?" he asked savagely.

"I do," Jason replied, even though he knew no such thing.

His chest cavity felt hollow, his heart suddenly leaden, the tired muscle squeezing uncomfortably and leaving behind a dull ache. These were symptoms Jason was intimately familiar with— hopelessness and despair. He'd experienced them often enough to know that they weren't to be ignored or dismissed. In the past, he'd managed to channel his misery into much-needed action, and he would do so now. That was the only way forward.

"Where are we going?" Daniel asked.

"I'd like to speak to Inspector Warren again," Jason said. "If Malcolm Briggs was known in this area before his arrest, Inspector Warren might be able to tell us something."

"If Malcolm Briggs went to prison and was freed just in time to discover that his beloved was about to marry another man, that would certainly put him in the frame," Daniel said.

"That's what I was thinking. But would someone like Malcolm Briggs ever leave prison?"

Due to public outcry, the death penalty, which had been the sentence for most crimes in the past, had finally been limited to only the most heinous offenses, like murder and treason, but in some ways, life in prison was an even crueler punishment than a quick death. The conditions inside the prisons were appalling. Many prisoners were ill and malnourished, since the prisons did not provide food and the inmates had to rely on either their families or the kindness of strangers for their daily bread. And the prisoners were made to perform manual labor for countless hours a day, not because the labor benefited anyone but because it was a way to make them suffer. Jason had heard from one of the doctors at the hospital he volunteered at that cranks were installed in prison cells and the inmates were forced to turn them for several hours a day. The jailers were able to tighten the cranks to make the task more difficult if they felt so inclined. By Jason's estimation, the physical effort that went into turning the crank would burn through whatever nutrients the prisoners were able to receive and eventually sent them to their graves. It was one way to keep the prison population down without executing the sentenced men outright.

"Perhaps he escaped," Daniel replied.

"Are there many successful breakouts?"

"No, but there are some. As you said, money is the ultimate motivator for some men, and there are guards who can be bribed to help a prisoner escape."

This theory was the first breakthrough they'd had in Rebecca's killing, and Jason hastened his step, eager to speak to Inspector Warren. Perhaps they were finally on the right track.

Chapter 18

If Inspector Warren was surprised to see them again so soon, he didn't let on. "Something else I can help you with, gentlemen?" he asked amiably when they walked into his office at the Covent Garden station house.

"Malcolm Briggs," Daniel said. "Ever heard of him?"

"Good Lord. How did you come by that name?" Warren asked.

"Sally Malvers, a childhood friend of Rebecca Grainger, mentioned him. Said Rebecca had gone off with Malcolm Briggs after her father died."

Inspector Warren nodded. "Now that you mention it, I think she might have been his sweetheart."

"Why didn't you say so before?" Daniel snapped.

"Haven't thought of Malcom Briggs in years," Inspector Warren replied.

"Please, tell us about him, Inspector," Jason invited.

"Would if I could," Inspector Warren said with a shrug of his meaty shoulders. "Malcolm Briggs was too big a prize for the likes of us. Best cracksman in London, by all accounts. Never met a safe he couldn't pop. When he was finally caught, took three constables to get the cuffs on him, and then it was straight to the Yard. If memory serves, it was John Ransome that finally put an end to Briggs' illustrious career."

"John Ransome?" Daniel asked, surprised that he didn't know this about his superior.

"Oh, yes. He was Inspector Ransome then, but Malcolm Briggs was the arrest that fast-tracked his career. I hear he's mighty full of himself these days. Too important for the likes of his old friends."

"You and John Ransome were friends?"

"John and I met when we were mere bobbies. In fact, I helped him out of a tight spot one night, and he bought me a pint to thank me. I thought we'd be mates forever after that, but John had ambition enough for three men. He was made chief inspector, married the commissioner's daughter, and now he's sitting pretty, poised to become the next commissioner of the Metropolitan Police Service when Commissioner Hawkins retires, while I'm still cleaning up scum in Covent Garden." Inspector Warren didn't bother to hide his bitterness, or more accurately, his jealousy.

"I had no idea Ransome was married to Commissioner Hawkins' daughter," Daniel said once they had left the station house and were headed for the nearest hackney stand.

"And with good reason. John Ransome wants to be judged on his own merit, not on the strength of his connections," Jason replied.

"A bit of nepotism never hurts," Daniel said snidely. "I wonder if Ransome's wife has an unmarried sister."

Jason's eyebrows lifted comically. "Is that the plan, then?"

"I'm sorry, Jason," Daniel said, and sighed heavily. "I'm just angry, and very frightened."

"I know, Daniel, but you must keep your wits about you. We're Charlotte's only hope."

Daniel nodded, unable to respond. He couldn't bear to think of Charlotte, so he had to focus on the case. Every little nugget of information was worth its weight in gold if it led them to his baby girl. He hoped John Ransome would be able to tell them something they could use.

An unnatural pall seemed to hang over the building when Jason and Daniel walked into the reception area of Scotland Yard. Even Sergeant Meadows, whose friendly face was meant to put visitors at ease, fidgeted nervously, his expression grim.

"Is Superintendent Ransome available?" Jason asked, wisely skipping the niceties in favor of a quick result.

"He is that," Sergeant Meadows replied, and jutted his chin toward Ransome's office. "Been in there for the past hour. Quiet as the grave."

That didn't much sound like John Ransome, and Daniel felt a tremor of foreboding deep in the pit of his stomach.

John Ransome looked up when Jason knocked on the doorjamb to get his attention. "Come," was all he said. He didn't seem overly surprised to see Daniel and did not comment on his presence.

As they took the guest chairs, Daniel's gaze slid to the two photographs laid out on the superintendent's desk. He fought down the nausea that threatened to overwhelm him. He was an inspector, a man who'd seen violent death, but it seemed he had yet to view it in this gruesome incarnation. The woman was half sitting, propped up against a column. Her head lolled to the side, her eyes wide open and her mouth slack. Her blue gown had been sliced open right down the center, the flesh beneath meeting the same fate. Glistening entrails spilled from her belly, pooling in her lap like uncooked sausages. It was absolutely grotesque.

Jason was staring at the images as well, his mouth slightly ajar, his face pale. "When?" was all he asked.

"Last night. Her remains were found in Covent Garden by a farmer who'd arrived early to set up his stall. She had been dumped at the center of the piazza."

"Dear God," Daniel said, unable to tear his eyes from the nightmare-inducing sight. "Did he kill her before he did…that?"

"Dr. Fenwick thinks she was strangled first, then disemboweled. Small blessing, that. I'd hate to think she was still alive for the final act."

"Who was she?" Jason asked.

"A prostitute who was often seen in Drury Lane. Amy something-or-other. No one was sure of her surname. She was seventeen," John Ransome added.

"Any witnesses?"

"The doxy that identified her said she'd seen her lead a customer toward the arcade. That was the last she saw of Amy before her own services were engaged. The man matched the description of Edward Marsh, from what she saw of him."

"Many men might fit such a general description. Do you believe this is the work of Edward Marsh?" Daniel asked.

"If it is, we now know several things," Ransome said, ticking off the items by folding down his fingers. "One, he's left Southwark. Two, he's still in London. And three, he's now armed with a knife."

"We also know that he will kill again," Jason said with unwavering certainty.

"Not if I have anything to say about it," Ransome said as his gaze strayed back to the photographs. "When I was at school, every Sunday we'd all be herded to church. It was an old, drafty building, always cold, always dim. The pews were so hard, I thought my arse would never regain feeling once I was allowed to finally stand. And Sunday after Sunday, a dotty old vicar would drone on about evil. He said the Devil was everywhere, and if we weren't careful, he'd take over the world. I thought the vicar was a fool who saw sin behind every bush. But when I see something like this," Ransome said, his gaze boring into the images, "I think he may have been right. I've seen many a victim of murder in my day, but I have never seen anything like this. This—" He jabbed his finger at the center of the photograph. "This is true evil. It exists, and it's contagious."

Daniel expected Jason to disagree, but Jason nodded, a faraway look in his eyes. "There are those who kill because they must, and there are those who take great pleasure in torture. I saw it during the war. Once sanctioned, there are certain individuals who relish the kill and inflict more damage than is necessary to vanquish not only the enemy but those who'd been left behind, defenseless women and even children," Jason said angrily. "And you're correct, Superintendent. It is contagious. Weaker men who might not have the courage to follow their urges will do so when given license to maim and kill by their leader, be he chosen by the army or by the men themselves."

"This is why I will not give him the satisfaction," Ransome said hotly. "He wants to see his work described in the newspapers, the victim depicted in all her gory horror. Well, I won't have it." Ransome slammed his fist onto the desktop. "I won't have it."

"The public must be warned," Daniel protested. "They have a right to know."

"And do you think they'll listen, Haze?" Ransome demanded. "Those who make their living by night can't afford to hide away, not even for a day. And those who're snug and warm in their pretty parlors don't care."

"Did the killer engage in sexual intercourse with Amy before killing her?" Jason asked.

Ransome looked up, his gaze still clouded with the horrors of the morning. "Hard to tell, given the lady's occupation. She might have serviced a dozen other punters before her killer chose her for death."

Jason inclined his head in agreement. There was no way to know if the killer had been driven by a desire for sexual gratification or simply for the pleasure of carving up a pretty young woman.

"Do you think Miss Grainger might have been murdered by this lunatic, Lord Redmond?" Ransome asked. "His first victim after attaining freedom?"

"I would like to reserve judgment," Jason replied. "There's quite a big difference between strangulation and strangulation followed by disembowelment. We might be dealing with two different culprits."

"Or perhaps we're dealing with the same man who was spooked or unexpectedly interrupted and had no time to complete his task," Ransome argued. "We've yet to establish a tangible connection between the two murders, so at this time, we will treat them as two separate crimes. Were you able to learn anything about Rebecca Grainger that might be of use?"

"Do you remember Malcolm Briggs?" Jason asked.

"Malcolm Briggs?" Ransome asked, his eyes widening in surprise. "Why would you ask about him?"

"It would seem that Rebecca Grainger went off with him after her father died. They might have been romantically involved," Daniel said with more bitterness than was professional. He was jealous of any man Rebecca might have felt affection for.

"I remember Malcolm Briggs quite clearly, but you can eliminate him from your inquiries," Ransome said. "He was a clever lad. Best cracksman in London. There were some who had his skill with a safe, but none had his speed. He was in and out in mere minutes, going over the rooftops with his loot and disappearing into the night like a plume of smoke."

"How did you catch him, then?" Daniel asked.

"We had a tipoff from an anonymous source about which house Briggs would hit. We assumed it was from one of his rivals, which made it legitimate, since no one wanted Briggs gone more than his competitors. Normally, Briggs was very careful, watching the place until he was sure it was safe to act. And he always had a trusted lookout, but that night, something distracted him. He never noticed the men on the roof, who hid behind the chimney stacks and waited for him to climb up. Caught him red-handed, his pockets full of valuables."

"Was he sentenced to life in prison?" Daniel asked.

John Ransome shook his head. "Briggs was sent down to Australia. Transportation of convicts to Botany Bay had all but ceased by that point, but ships were still going out to Western Australia and continued to deliver convicts until two years ago, when the practice was abolished."

"Could Malcolm Briggs have escaped and returned to England?"

"Briggs never made it," Ransome replied. "The ship, *Verity*, she was called, sank off the coast of Agadir in March of sixty-five. All souls lost."

Jason had just opened his mouth to ask a question when there was a commotion in the foyer, men's voices raised in obvious distress. Ransome shot to his feet, probably fearful that another victim had been found, and hurried from his office. Jason and Daniel followed him out to the duty room. Sergeant Meadows was admonishing Constables Putney and Napier in an urgent whisper, begging them to be quiet and make their way to the basement, but it was too late.

Daniel stared at the bundle in Constable Napier's arms. It was wrapped in a blanket, but it was definitely a child. A long black curl escaped from the binding, snaking downward and dripping water onto the flagstones. It was a girl, a little girl.

Grabbing onto the polished counter for support, Daniel shut his eyes to keep the room from spinning. His life had never been easy, but these past few days, it had turned into a nightmare he couldn't seem to wake from.

"Daniel, take a seat," Jason said firmly. "Sergeant, some water please."

Daniel was led to a bench set against the wall and made to sit down, a cup of water thrust into his hand.

"Drink," Jason said.

"Is it… Is…?" Daniel couldn't bring himself to speak the words.

"We don't know, sir," Constable Napier replied. He looked like he was about to burst into tears. "We've never seen your daughter."

"This little girl was pulled from the Thames not an hour since," Constable Putney interjected. "She fit the description," he added apologetically. "So we brought her here."

"Take the child downstairs to the mortuary. I'll be right there," Jason barked.

Daniel set the cup down and made to rise, but Jason placed a hand on his shoulder and forced him back down. "No," he said.

"I need to see for myself, Jason."

"You do not."

Daniel found that he was actually grateful not to have to look at the child's corpse. He leaned his head against the wall and shut his eyes again, images of Charlotte, laughing and playing, passing before his eyes as Jason's footsteps receded toward the stairs.

The duty room was quiet. Sergeant Meadows was behind the counter but didn't utter a sound, and John Ransome had followed Jason down to the mortuary. Daniel felt himself drifting, his thoughts scattering like marbles on a cobblestone street, but that was preferable to cold, clear thinking. He simply couldn't allow himself to imagine a life without Charlotte in it. He was coping with the death of Sarah, but he would never be able to accept the loss of Charlotte. Not ever.

Harriet. The thought dropped into Daniel's head quite unexpectedly. Harriet didn't know her granddaughter was missing. She was going about her days in blissful ignorance, having no inkling that her life might be upended once again, whatever was left of her heart torn out of her chest. Daniel decided he wouldn't tell her anything until he knew for certain. He would spare her the pain for as long as he could.

The sound of footsteps jolted Daniel out of his stupor. He forced himself to open his eyes and look toward the stairs. Jason was walking toward him, his expression grim.

"Oh dear God," Daniel moaned. He gulped air, but no oxygen reached his lungs, and dark spots began to dance before his eyes. He grabbed onto the bench, digging his fingers into the unforgiving wood in the hope of anchoring himself to the moment.

"Daniel, did you hear me?" Jason asked. He was standing before Daniel now, his voice gentle as he called to him.

Daniel shook his head, unable to form any words.

"It's not Charlotte," Jason said. "Daniel, it's not Charlotte," he repeated to make sure Daniel had heard.

"How did the child die?" Daniel croaked, his throat constricted by a huge lump that made it difficult to speak.

"I believe she was strangled, but I can't tell for certain without performing a postmortem."

"Jason, there's no time," Daniel cried. "We must find Charlotte."

"Dr. Fenwick will see to the child," Jason replied. "We will continue with our inquiries."

Daniel's breathing eased, and he did his best to focus on Jason, but then remembered what Ransome had told them just before the constables had arrived. "Jason, Malcolm Briggs is another dead end. Where do we go from here?"

"I don't know, but we must persevere. Someone knows something, and we will find them."

"When?" Daniel cried. "It might be too late for Charlotte. Just because that child in the mortuary is not my daughter doesn't mean she's still alive."

Jason nodded. To argue would have been pointless since he knew as well as Daniel what could happen to a child in a city the size of London. "Daniel, you're in no condition to continue today. You must go home and rest."

"You think I can rest?" Daniel cried.

"You are no good to Charlotte if you're coming apart at the seams," Jason said. "I will collect you tomorrow at eight."

Every fiber of Daniel's being wanted to argue, to demand that they carry on, but they had no fresh leads, and Jason looked exhausted, his skin grayer than Daniel could ever recall seeing, and deep shadows smudged the skin beneath his eyes. This investigation was taking a toll on him, and Daniel knew that what Jason feared was that he would fail both him and Charlotte.

"All right," Daniel rasped. "We will continue tomorrow."

Daniel saw Jason to a cab, then set off on foot. He had no reason to rush home, and he needed to walk off his fear and frustration.

Chapter 19

It wasn't a long ride, but Jason was grateful for a few minutes of solitude. As soon as he got home, Katherine would ask him endless questions and do her utmost to help, but there was nothing she could do, and he would not tell her about the latest developments before he had to. The grisly death of the young prostitute and the bloated body of the child he'd just examined were not suitable topics of conversation, not even with his sensible and sympathetic wife. He loved Katherine too much not to spare her the horrors he had witnessed today, and all he wanted was to put the memory of the dead from his mind. But there was still the living to contend with.

Now that Jason had time to think on it, he wasn't at all sure how he felt about seeing Elias Garfield again. A part of him thought that their shared past didn't matter, and he had to treat Elias as nothing more than the director of the Pine Grove Asylum, but the greater part had other ideas. Instead of the well-appointed office, Jason's mind conjured up images of Elias as he had known him during the war, both on and off the battlefield. He saw Elias sitting on a fallen log, smoking a cheroot, a grin spreading across his face when he saw Jason coming toward him, and the emotions passing over his face as he closed his eyes and listened to Liam Donovan sing. Elias had loved those old Irish ballads, and Liam's warm voice and melodic Irish lilt had added to the heartfelt delivery and brought Elias to tears more than once.

Jason could almost smell the smoke of the campfires and feel the heat of those long southern nights. He also remembered the mosquitoes and the humidity that had made him feel like he was melting in his woolen uniform, and the chirping of crickets that had driven him mad as he tried to sleep. But the memory that pushed its way to the forefront was that of Elias standing before the makeshift operating table in a canvas tent they'd used as a field hospital. Elias was dressed in a blood-splattered smock, his hair pushed beneath a linen cap to keep the sweat from dripping into his face, a scalpel glinting in his hand. Jason was at the other table, his own scalpel bloodied and nearly dull as he operated on one wounded soldier after another until he thought his fingers would cramp with fatigue and he wouldn't be able to make a clean incision.

Elias's hand had always been steady and sure, despite the chaos just beyond his canvas sanctuary. He'd had the uncanny ability to completely ignore the sounds of battle, blocking out cannon and gun fire, the screams of men and horses, and the endless parade of wounded men that were delivered to the hospital tent and triaged by a sergeant who'd been a medical student before the war broke out. Elias had done his best never to cause any unnecessary suffering to the men he'd operated on, and he had saved more men than he'd lost. Did Elias miss surgery? Jason wondered. Once a surgeon, always a surgeon, his medical school mentor used to say, and Jason knew it to be true, if only for himself.

Was it enough for Elias to sit in his office and perform mostly clerical duties? And what of his private life? Elias's hunger for pleasure had always been larger than life. He'd eaten heartily, drunk too much when he wasn't working, and squired more women than any other officer of Jason's acquaintance. It wasn't the shy, blushing debutantes that had appealed to him. Elias had liked his women willing and experienced and wormed his way into more than one man's marriage bed. Had he finally settled for one woman, or was he working his way through London society, bedding bored matrons and making enemies of their husbands?

And what of the thieving? Had taking valuables off the dead been some sort of life-affirming thrill, or was Elias someone who stole to fund his comfortable lifestyle? Was Elias Garfield a man who felt useless and directionless now that he was a civilian? It was difficult to tell from such a brief meeting, but Jason was sure of one thing. The man Jason had met today was not the man he had known during the war, and he realized that while some had only wanted the war to come to an end so they could return to their families, Elias Garfield had thrived on life-and-death situations and had felt the most alive when he'd thought he was about to die.

The hansom pulled up before Jason's house, and he paid the cabbie and walked up the path to the front door.

Chapter 20

Monday, March 8

Sunrise found Jason in the drawing room, staring balefully out the window. He'd woken several times during the night, his heart pounding, and his forehead damp with perspiration. It had been a long time since he'd been troubled by nightmares, but a day like yesterday would leave its mark on even the most hardened of cynics. Jason's tortured brain had conjured up images of the poor little girl they'd pulled from the river, of the lifeless infant he'd pulled from Sally's heaving body, and of Amy, whose entrails had slithered after her as she walked across the Covent Garden piazza in search of help, her eyes rolling with pain and animal-like terror. Unable to go back to sleep for fear of resurrecting the horrors that haunted him, Jason had gone downstairs and settled in his favorite chair, determined to think through the case logically and methodically, but try as he might, he couldn't see any new angle or think of where to start once he collected Daniel.

He wasn't sure how much they would accomplish if he didn't come up with a plan, and worried about wasting time they didn't have. With every passing hour, the chances of finding Charlotte alive diminished considerably, and the trail grew even colder. Malcolm Briggs was dead. Leon Stanley had no motive that they knew of. There had been no word from Tristan Carmichael, who was a long shot anyway. And Edward Marsh was out there, probably hunting for his next prey. If Marsh had been the one to take Charlotte… Jason couldn't allow his thoughts to stray in that direction because if they did, he would come hopelessly undone.

"Can I get you some coffee?" Mrs. Dodson asked as she poked her head into the room.

"Please," Jason replied, overcome with gratitude for Mrs. Dodson's thoughtfulness. "In fact, I'll come to the kitchen, if you don't mind. I could use a bit of company."

"You're always welcome," Mrs. Dodson replied, smiling at him in her motherly way.

Jason missed their talks, but now that he had a wife to share his troubles with, he didn't confide in Mrs. Dodson as often as before. Still, Mrs. Dodson was a comfort, and a strong cup of coffee wouldn't come amiss either, especially as he had yet to figure out the workings of the range if he were to make some himself.

Jason followed Mrs. Dodson to the basement kitchen and sat at the scrubbed pine table. He watched as Mrs. Dodson went about her morning routine, lighting a fire in the cast-iron stove before going to the larder to collect the items she needed to prepare breakfast. She spooned coffee into the linen filter she used and affixed it to the coffee pot, then, once the stove was hot, put water on the boil and went about toasting bread.

"I'll fry you an egg, shall I?" Mrs. Dodson asked. Jason always took protein with his breakfast in order to ward off the weakness and dizziness brought on by bouts of hypoglycemia.

"Thank you."

Jason found that he felt less anxious, the mundane domestic tasks reminding him that life went on no matter what happened. His mother had always said that the kitchen was the hub of the house, and he tended to agree, even though he didn't venture downstairs as often anymore.

Mrs. Dodson brewed the coffee and set the silver coffeepot on the table before adding a jug of cream and a bowl of sugar cubes. She then cracked two eggs into a skillet and cooked them for a few minutes before serving them to Jason with toast, butter, and a pot of her own orange marmalade.

"Where's Kitty?" Jason asked, referring to their young scullery maid.

"I suggested she have a bit of a lie-in," Mrs. Dodson replied. "I like to have the kitchen to myself before she starts banging pots and asking me endless questions." Mrs. Dodson smiled affectionately. "I think our Kitty has her eye on my job. It's time I started teaching her. I won't be around forever, you know."

The possibility of the Dodsons retiring had never occurred to Jason. They were so much a part of the household, he thought they'd be around forever, but he supposed they had earned their rest.

"But you didn't come down here to talk about Kitty," Mrs. Dodson said, eyeing Jason knowingly.

"No," Jason admitted. "Won't you join me for a cup of coffee?"

"Don't mind if I do."

Mrs. Dodson fetched a clean cup and saucer, settled herself at the table, and helped herself to coffee, pouring cream with a generous hand, then adding two sugars.

"Never thought I'd learn to like the stuff," she said, "but one does develop a taste for it, doesn't one?" She watched Jason over the rim of her cup, her shrewd eyes missing little. "Tell me what's on your mind, Captain," Mrs. Dodson invited, using the title that was closer to Jason's heart.

And Jason did. He told her about the case and about his nightmares, and about his fears for his own family.

"You haven't been troubled by nightmares since you first arrived in England," Mrs. Dodson observed. "It isn't right what they're asking of you."

"How do you mean?" Jason asked. Despite his misery, he was hungry and tucked into his breakfast.

"They should have asked someone else to take the case, is all I'm saying," Mrs. Dodson explained, her indignation apparent. "If you don't find that little girl, you'll carry the guilt with you for the rest of your days. And Daniel Haze might say he won't blame you, but he will. He'll think you should have done more, tried harder."

Mrs. Dodson's observations went straight to the heart of the matter. Jason hadn't even realized how deeply he feared that Daniel would blame him if he failed to get Charlotte back. The knowledge was enough to paralyze Jason with crippling fear of his own inadequacy, but he couldn't afford to focus on his own feelings. Time was short.

"I don't know what to do, Mrs. Dodson," he confessed. "I'm in possession of a number of random facts, but they don't form a cohesive narrative. And why would Rebecca's killer, assuming he's not Edward Marsh, take Charlotte? To what end?"

"If you could answer that, then you'd have your man," Mrs. Dodson observed.

"What makes you say that?"

"The child seems to be at the center of this case, doesn't she? Otherwise, whoever murdered Miss Grainger would have left her where he had found her."

"I'm not sure about that," Jason replied. "And perhaps he did leave her where he'd found her and we just haven't discovered her remains yet."

"Why kill an innocent little girl? There must be a reason. And if that monster, Edward Marsh, had butchered her, he'd have left her remains for everyone to see as he had done with his previous victims," Mrs. Dodson pointed out.

"I can't see that anyone would have anything to gain by murdering a child, but there are some depraved people in the world." Edward Marsh may not have sought a child to murder, but if one got in his way…

"You have to find her, Captain. Dead or alive," Mrs. Dodson said. "Because if you don't, Daniel Haze will go mad. It's bad enough that he lost his son, then his wife, but at least he got to bury them, to say a proper goodbye. If he never knows what became of that little girl, he'll lose all reason and possibly go the way of Sarah."

"I know, Mrs. D.," Jason replied. "But I'll be damned if I know where to look next."

Mrs. Dodson finished her coffee and set down her cup. "Talk to the staff. Servants always know more than they're saying."

"You mean Daniel's maidservant, Grace?"

"I mean the servants at Abel Grainger's house. If Miss Grainger had lived there for a time before seeking employment, they must know something of what she got up to."

"And what do you think she got up to?" Jason asked.

"There was a sweetheart, wasn't there?" Mrs. Dodson asked, raising one brow suggestively.

"He was sent to Australia and died on the way."

"Maybe there was more than one sweetheart. A woman is allowed to look for happiness after a bereavement."

Jason nodded. "Thank you, Mrs. D. I will certainly speak to the staff and Rebecca's grandfather. Perhaps Daniel was too overwrought to ask the right questions."

"You just keep a cool head, Captain, and you'll get to the bottom of this tragedy. You just keep a cool head," Mrs. Dodson reiterated, and pushed to her feet. "Time I got on with my work. Her ladyship will be expecting her morning tea in a quarter of an hour."

"I'd best get dressed," Jason said, realizing the time once Kitty appeared in the doorway, her cheeks reddening when she spotted Jason wearing nothing but his dressing gown.

"Good morning, Kitty," Jason said.

"Mornin', sir," Kitty muttered. She scurried past him and grabbed the coal hod, her gaze fixed on the flagstone floor.

Jason thanked Mrs. Dodson for both the meal and the advice and went upstairs to shave and dress. Henley would have laid out his clothes by now, and it was time he got ready. He also wanted to spend a few minutes with Katherine and Lily before he left for the day and have a word with Joe. He didn't want Joe to tell Micah about Rebecca and Charlotte when he picked him up from school. He'd speak to Micah himself once Micah was back in London.

Jason was coming down the stairs after visiting the nursery and enjoying a morning cuddle with Lily when loud banging on the front door reverberated through the house. Dodson, his expression one of outrage at the impertinence of someone calling at such an uncivilized hour, hurried toward the door, keyring in hand. He unlocked the door and was probably about to give whoever had dared to show up on the doorstep at half past eight a stern talking to when Jason heard Constable Napier's agitated voice.

"You must come now, your lordship," Constable Napier cried from the doorway.

"What happened, Constable?" Jason asked as he hurried across the foyer toward the young man.

"It's Leon Stanley, sir. He's been murdered in his bed. A chambermaid found him this morning when she went to bring up his breakfast."

"Has Inspector Haze been notified?" Jason asked as he followed Constable Napier into the chilly, gray morning. It was no use pretending that Daniel wasn't investigating the case alongside Jason. Despite Ransome's directive, no one expected him to remain at home, not even Ransome himself.

"Not yet, sir. I came to get you first, on account of you being in charge. Shall I fetch him?"

"Dodson, please ask Joe to collect Daniel and bring him to the Charing Cross Hotel as soon as possible," Jason called over his shoulder to Dodson, who looked distinctly worried. He didn't think a man of Jason's standing should involve himself in the sordid affairs of the police, but Daniel Haze was a friend, and Charlotte was Jason and Katherine's goddaughter and Lily's playmate. If this was personal for Jason, it was personal for Dodson as well.

"Yes, sir. Leave it with me, sir," Dodson called out as Jason climbed onto the bench of the police wagon.

As the cumbersome conveyance drew away from the curb, Jason reflected that if someone had seen fit to kill Leon Stanley, then the motive pointed squarely at Rebecca Grainger rather than a desire for revenge against Daniel or Jason, but his supposition did little to lift his spirits, nor did it explain the purpose of Charlotte's abduction. Jason prayed that Charlotte wasn't simply collateral damage in a scheme to murder Rebecca because that would render her useless to her kidnapper and drastically reduce her chances of survival.

Chapter 21

The police wagon was met at the entrance to the Charing Cross Hotel by none other than the manager, Mr. Crosby, who directed Constable Napier to drive the conveyance around the back and find an unobtrusive spot behind the kitchen to avoid the sort of negative attention any respectable hotel would wish to avoid. Mr. Crosby then asked Jason to accompany him inside. The manager was a man in his mid-to-late forties with carefully oiled sandy hair, a neatly trimmed beard, and anxious blue eyes. He was smartly dressed and had an enviable posture that conveyed self-assurance and rigid discipline.

Mr. Crosby invited Jason into his office on the ground floor and firmly shut the door before coming around to settle behind his desk. The few items on the surface were arranged with military precision, and the polished surface gleamed in the morning sun, not a stray speck of dust to be seen or it would probably be instantly vanquished by the desk's owner.

"Do sit down, Inspector," Mr. Crosby said, and smiled, but the gesture did nothing to soften the tension in his face.

Jason was about to tell Mr. Crosby that he wasn't really an inspector of the police but then decided not to bother with unnecessary explanations. He had been given leave to investigate the case, and to undermine his own authority would serve no purpose.

Mr. Crosby clasped his hands and took a deep breath, all the while taking Jason's measure. In his position as manager, the ability to read people was necessary, and he was probably proficient in figuring out how to handle any difficult situation. Having settled on an approach with a barely perceptible nod, he began.

"Inspector, I know you have a job to do, but so do I. And my job is to make sure that our guests feel safe and comfortable and will consider staying with us again should they find themselves in London. Knowing that a brutal murder had taken place while they were at their most vulnerable will not only spread panic but ruin the reputation of the hotel and put respectable guests off, possibly forever. I implore you to go about your business with the utmost discretion." He gave Jason an apologetic look. "I'm afraid I turned the police photographer away. I can't allow him in the building."

"Mr. Crosby, it is not my purpose here to either undermine the reputation of your hotel or terrify the guests. You may have one of your employees bring up Constable Napier, and Inspector Haze when he arrives, by the servants' stairs, and I will interview the staff in a place of your choosing. No one need know, unless there's a threat to public safety, in which case I won't hesitate to issue an alert."

Since Jason had no idea which photographer had been sent or where he had gone, he decided not to worry about photographing the crime scene at present.

"Do you believe there is a threat?" Mr. Crosby asked. Given his shock, Jason realized that the thought had not occurred to him, and he had assumed this was an isolated incident.

"I can't offer you any reassurances until I've had an opportunity to examine the crime scene and speak to the staff."

"Fair enough," Mr. Crosby said, sighing with resignation.

"Do members of the staff know what has happened?"

Mr. Crosby shook his head. "They do not. They will gossip, and before long everyone will know there's been a murder at the hotel and I will have journalists camped out at my door, fishing for details and trying to bribe the maids into taking them up to the room so that they can take a photograph of the murder scene."

"What exactly occurred?" Jason asked Mr. Crosby, who had reached for the crystal decanter on his desk and poured some water into a matching glass.

Jason knew nothing beyond the fact that Leon Stanley was dead. Was it possible that his death had been a suicide rather than murder, and someone, probably Mr. Crosby himself, had arrived at a premature conclusion and alerted Scotland Yard? Leon Stanley had loved Rebecca Grainger and had been about to marry her and whisk her off to his ranch in Argentina. Perhaps her death had robbed him not only of the woman he had loved but of hope for the future and the family he'd looked forward to starting with his beautiful young bride. Most people found a way to cope with their grief, but perhaps Leon Stanley had given in to despair, more so because he was alone and had no one to support him in his grief.

Of course, there was another possibility if the death had indeed been a suicide. Leon Stanley might have murdered Rebecca in a fit of rage and found himself unable to live with the consequences of his actions. Jason considered that for a moment. He hadn't met Leon Stanley so couldn't speak to his character, but it was possible that he had met Rebecca during her walk with Charlotte, and she had shocked him by informing him that she had changed her mind either about the wedding or the upcoming move to Argentina. That might have angered Leon Stanley enough to strangle her, but if that were the case, what had he done with Charlotte?

Jason turned his attention to Mr. Crosby, who began to speak, having taken a sip of water and cleared his throat.

"Mr. Stanley had a standing order for breakfast. Seven o'clock sharp. Two fried eggs, kippers, toasted bread, butter, and strawberry preserves. And a pot of coffee," he added. "When the chambermaid delivered the breakfast tray, she found Mr. Stanley dead."

"How did she know he was dead?" Jason asked.

Mr. Crosby's brows rose in surprise at the absurdity of the question. "How did she know?" he sputtered. "Mr. Stanley was lying in bed, his throat slit, the bedlinens soaked with blood. Thankfully, the young woman had the presence of mind to shut the door behind her and come directly to me instead of running down the corridor screaming in her distress and alerting all and sundry that a murder had taken place only a few yards from where they were sleeping."

Leon Stanley might have slit his own throat, but the chambermaid who'd found him would not have had the presence of mind to make that determination even if she was observant enough to notice certain details, such as a bloodied knife that might have slipped from the man's hand as he lost consciousness. And Jason hoped that Mr. Crosby had not taken it upon himself to go up to the room and disturb whatever evidence was there to find.

"Did you enter the room after the chambermaid alerted you to Mr. Stanley's death?" Jason asked.

"Yes, but I did not approach the bed, nor did I disturb anything," Mr. Crosby said defensively. "I needed to make certain the man was beyond help and that it was, indeed, Mr. Leon Stanley."

"And was it? How could you be certain?"

"I have conversed with Mr. Stanley on several occasions over the past few weeks, and the victim is most definitely Mr. Stanley."

"What did you make of him?" Jason asked.

He thought Mr. Crosby was the sort of man who assessed every guest the moment they walked through the door and arrived at certain conclusions about how they were to be handled. Some guests required a minimum of attention, while others would find endless reasons to complain and would do so very loudly and publicly. Jason had met a few individuals of that nature on the crossing to England and had made it a point to steer clear of them and their endless outrage, especially where Micah was concerned. There were those that didn't think an Irish boy who was clearly not related to Jason should be staying in a first-class cabin and must be sent down to steerage to undertake the voyage with his own kind. It had taken a well-aimed and rather cutting rebuke from Jason to get the loudest of Micah's critics to finally pipe down if she didn't care to have her own background examined and discussed.

Mr. Crosby took another sip of water. "Mr. Stanley was a likable chap," he said. "I got the impression that he was clever, practical, and mild-mannered."

"Did you ever see him with a lady?"

"Yes. Mr. Stanley was to be married in a few days." Mr. Crosby looked genuinely upset. "His intended was murdered on Saturday. Miss Grainger was a lovely young woman. Had a smile that could light up a room."

"Yes, she did," Jason agreed.

"Did you know her in life?" Mr. Crosby asked.

"Yes, I knew Miss Grainger rather well, and I'm deeply saddened by her death."

"Mr. Stanley was heartbroken, but as I said, he had a rather stoic nature and did not give in to his grief. He was, however, determined to remain in London until the case was solved and Miss Grainger's killer executed."

Jason thought this information bore further examination. If Leon Stanley had murdered Rebecca, it would have been in his interests to leave London as soon as possible, before suspicion fell on him. The fact that he hadn't fled spoke in his favor but didn't exonerate him entirely. His guilt might have pushed him over the edge in the end, prompting him to take his own life.

"Did Mr. Stanley speak to you of Miss Grainger's death?" Jason asked.

"I found him drinking alone on Saturday night. As a manager, you instinctively know who wishes to be left alone and who would appreciate a spot of company, so I offered to buy him a drink and joined him for a few minutes. He told me what had happened. For what it's worth, Inspector, I felt his grief was genuine."

"Genuine?" Jason echoed.

"Yes."

"Did something in Mr. Stanley's behavior lead you to believe that he might not have had authentic feelings for Miss Grainger?"

Mr. Crosby looked mildly uncomfortable. "They became betrothed after rather a short acquaintance, so I assumed the arrangement was of a more practical nature than based on any real depth of feeling."

"I see," Jason said. "And had you had an opportunity to observe Miss Grainger's attitude toward Mr. Stanley when you saw them together?"

"She was alluring and vivacious, but I got the impression that her charm was feigned. Mr. Stanley, however, was noticeably smitten."

"What made you think her affection for Mr. Stanley wasn't genuine?" Jason asked.

Mr. Crosby looked uncomfortable, as if he didn't wish to speculate on the motives of a woman who was deceased, but Jason was interested in his opinion and waited patiently for him to respond.

"Miss Grainger was an attractive young woman, but she was in her mid-twenties, if I'm not mistaken, and I believe she was a governess. A woman of her years and social position would be a fool to pass up an opportunity to marry a man who was not only wealthy, attractive, and pleasant in his personality, but also unencumbered by children from a previous marriage. Even if Miss Grainger wasn't romantically in love with him, she would love the life that he gave her and would no doubt do her utmost to be a good and loving wife to him."

Jason nodded again. He agreed with Mr. Crosby's assessment. Rebecca Grainger had been ready to marry Daniel until something better came along and very quickly transferred her ambitions onto Leon Stanley. She had known him in the past, but Jason very much doubted she had given him another thought until he sought her out upon arriving in London.

"How did you notify Scotland Yard of Mr. Stanley's death?" Jason asked.

"I sent one of the porters with a message. And before you ask, no, the porter did not know what had happened. I gave him a sealed envelope and asked him to return directly once he had delivered it."

Mr. Crosby shot Jason a searching look. "Are the two murders connected?"

"I'd be surprised if they weren't," Jason replied, but he had no wish to discuss the investigation with the hotel manager. "What is the name of the chambermaid who found the body, and where is she now?" he asked instead.

"Her name is Bridget Connelly, and I have asked her to wait in one of the empty rooms. She'd had a shock and needed to rest, and I needed to keep the information contained."

"Very wise of you," Jason said. "I'd like to go up now."

"Of course. I'll just instruct one of the bellboys to bring your constable up the back stairs," Mr. Crosby said as he sprang to his feet.

It was obvious that he wanted nothing more than to have the ordeal over with and return to his normal routine. Taking the body out might prove problematic, but Jason was sure that Mr. Crosby already had a plan and would put it in motion as soon as Jason left him to do his job.

Chapter 22

Once Mr. Crosby had issued instructions to the bellboy, they ascended to the fourth floor. Unlike the elegant foyer and the well-appointed public rooms downstairs, this floor was simple to the point of being spartan. The floor was lined with a carpet runner, and there were no paintings or flowers to brighten the windowless length of the corridor. Simple frosted-glass gas lamps affixed to the walls gave off just enough light to see comfortably but not to illuminate the corridor to the point of brightness. There were about twenty doors in total, ten per side. Mr. Crosby unlocked the door to number 415 and led Jason inside.

The room was just what Jason had expected after traversing the length of the corridor. There was a single bed with a plain wooden headboard and footboard, a narrow wardrobe, and a washstand. A table big enough for one and a single chair were the only other items of furniture. The curtains were made of cheap muslin, and there was no carpet on the floor, just an oval woven rug next to the bed, where the victim's slippers still stood in readiness. This was a room for the solitary traveler and was probably one of the cheapest rooms at the hotel, unless there were a few guestrooms tucked into the attic and reserved for lady's maids and valets, who didn't warrant anything better as far as their masters were concerned and could share with a stranger if the rooms were big enough for two.

The room had no water closet, so Leon Stanley would have used the communal facilities at the end of the hall, which would account for two of the twenty doors, one room containing a commode and the other a bathtub and washstand. A tray with Leon Stanley's breakfast stood on the table where Bridget Connelly had left it several hours ago, and the aroma of coffee and kippers overlayed the metallic scent of blood and the putrid smell of death. The window was closed, the curtains open and the sun streaming onto the congealed eggs and the body in the bed.

Jason stopped just inside the room and held up a hand to stop Mr. Crosby from going any further. First impressions were important, and he needed a moment to simply look. The first thing he noticed was that three items were arranged on the washstand: Leon Stanley's watch, which looked to be made of solid gold, a leather billfold that bulged with notes, and a small velvet box that had been left open to reveal a thin gold band, presumably Rebecca's wedding ring. If this was a murder, the killer had made sure the police knew robbery wasn't the motive.

Jason continued his appraisal of the room. There was no blood on either the doorknob or the floor, but the water in the basin was crimson, and the towel that hung on a hook near the washstand was covered in dried blood. Leon Stanley would have been in no position to wash his hands after he'd sliced his throat, but whoever had done it had washed off the blood before leaving the room and had most likely taken care to protect his or her clothing at the time of the attack. The wall next to the bed had not fared well. The pale-yellow paint was splattered with arterial blood.

"Stay back, Constable," Jason said to Constable Napier, who'd entered the room and looked like he was about to go charging toward the victim.

"Yes, sir."

Jason left the two men by the door and walked over to the bed. Leon Stanley lay on his back, his eyes wide open and staring at the ceiling. His expression was one of surprise rather than agony or terror. The cut across his throat gaped like a partially open mouth, the blood on the neck and the linens brown and completely dry. Jason bent over the corpse and examined the wound. It appeared to be deeper on the left side of Leon Stanley's neck, which indicated that the cut was made from Jason's right to his left with more pressure applied to the weapon at the moment of incision, meaning the killer was right-handed.

Jason's supposition that Stanley had been murdered was further supported by the lack of a weapon. Had Leon Stanley cut himself accidentally, washed his hands, and wiped them on the towel, then decided to lie down and slit his throat, the knife would be close to the body, either on the bed or on the floor below.

Given the position of the body and the expression on the victim's face, Jason thought that the man had been taken by surprise, the attack taking place after he'd gone to bed. He'd probably been woken from sleep by the pain. He wouldn't have had time to try to save himself or call for help since once the carotid artery was severed, he'd have only moments to live. The killer didn't appear to have been interested in a confrontation, only a quick death, and given the appearance of the body and the fact that the blood had completely dried, the attack must have taken place last night rather than in the early hours of the morning.

Looking down, Jason continued his examination. The corpse was wearing a nightshirt and was neatly tucked in. Either Leon Stanley had somehow tucked himself in before going to sleep or the killer had done that after the man was dead, which was an odd thing to do given the brutality of the attack. Perhaps the blanket had been meant to conceal something. Jason pulled away the woolen blanket, suddenly certain that he was going to find other injuries.

Jason sucked in his breath when his gaze came to rest on the man's genitals, or what would have been his genitals had there been anything left. The shirt had been pushed up and the penis and scrotum neatly sliced off. Although there was some blood, the amount was minimal since the amputation must have taken place postmortem. Looking carefully over the rest of the body, Jason saw no other wounds, so he covered the man and pulled the counterpane over his face.

Mr. Crosby and Constable Napier were silent and pale, their eyes wide with shock at what they had just seen. It was one thing to murder a man and quite another to emasculate him. Such an act spoke of personal hatred and a desire to humiliate, even if the victim was dead and unable to appreciate what had been done to him.

"Did he know?" Constable Napier finally asked, not bothering with the specifics. Jason understood what he wished to know.

"No, Constable. He was already gone."

"Well, thank the Lord for that," Constable Napier gushed. "At least he was spared that horror. I can't imagine why someone would do such a thing, especially to a corpse."

Jason could imagine why, but not necessarily how, at least not how the killer had disposed of Mr. Stanley's genitalia. He looked under the bed and found the answer to his question. The chamber pot beneath the bed, which was probably placed there for those guests who didn't care to leave their room in the middle of the night to use the public toilet, was half full of urine, the amputated parts floating in the liquid. Jason pulled the pot out from beneath the bed and heard the sounds of retching as Mr. Crosby emptied his stomach onto the floor, the vomit splattering Constable Napier's trousers and Mr. Crosby's polished shoes.

"Dear God," Mr. Crosby exclaimed between deep gulps of air. "Why did you do that?"

"Because it's evidence, and I can hardly leave it here," Jason replied calmly. "Besides, I highly doubt you would want one of the chambermaids to find this."

Mr. Crosby saw the truth of that and nodded vigorously. "We can't allow the guests to see this horror," he cried.

"We will take the body down using the back stairs, but we will need help. Do you have a trusted man you can spare?"

"Eh, yes. I will be right back."

While Mr. Crosby went for help, Jason carefully wrapped the body in the blanket so that no part of Mr. Stanley was visible. He then examined the contents of the chamber pot more closely and covered the pot with its lid before Mr. Crosby returned with a strapping young porter in tow.

"Mr. Stanley suffered heart failure, Billy," Mr. Crosby said to the young man. "He passed in the night."

"So why are the police here, sir?" asked Billy, who was clearly smarter than he looked. He had to have noticed the blood on the wall, but wisely didn't comment.

Mr. Crosby looked momentarily taken aback but recovered admirably. "It's because Mr. Stanley was visiting from Argentina and had no family in London. The police will follow the necessary procedure to send his body home to his family."

"Oh," Billy said. "And you don't want any of the guests to see his body, right?"

"Right," Mr. Crosby said. "Now, help the constable carry Mr. Stanley's remains to the police wagon."

"Yes, sir," Billy replied with obvious reluctance.

Constable Napier and Billy took hold of the body and carefully maneuvered it out the door and toward the service stairs. If anyone saw them, they might think they were simply carrying a heavy carpet, if not for the fact that one of the men was in police uniform. Luckily for Mr. Crosby, no guests happened to be in the corridor, and the two men disappeared through the door unnoticed.

Jason handed the lidded pot to Mr. Crosby. "I trust you can dispose of this?"

"I thought it was evidence," Mr. Crosby said, staring at the pot with obvious disgust.

"I've seen all I need to see," Jason replied.

Mr. Crosby nodded and accepted the offending article, then immediately shoved it back beneath the bed. "I will see that this is dealt with."

"Good. Now I would like to speak to Bridget Connelly."

There was an urgent knock on the door, and Daniel was admitted into the room, a fresh-faced bellboy hovering behind him and craning his neck to get a better look at what all the fuss was about. His curious gaze fell on the blood-spattered wall, and his mouth opened in shock before Mr. Crosby shut the door in his face.

Daniel looked like he wanted to ask questions, but Jason gave him a look that said, *We'll speak later. In private.*

Daniel nodded and remained silent, scanning the room, and recording every detail for future analysis. Mr. Crosby opened the door, peered into the corridor to make certain no one was about, then opened the door wider to allow Jason and Daniel to pass and locked it behind him with a sigh of relief. For the moment, disaster had been averted.

Chapter 23

Bridget Connelly was no older than eighteen, a striking young woman who seemed to relish her unexpected period of rest. Jason thought he noticed a spark of amusement in Bridget's green eyes when she faced Mr. Crosby. This was not a terrified chambermaid but one who had probably used the time alone to consider her options. Her apron was clean and crisp, and her cap was set on her hair like a tiara. Whatever Bridget had been doing, she hadn't been lying down.

"Miss Connelly, these men are from Scotland Yard. They'd like to ask you a few questions," Mr. Crosby said. "Please answer them to the best of your ability."

"Of course I will, Mr. Crosby. You can count on me, but I wouldn't say no to a cup of tea and something to nibble on. I've missed my breakfast," Bridget said pointedly. She had a lovely Irish lilt that reminded Jason of Micah's sister, Mary Donovan. In fact, with her red hair and heart-shaped face, she resembled Mary more than Jason had initially noticed.

"I will have some breakfast sent up," Mr. Crosby said. "Gentlemen, would you care for tea or coffee?"

"No, thank you," Daniel said after looking to Jason, who shook his head.

"Would you like eggs and kippers, Bridget?" Mr. Crosby asked solicitously.

Bridget looked momentarily taken aback, probably because all she normally got was a bowl of porridge, but recovered herself admirably. "That'd be grand, Mr. Crosby. And some toasted bread, butter, and a dish of the strawberry preserves, if you would be so kind."

Mr. Crosby nodded and left the room, although it was clear from his demeanor that he would have liked to stay and hear

Bridget's account for himself, if only to make sure that she didn't say anything defamatory about the hotel.

The room was a step above Leon Stanley's room. It was painted a cheery yellow and had matching damask curtains pulled back with tasseled ties to reveal the lace panels beneath. There was a four-poster bed, a handsome wardrobe, and a seating area with a settee, two chairs, and a low table arranged on a carpet in shades of blue, yellow, and gray. It was a room for a guest who was willing to pay for finer accommodation without breaking the bank and reserving a suite. The fact that Mr. Crosby had locked Bridget in such a room spoke volumes to Jason, and clearly to Daniel, who smiled kindly at Miss Connelly.

"This is a lovely room," he said.

"Had to stumble over a dead body to land in the lap of luxury," Bridget said with a smirk. She didn't seem in the least intimidated or distressed about the morning's events. "Do sit down, gentlemen," she invited, and settled on the settee, arranging her skirts as if she were a young matron entertaining her guests rather than a chambermaid who'd found a mutilated corpse.

"Can you tell us what happened this morning, Miss Connelly?" Jason invited.

Bridget made a show of thinking. "Well, I arrived at six sharp to start my shift. By six-fifty, Mrs. Hawley—that's the cook—had Mr. Stanley's breakfast ready and told me to take it up to his room. My stomach was growling at the smell of that food," Bridget confessed, "and I was looking forward to having my own breakfast later on. It's included with my wages," she explained. "Except the employees only get porridge and tea. Still, better than nothing, I always say."

Any meal a girl in her position didn't have to pay for would be a godsend, although Jason was sure that Mr. Crosby figured the cost of the food into the staff's wages.

"Please, go on," Daniel said. It was obvious he didn't really care about Bridget's dissatisfaction with her job and wanted to hear about what had transpired later.

"Well, I came upstairs and opened the door."

"Was the door locked?" Jason asked.

Bridget stared into the middle distance as she tried to recall. "Now that you mention it, no, but I thought Mr. Stanley had left it that way so that I could deliver his breakfast."

"Then what happened?" Daniel asked.

"I walked in and saw him lying there. At first, I thought he was sleeping."

"You didn't notice that something was wrong straight away?"

"The room was in near darkness, Inspector, with only the light from the corridor to light my way."

"Was there any evidence of a struggle?" Jason asked.

"Not that I saw."

"So what did you do?"

"I set the tray down, drew the curtains, and turned to leave," Bridget explained. "I wanted to get out before Mr. Stanley woke. It was only when I turned around that I saw the blood."

"Why did you want to leave before Mr. Stanley woke?" Daniel asked.

Bridget gave him a derisive look clearly meant to highlight his monumental ignorance. "When a woman goes into a man's bedroom, Inspector, she puts herself at risk every time."

"Have guests at the hotel ever troubled you in that way?" Jason asked.

"Of course they have," Bridget replied, her angry gaze telling them just how little they understood of her reality. "Happens at least once every bloody day."

"And does Mr. Crosby look after his staff?"

"Mr. Crosby is fair, I'll give him that, but it's this hotel and his own reputation he cares about. Chambermaids are not hard to come by, so it's not wise to make too much of a fuss about a pinched bottom or a disgusting proposition."

"Miss Connelly, it is my understanding that you shut the door behind you and went directly to Mr. Crosby's office. That's rather an odd reaction to finding a body," Jason said. "Were you not frightened?"

Bridget shrugged. "I've seen plenty of dead bodies, sir. It's not the dead I'm afraid of, it's the living."

"How did you come to see so many dead bodies?" Daniel asked.

"My father is an undertaker, sir, as was his father before him. I was expected to help in the family concern."

"So why aren't you helping in the family business now?"

"My da and I had a difference of opinion," Bridget said tartly. "I was invited to leave and never to return."

"What was this difference of opinion?" Daniel probed.

Bridget turned up her pert nose. "Not that it's any of your affair, but it was about a lad I wished to marry."

"Was he unsuitable?"

"You could say that, Inspector. My father would not tolerate a Protestant son-in-law."

"Did he leave you, then, your young man?" Daniel asked.

Bridget looked momentarily surprised. "Leave me? Of course not. Rory is one of the waiters at the restaurant downstairs. We're to marry in June."

"Well, best of luck to you both."

"If I play my cards right, I won't need luck."

Jason could see the determination in her gaze. Bridget had a plan, and it went beyond spending a few hours in a nice room and getting eggs and strawberry preserves for breakfast.

"Be careful, Bridget," Jason said. "Mr. Crosby is not a man to be crossed."

"Dear me. Who said anything about crossing Mr. Crosby?" Bridget asked, all innocence.

Jason didn't bother to reply. Bridget Connelly looked perfectly capable of figuring things out for herself.

"Enjoy your breakfast, Miss Connelly," he said as a young man, whose eyes glowed with affection, walked through the door, a tray balanced on one hand. Bridget's response was instant and genuine, and Jason smiled at the young lovers, hoping life wouldn't be cruel to them.

Leaving Bridget to her meal and her beau, Jason and Daniel returned downstairs, where Mr. Crosby was speaking to a guest, smiling as if nothing untoward had happened upstairs.

"A moment of your time, Mr. Crosby," Jason said once the man had finished and wished the guest a pleasant day.

"Of course. Let's speak in my office." Once they were settled, Mr. Crosby leaned forward, eager to hear their conclusions.

"Mr. Crosby, I can't be certain without performing a postmortem, but based on the state of the body, I believe Mr. Stanley has been dead for ten to twelve hours, which would mean that he was murdered yesterday evening. Did anyone hear or see anything suspicious last night?"

"Not that I know of. The night manager, Mr. Higgins, came on duty at eight o'clock and remained until eight this morning. I usually arrive at seven so that I can speak to him before he departs, and then I take breakfast in my office. I questioned Mr. Higgins after Bridget Connelly informed me of what had happened, but he said he hadn't noticed anything out of the ordinary. All the guests who came to the reception desk were staying at the hotel and had stopped by only to retrieve their keys. Only one new guest checked in last night, at half past seven. The gentleman, Mr. Brand, had written for a reservation and paid for two nights. He had breakfast in the dining room this morning while I awaited your arrival. He asked for a cab to take him to the British Museum not half an hour ago."

"The killer might have entered through the servants' entrance," Jason pointed out. "Did anyone notice anyone who didn't belong there?"

"The hotel is very busy at that time of the evening since many of our guests choose to dine on the premises. There are cooks, waiters, busboys, and chambermaids turning down the beds and responding to any summons from guests who are in need of something or wish to order food or drink to be brought to their room. I'm sorry, but it's impossible to tell if someone had found their way in."

"So, if someone wished to enter the hotel, all they would have to do is walk either through the front door or the back door and make their way to the fourth floor," Daniel observed.

"I'm afraid that is correct. This is not a prison, Inspector. We don't stop people at the door and ask to check their credentials or require them to present proof that they are staying at the hotel. There are those individuals who wish to have a drink at the bar or a meal at the hotel restaurant while they wait for their trains. The only instruction the doorman and the reception staff have is to turn away any whores that try to solicit for business in the foyer."

"And if a man wants to take a prostitute up to his room?" Jason asked.

"He may do so. We can hardly demand that he send her away." Mr. Crosby fixed Jason with a speculative stare. "Do you think Mr. Stanley was murdered by a woman?"

"Given that his genitals have been severed, I think that's a distinct possibility."

"Revenge?" Mr. Crosby asked. "Perhaps he was already married, and his wife discovered that he was about to take a new bride and take her to Argentina, where no one would be the wiser."

"Perhaps," Jason agreed. "But we don't have anyone who can verify that at the moment."

"Was Miss Connelly of some assistance?"

"She was," Jason said. "A clever young woman."

"Too clever for her own good, if you ask me," Mr. Crosby grumbled.

"What about the rest of the staff? Would there be any value in interviewing them?" Daniel asked.

"All those on the premises last night left after their shift ended at midnight," Mr. Crosby said. "If you wish to interview them, you must return at four o'clock. However, I would ask you not to. News of the murder will incite panic, and I very much doubt any of them could tell you anything. The turnover of staff is rather high, so it's not unusual to see an unfamiliar face," he confessed.

"Why is that?" Jason asked.

"Because the hours are long, and the pay is low. I do not determine the wages," Mr. Crosby hastened to add. "I'm the manager, not the owner."

"And the owner?"

"Is not currently in London. He and his wife are on holiday. In Florence," Mr. Crosby added wistfully. "Well, if there's nothing else, gentlemen, I must return to my duties."

"By all means," Jason said. "We'll let you know if we require anything further. Thank you for your cooperation, Mr. Crosby."

"What do you intend to do next?" Daniel asked once they returned to the foyer.

Jason glanced at the clock mounted above the reception desk. It was nearly noon. "Let's get something to eat. We have much to discuss."

Chapter 24

They settled on a chophouse near Charing Cross Station and placed their orders. Daniel opted for the steak and ale pie, while Jason ordered fillets of beef with roasted potatoes. As they waited for their drinks and food to arrive, Daniel glanced out the window at the congested street beyond and marveled at the fact that he was sleeping, eating, and generally functioning as a human being while Charlotte was out there somewhere, possibly experiencing untold torment. He supposed it was normal that he would cling on to life, especially if that meant he could do something to rescue his beloved child, but there was something utterly obscene in the normality of the scene and his actions within its context.

Daniel's reverie was interrupted by the waiter, who silently placed their pints before them. Daniel took a long pull of ale and turned to Jason, eager to hear his thoughts. "You look positively elated," he said, noting Jason's look of satisfaction.

"Elated is rather a strong word, given that a man has just lost his life, but I am pleased, if that is the correct sentiment in this case."

"What are you pleased about?" Daniel asked. He should have been able to figure it out for himself, but his mind felt like sludge, his brain still unable to make the most basic of connections.

"The murder of Leon Stanley proves beyond a shadow of a doubt that Rebecca Grainger wasn't a random victim. Whoever killed Stanley had most certainly murdered Rebecca as well, and the fact that the man's genitalia were severed is proof that this was a crime motivated by strong emotion and a desire for revenge."

"Sexual jealousy," Daniel said, fighting through the fog to concentrate on what Jason was suggesting.

"Precisely. The killer was hurt and angry and would rather murder two people in cold blood than allow them to marry. I can't see that Edward Marsh had anything to do with either death, and to be honest, I'm relieved that the two cases are not connected."

"I'm not sure what's worse, to be chosen at random or to have inspired such boundless fury in someone you know and possibly even trust."

"The end result is much the same, but it does make it easier from an investigative perspective. At least if there's a discernable motive, we can work to unravel the events that led up to the murder."

"To do that, we'd need clues," Daniel replied sourly. "Could Leon Stanley have been murdered by a woman?"

"Yes, but it would have to be a daring, decisive woman."

"What led you to that conclusion?"

"The cut to the throat is straight and deep, made in one fluid motion. There were no ragged edges as one would expect to see if the killer had fumbled or hadn't pressed down the weapon hard enough. Likewise, the genitalia were removed with a steady hand. I would go so far as to say that the precision of the attack resembles the work of a surgeon. Or a butcher."

"But it could also have been a man?" Daniel asked.

"Yes, it could have been a man. There's nothing obvious to suggest either. We do know that the killer had entered the hotel unchallenged, went up to Stanley's room, slit his throat, then mutilated him."

"That's rather obvious, wouldn't you say?" Daniel grumbled. He agreed with Jason's conclusion that Edward Marsh was probably not their man, but they were no further along in identifying the culprit than they had been last night.

Jason waited while the waiter set down their plates, then continued. "Leon Stanley was murdered in bed, and given the expression of surprise on his face and obvious lack of a struggle, I'd say he was asleep when the killer entered his room."

"So what does that prove?"

"It proves that whoever did this has the ability to remain calm despite their all-consuming rage. This wasn't a crime of passion, this was a well-thought-out plan. Perhaps the killer had even obtained a key to Leon Stanley's room and entered in the dead of night, when no one would be in the corridor."

"Unless a guest was headed to the water closet."

"If the killer had the key to the room, any person headed to the communal water closet would simply assume that the killer was one of the guests returning to his or her room. There is something else as well," Jason mused, his beef fillets ignored. "Rebecca was strangled, but Leon's throat was slashed."

"So?" Daniel asked as he sampled his pie and found it satisfactory.

"So, the murder of Rebecca Grainger was most likely not premeditated. It might have been a result of a heated argument, whereas the murder of Leon Stanley was carefully planned and executed."

"Jason, despite all these very valid observations, we're back to the starting point. We know nothing of either Rebecca or Leon's romantic history. Malcolm Briggs was said to be Rebecca's beau, but he's dead, and we know of no other man who was courting her, except me. So, given what we've learned of the killer's emotional state and criminal ability, by rights I should be your prime suspect, a callously rejected lover who would rather see the object of his affection and her betrothed dead than allow them a moment of marital happiness."

Jason gave Daniel a despairing look. "Unless that was a clumsy attempt at a confession, I suggest you shelve that sort of thinking and help me solve this case. Whoever killed Rebecca and Leon knew where to find them and what they were planning, so it stands to reason that it wasn't someone from the distant past who just happened upon them."

"Leon Stanley had only just arrived in England a few weeks ago," Daniel pointed out.

"Given his choice of room, I would have to conclude that he couldn't afford to remain for very long or splurge on more luxurious accommodation. He admitted that his reason for returning to England was to find a bride. He had fond memories of Rebecca Levinson, as he knew her, and wished to look her up, but I very much doubt that she was the only woman he'd had in mind. Perhaps he had approached several ladies of past acquaintance to see if any of them were still unmarried and would make for a suitable partner. In any case, he was under a time constraint since the longer he stayed, the more expensive his scheme to find a wife would become."

"And Rebecca?"

"As far as we know, Rebecca didn't have any other suitors, but we also know that she was good at keeping secrets. The one person she seemed to trust was Mrs. Linnet. I wager the woman knows more than she told you."

"So your plan is to speak to Mrs. Linnet?" Daniel asked, deeply disappointed that this was the best Jason could come up with.

He could hardly blame Jason. He'd come up with a plausible theory, but they had nothing factual to back it up. The killer could be a man or a woman, a person skilled at killing or just someone who was angry enough to strangle Rebecca with their bare hands and execute Leon Stanley and mutilate him without getting caught. They might have walked in through the front door of the hotel or used the employee entrance, and they may have had a key or skillfully picked the lock. The killer had got away without arousing suspicion and could even now be on their way to some unknown destination, safe in the knowledge that no one was on their trail. Speaking to Abel Grainger's housekeeper could hardly shed enough light to point Daniel and Jason in the right direction.

"We'll start with Mrs. Linnet," Jason said.

"And if she knows nothing?"

"I suppose we'll have to return to the hotel tonight and interview the staff to see if they noticed anything suspicious last night."

Daniel stared down at his plate, unable to meet Jason's gaze. Jason wasn't ready to admit it, but he'd hit a brick wall in the investigation and Charlotte was as good as dead, if she wasn't dead already.

Chapter 25

Once Daniel had introduced Jason as Dr. Redmond, as was their custom when investigating a crime in order to avoid unnecessary awkwardness from witnesses who felt intimidated by Jason's rank, Mrs. Linnet led them into her private parlor and shut the door firmly behind her.

"Mr. Grainger is resting, the poor man," she said as she invited them to sit down. It was a pleasant room, well-appointed and comfortable. "He's distraught over the Rebecca's death. He thought he had time to make things right between them, but now she's gone, and he's all that's left of what was once a loving family."

"Mrs. Linnet," Jason began, doing his best not to look in Daniel's direction. The hopelessness in Daniel's gaze tore at his heart, and he prayed that Mrs. Linnet would tell them something they could use. "We believe Rebecca was murdered by someone she knew, someone who was upset about her forthcoming marriage."

"But who would care?" Mrs. Linnet protested. "Rebecca was free to marry where she pleased."

"Perhaps it was Mr. Stanley who wasn't," Jason suggested. "Do you know if he had been married before or had approached any other ladies since his arrival in London?"

"Dear me, how would I know that?"

"Did Rebecca love him?" Jason asked.

Daniel looked away. The question must have cut him to the quick. He had thought Rebecca loved him, but he'd been wrong. Perhaps Leon Stanley had been led to believe the same thing by a woman who was simply looking to better her situation through marriage.

"I really couldn't say," Mrs. Linnet replied, but Jason noticed the guarded look that came over her features.

"Mrs. Linnet, where did Rebecca go after her father died? We cannot account for three years of her life," Jason tried again. "I know you feel compelled to protect Rebecca's privacy, but unless we know more about her life, we'll never catch her killer or find Charlotte Haze."

Mrs. Linnet's gaze betrayed her emotion. "So she's still missing, then, the poor little mite?"

"She is."

Jason didn't need to spell it out for Mrs. Linnet. She understood the implications well enough.

Mrs. Linnet sighed, as if expelling every last reservation. "When Rebecca came to us, she was in a bad way. Oh, she had fashionable gowns and some money of her own, but she was broken, the poor dear. She wouldn't tell her grandfather where she'd been, only that she wanted to stay."

"Was she still grieving her father?" Jason asked. He had a fairly good idea why Rebecca had been so distraught, but this was a way to test the extent of Mrs. Linnet's veracity.

Mrs. Linnet shook her head. "She was grieving her sweetheart."

"Malcolm Briggs?" Daniel demanded, clearly still jealous of a dead man.

Mrs. Linnet nodded. "Malcolm Briggs was a criminal, a safe breaker, but Rebecca loved him. The loss of him…" Her voice trailed off, but then she gathered herself and continued. "Malcolm was arrested, tried, and sent to Australia. He promised Rebecca he'd find his way back and asked her to wait for him, but for all her tender feelings, she was a pragmatic girl."

Mrs. Linnet's gaze slid toward the window, where a pretty red bird was singing its heart out in a nearby tree. "She knew she'd never see him again," she said at last, still not looking at either man. "Just as she knew it was her one chance to get away from a life where people died by violence every day. It was then that she decided to rid herself of the child." Mrs. Linnet's expression betrayed the guilt she felt at divulging the secrets of the young woman who had trusted her.

"Rebecca was pregnant when she came to you four years ago?" Jason asked.

Mrs. Linnet nodded. "Mr. Grainger never suspected, Lord bless him. Oblivious as a babe in arms," she added. "But I knew straight away. A woman who's had children of her own can always recognize the signs."

"How did Rebecca rid herself of the child?"

Women had been self-aborting since the beginning of time, but Jason had to wonder how a young woman like Rebecca Grainger would go about it without the assistance of a trained midwife or someone who was skilled in the use of herbs that would cause the womb to contract hard enough to expel an unwanted child. Most women, like Sally Malvers, went through the pregnancy and delivered their children, whether they wanted them or not, either because they believed an abortion to be a sin against God or they simply didn't have the resources to avail themselves of the alternative.

"We never discussed it," Mrs. Linnet said, "but I was there when she needed my help. I looked after her."

"How far along was she?" Jason asked.

"About two months."

"And are you sure she didn't lose the baby naturally?" Daniel interjected. "Such things do happen, especially when the expectant woman is under undue stress."

"I'm sure, Inspector. She waited until Mr. Grainger went out for the day and executed her plan. It was important to her that he never know what she had done."

"Why?" Jason asked.

"Why what, Dr. Redmond?" Mrs. Linnet asked.

"Why did Rebecca wish to rid herself of the child? She had presumably loved the father, and her grandfather could have easily helped her to hide the pregnancy and then find a good home for the baby if she didn't intend to raise it herself."

The question seemed to stump Mrs. Linnet. She shrugged her rounded shoulders delicately. "I can only presume that she wanted no ties to her past life. A bastard child does alter one's prospects, doesn't it?" It was a question that required no answer, so they moved on.

"Was it once Rebecca had recovered that she decided to seek a position as a nursemaid?" Jason asked.

"Not straight away, no. Rebecca kept to the house for weeks. I don't believe she ever regretted her decision, but she did mourn the loss of her child and the life she might have had with Malcolm. But eventually, her spirit won out. She was a young woman who needed to find hope in her present situation, so she consented to attend several intimate society gatherings with Mr. Grainger. That was all the encouragement he needed."

"Were there any serious contenders for Miss Grainger's hand during those days?" Jason asked.

"There were a few gentlemen who had expressed an interest, but Rebecca's polite rebuffs drove them away. There's no shortage of eligible young ladies in London."

"Was there not a single gentleman Rebecca had made a lasting connection with?" Daniel asked.

"There was one. Peter Hunt. Peter had suffered a bereavement, and although he was out of mourning, he was still grieving the loss of his fiancée. Rebecca and Peter struck up a friendship, but once Rebecca realized Peter had designs on her, she refused to see him."

"Might this Peter Hunt have been so deeply wounded by her rejection that he would be driven to a murderous rage?"

Mrs. Linnet smiled sadly. "Peter was a kind and gentle man. He was deeply hurt, to be sure, but he had since married and was a father to two beautiful children. He never held a grudge against Rebecca. He understood."

"You're speaking of him in the past tense," Jason pointed out.

"Peter died a few months ago. Consumption. He had been confined to a sanitorium, where he had spent the last few months of his life. I do have an address for his widow, but only because she had sent the master an invitation to Peter's funeral."

"Another dead end," Daniel said bitterly, earning himself a look of reproach from Mrs. Linnet.

"It was after Rebecca had refused Peter that she decided to find a position. She had no desire to be married, at least not then, and knew that her grandfather would not respect her wish to remain single. As with Nellie, Mr. Grainger had tried to impose his own will on the situation. Rebecca's decision caused a rift between them."

"But they eventually reconciled," Daniel said.

"They did. Mr. Grainger was her only living relative, and she understood that his actions had been motivated by love and a desire to see her settled before he passed."

"Were they close?" Jason asked.

"They were coolly polite."

"But Rebecca confided in you when she came to visit," Daniel said.

"She did. She needed someone to talk to, and I was there to listen."

"And what did she tell you about Mr. Stanley?" Jason probed.

"She admired him."

"Why?" Daniel demanded with more belligerence than necessary.

"Mr. Stanley had not had a good start in life, but he'd turned things around and become a prosperous rancher. And he wanted to give Rebecca the world."

"And is that what Rebecca wanted?"

"She wanted security, Inspector Haze. She wanted safety. And she thought she had found that with Mr. Stanley. She thought he'd look after her."

"Do you know if Leon Stanley had any family?" Jason asked.

"His widowed younger sister, Emmeline, lived with him at the ranch. Rebecca mentioned that it was Emmeline's idea that Leon return to England to find a wife."

"Did Rebecca know Emmeline?" Daniel asked. Clearly that was another tidbit Rebecca had never mentioned.

"Yes. They knew each other before, and Rebecca looked forward to seeing Emmeline again."

"And does Emmeline have any children?" Jason asked.

"No."

"Thank you, Mrs. Linnet," Jason said, and stood to leave.

Daniel followed him outside and exploded as soon as they were out of earshot of the house. "None of this helps," he exclaimed. "Malcolm Briggs is dead. Peter Hunt is dead. Leon Stanley's sister has no son who might have followed his uncle to England and knocked him off before he could produce an heir to his ranch. What now?" He tried valiantly to control himself, but tears misted his eyes, and Jason felt overwhelming sympathy for him. "Jason, it's been three days. Charlotte—" He turned away to hide his grief.

Jason laid a gentle hand on Daniel's shoulder. "I know," he said quietly. "I know." Pulling out his pocket watch, Jason consulted the time. It was only past two, but they had no viable leads to pursue. "Let me take you home, Daniel."

Home was probably the last place Daniel wanted to be, but he could hardly fault Jason for calling it a day. They had no suspects and no clues, even if they had arrived at a possible motive. They had reached the end of the line, at least for today.

Daniel nodded, and the two men walked toward the nearest hackney stand in an uneasy silence.

Chapter 26

Jason was in a grim mood when he returned home, made grimmer still by a note that had been delivered for him not an hour before. The missive was from Tristan Carmichael, who stated that he had asked around, as promised, but no one knew anything about the abduction or whereabouts of Charlotte Haze. Despite his dislike for the man, Jason believed him and thought the man had no reason to lie to him. No part of what he'd learned so far implicated Tristan Carmichael in Rebecca's murder.

Dropping the note back onto the silver salver in Dodson's hand, Jason momentarily wished he could lock himself in the study so he could think things through uninterrupted, but he could hardly refuse to greet Micah or speak to Katherine. A part of him wanted to ask for her thoughts on Rebecca's decision to abort her child, but the part that was a Victorian gentleman of breeding begged him not to burden his wife with such shocking disclosures. Katherine would be devastated to learn that the woman she had considered a friend had not been what she believed her to be and had done things Katherine could never approve of, either as a vicar's daughter or simply a woman of unimpeachable character.

Taking a deep breath to center himself, Jason headed for the drawing room, where Micah sat reading by the fire, his hair nearly the same color as the flames in the hearth. In the past, Micah would have rushed to Jason, eager for a fatherly hug, but he was no longer the little boy Jason had taken in after his father and brother had died at Andersonville Prison. He held out his hand, and Jason took it and shook it as if Micah were one of his colleagues at the hospital and not the child he'd come to love. He reflected that Micah seemed to have matured a little more every time Jason saw him, and when he said, "Hello, Captain," using Jason's military rank as usual, his voice sounded gravelly and deep. Jason took in the russet hair that shadowed Micah's upper lip and pale cheeks and suddenly, he saw the man Micah was going to become— the young man he had become already.

"It's good to see you, Micah," Jason said with feeling. "How was the journey down?"

Micah shrugged. "Fine. I thought you were coming to get me."

"I'm sorry," Jason said, suddenly very tired. "Something's come up."

Micah gave him a searching look, his blue eyes appraising Jason with almost the same eagle-eyed intensity that Katherine's normally did when he was on a case and she was worried for his safety. "A new case?"

"Where's Katherine?" Jason asked instead.

"In the nursery with Lily."

For a moment, Jason was almost glad that Katherine wasn't there to hear about his spectacular failure, but she'd come down soon enough and ask him point-blank if he'd made any progress. Needing Dutch courage, Jason poured himself a large whisky and collapsed into a wingchair, too distraught to talk about the case.

Micah seemed to sense his mood and didn't ask any questions. He regarded Jason for a long moment, his gaze that of a full-fledged adult, not a boy of fourteen, and asked, "Would you like a game of chess? That always made you feel better when you were in low spirits."

"Thank you, Micah, but I don't think I'd be able to concentrate."

"I might be able to help if you tell me what's troubling you."

Jason sighed and took a gulp of whisky. It burned its way down with satisfying intensity as Jason considered Micah's offer. He would find out what had happened sooner or later, and then he'd resent Jason for treating him like a child and not telling him the truth.

"Rebecca Grainger was murdered on Saturday. Charlotte was with her at the time, and no one has seen her since. We believe she has been abducted. Superintendent Ransome has put me in charge of the case, since Daniel is in no mental state to head up an investigation into his daughter's disappearance and Rebecca's murder. And then Rebecca's fiancé, Leon Stanley, was murdered last night, his throat slashed as he slept." Jason left out the rest. Neither Micah nor Katherine needed to know that.

Micah's mouth dropped open, and his eyes filled with tears, but he blinked them away determinedly. "Jesus, Mary, and Joseph," he sputtered as he shook his head in disbelief. "Poor Inspector Haze. He must be beside himself."

"He is hanging on by a thread."

"If anyone can find Charlotte, it's you, Captain," Micah said, his loyalty nearly bringing Jason to tears. "You'll get her back."

Micah looked at Jason in a way that told him he needed to be reassured that Jason would indeed bring Charlotte back safely, but Jason could offer no such guarantee.

"Nothing about this case adds up, Micah," Jason exclaimed, venting his frustration at last. "I have two murder victims, a missing child, and a number of random facts, but no hard evidence and not a single living suspect."

"All your suspects are dead?" Micah asked.

"Essentially, yes."

"And do you think Charlotte…" Micah couldn't finish the sentence.

"Something inside me believes that Charlotte is still alive, but I don't know if it's some sort of instinct or simply hope."

"I think you know when someone is dead," Micah said, his voice flat. "There's just this…" His voice trailed off as he tried to marshal his thoughts. "It's as if you can sense their spirit, even if they are miles away, and then suddenly you can't. There's nothing but a dense emptiness."

Jason considered Micah's words and tried to recall whether he had known his parents were dead before he'd learned of the train accident that had claimed their lives. He couldn't remember. He had been in prison in Georgia when his parents died. He'd been so ill toward the end of his imprisonment that he had been beyond caring if he lived or died. The only person that had kept him tethered to this world was Micah, who'd been left orphaned and was the only child at the prison, having been a drummer boy for his regiment and taken prisoner with the rest of the soldiers.

"You knew your parents were dead," Micah announced.

"Did I?"

Micah nodded. "I remember you saying so, but you were so delirious, I thought you were ranting. But you knew," Micah insisted.

Jason decided not to ask if Micah had thought Mary was dead when they couldn't find her after the end of the war. Mary was well now and living in Boston with her family. That was all that mattered.

"If you don't feel Charlotte is dead, then she isn't," Micah insisted. "You have to find her, Captain."

Jason tossed back the rest of his whisky and turned to set the glass on the occasional table at his elbow. He was just about to turn back to face Micah when something caught his eye. That morning's edition of *The Times* was lying on the table, no doubt left there by Katherine. Many a husband forbade his wife to read the news for fear that she might become afflicted with an opinion of her own, but Jason supported Katherine's desire for knowledge, and they often discussed current events over dinner and laughed at the silly incidents mentioned in the society columns. As much as Katherine enjoyed the political articles and commentary on social reform or lack thereof, she always turned to the society page after perusing the more serious fare, more to distance herself from the distressing news of the day than because she was genuinely interested in who had been seen where and with whom. Today's newspaper was folded in half, the society column displaying the heading:

A SÉANCE IN BELGRAVIA

Jason reached for the paper and scanned the short article. He was on his feet in seconds, hurrying from the room.

"Captain, where are you going?" Micah called after him. "What shall I tell Auntie Katherine?"

"Tell her I'll be back soon," Jason called over his shoulder.

He was outside a few minutes later, and not wishing to bother Joe, who was no doubt in the kitchen enjoying a cup of tea and a slice of cake after hours on the road, went in search of a cab.

"Twenty-five, Belgravia Square," Jason called out to the cabbie as he climbed into the first available conveyance.

The distance between Jason's home and the address in Belgravia was no more than a few miles, but the workday was drawing to a close, and there was the usual amount of late afternoon traffic. For once, Jason didn't mind. Even if the ride took an hour, he'd still get to Belgravia well before the start of the séance, and the delay gave him much-needed time to think. Blocking out the noise from the street, Jason returned to the interview with Mrs. Linnet. None of what she'd told them was really surprising, given what they already knew of Rebecca's past, but there was one thing that gave him pause. A long, pregnant pause.

Had Jason not been personally acquainted with Rebecca, he might have come to other conclusions, but he had known her since she had first taken up the position as Charlotte's nursemaid. Rebecca had been pragmatic to a fault, the sort of person who eschewed rash actions undertaken in the heat of the moment. The fact that she had decided to abort her baby didn't square with what

Jason would expect her to do. To kill an unborn child was not only dangerous and ofttimes fatal but extremely painful and also heart wrenching, especially if that child was the only reminder of a man the woman had loved.

Malcolm Briggs had vowed that he would escape and find his way back to England, and if Rebecca had undertaken the decision to rid herself of the child in the first trimester, she probably hadn't even known he had died. News of the ship's fate would have taken weeks if not months to reach London, given that it had gone down off the coast of Africa. So why had Rebecca decided to abort? Was it because she had desperately wanted to sever all ties to Malcolm Briggs, or was there another reason? Had she not loved Malcolm, or had she loved him and was terrified that he would return and find that she'd had a child? That would only be a problem if the child hadn't been Malcolm's and he'd know it.

How long had Malcolm Briggs been in prison before he was sent to Australia? If he had been in prison longer than a few months, then the child had definitely not been his, unless Malcolm and Rebecca had somehow managed to copulate during his imprisonment. If Malcolm had managed to find a sympathetic guard who could be bribed to allow the lovers a few minutes of privacy, then Jason's theory that the child wasn't Malcolm's went right out the window. Whoever the father was, Rebecca had clearly thought her decision through and had waited until she was safely at her grandfather's house, where Mrs. Linnet could look after her should things go wrong and summon a physician. That was probably the only reason Rebecca had gone to Abel Grainger's house. She had needed a safe place. Once she miscarried, she had stayed for a while but ultimately discovered that she had no interest in the life her grandfather wanted for her and chose independence over security.

As the hansom turned into Belgravia Square, Jason was forced to abandon his speculation and focus on the task at hand.

Chapter 27

Jason alighted before number twenty-five and took stock of his surroundings, since he'd never actually visited the square but had heard much about its charms. Belgravia Square was one of the priciest and most coveted addresses in London, the gleaming, white-stuccoed facades solid and imposing against the pale lavender of approaching twilight. The air smelled fresh and clean, and birds chirped happily in the private garden at the center of the square. Many of the windows were lit against the oncoming darkness, casting rectangles of golden light onto the street beyond, except where the curtains had already been drawn and the light filtered through colorful and probably very expensive fabric. Except for a sleek, yellow-bodied carriage that rolled past Jason and pulled up before one of the corner mansions to deposit two beautifully attired ladies, mother and daughter judging by their ages, no one was about.

The families that called Belgravia Square their home hid behind an army of servants and well-trained gatekeepers, and only Jason's rank would induce them to ignore his rudeness and allow him admittance, if only long enough for him to state his business and leave. Jason asked the cabbie to wait and marched up to the black-painted front door. A pompous but surprisingly young butler answered the door, his expression of sycophantic deference instantly changing to one of surprise and then hardened resolve. Jason had not been invited to the gathering that was to take place in Lady Cosgrove's salon that evening, and he would be turned away.

"How can I help you, sir?" the butler asked irritably, all the while blocking the door just in case Jason decided to force his way in.

"Lord Redmond to see Lady Cosgrove." Jason handed the butler his card and waited for the man to glance at it to judge the quality of the paper and the Kensington address printed across the front.

His expression softened infinitesimally, but he did not step aside. "I'm afraid her ladyship is not at home to visitors, my lord."

"My business with her will only take a moment. It's of the greatest urgency," Jason said.

"I'm afraid I'm going to have to ask you to leave, your lordship. Her ladyship is expecting guests."

"Yes, I'm aware of that." Jason extracted his temporary warrant card from the pocket of his coat and held it up to the butler's nose. "I need to speak to Lady Cosgrove. Either let me in, or I will return with reinforcements after her ladyship's guests have arrived and cause a disruption which will no doubt be covered in the papers tomorrow, and in great detail," Jason added for good measure.

The butler's gaze turned hard, his anger at being put in this position obvious. He had to decide whether to incur the wrath of his employer or to expose the family to possible scandal when the ruffian on the doorstep returned with uniformed constables, who were sure to make enough of a commotion to attract the attention of everyone within hearing distance. Having made his choice, the butler moved aside, allowing Jason to step into the black-and-white-tiled foyer. A sizeable flower arrangement stood on a round table at the center, the lilies giving off a funereal scent that reminded Jason of occasions he would prefer to forget.

"Please wait here, *your lordship*," the butler said testily, probably assuming he had been lied to and Jason was really nothing more than some jumped-up inspector, or worse yet, a journalist. "I will inform her ladyship you wish to have a word."

Lady Cosgrove was no older than thirty-five, with fair curls artfully arranged about her pale face and wide blue eyes. She wore a gown of lavender accented with a silver fichu and matching cuffs. Jet beads hung about her throat and swayed hypnotically from her earlobes. Lady Cosgrove was still in half-mourning for her husband, who'd been beaten to death in the Tuileries Garden in Paris two years ago when he was returning to his hotel in the early hours of the morning. A robbery gone wrong, or so the newspapers had suggested at the time.

"Lord Redmond, it's a pleasure to meet you," she said, smiling at him pleasantly, but Jason could see the effort it took for the lady to remain civil and not chuck him out of her presence. She was clearly trying to avoid a scene.

"My lady, please forgive me for barging into your home this way. I would not have dared had it not been a matter of life and death."

"Whose life and whose death?" Lady Cosgrove asked, a spark of interest igniting in her lovely eyes.

"A small child. My goddaughter."

"How can I possibly help?" Lady Cosgrove asked, her feathery brows knitting in confusion.

"You're hosting a séance this evening," Jason began.

"Yes. I hope to contact my late husband."

"And I wish you the best possible outcome, but I must speak to the medium before you begin."

"The medium?" Lady Cosgrove repeated, clearly stunned by the request.

"Mrs. Lysander and I are acquainted," Jason explained. "Please, Lady Cosgrove. It'll only take a minute, and then I will leave you to the night's entertainment."

That was hardly the right word to use when referring to someone's enduring grief and a desperate need to see their loved one just one more time, but Lady Cosgrove hardly seemed to notice Jason's clumsy mistake.

"Eh, yes, of course. Come this way, my lord."

Lady Cosgrove wanted him gone; that was obvious, but she was too gracious a person to simply evict him from the premises, especially when he had played on her feminine sensibilities and made her feel that a child might die if she refused to help. Jason suspected she thought he was quite mad, but it made no difference. He'd got his way; that was what mattered.

After knocking on the door of a small parlor to alert the individual within, Lady Cosgrove pushed it open. Alicia Lysander stood by the window, looking out at the dusky sky beyond. She was dressed all in black, as before, and her dark hair was gathered at her nape in a simple but elegant chignon. She turned, her mouth opening ever so slightly in surprise before she hastily shut it and lifted her chin defiantly.

She hadn't changed much since Jason had seen her last, more than a year ago, her exotic beauty, a gift from her Indian mother, even more pronounced when compared to the fair features of Lady Cosgrove. The two women were like some mythical representation of day and night, or innocence and experience, for no one who gazed upon Alicia Lysander could mistake her for anything but a woman of the world.

"Lord Redmond," Alicia Lysander said with an amused half-smile. "I did wonder when we'd meet again."

In the past, Jason might have questioned a medium's ability to predict a meeting between them, but having conversed with Alicia Lysander at length in the course of a previous case, Jason understood that she was not a fortune teller but a conduit between two worlds, a woman who made no pretense to knowing what lay ahead. And that suited him just fine. It wasn't the future he'd come to ask about.

"If we might speak in private, Mrs. Lysander."

"From your unscheduled appearance here, I can only surmise that you need my help," Alicia Lysander said, still smiling that maddeningly sardonic smile.

"I do."

Alicia Lysander nodded. "My lady, if you would permit us a moment."

"Of course," Lady Cosgrove said, and retreated, shutting the door behind her. Jason suspected she would not go far but hover within hearing distance to find out what was said, but he wasn't troubled by her curiosity. All his attention was focused on the psychic.

"Where's your assistant?" Jason asked, wondering if Constantine Moore was about to come barreling into the room, ever protective of his partner and paramour.

"He had an errand to run. I doubt he'd be pleased to see you." Alicia Lysander walked over to an elegant apple-green settee and sat down, folding her long-fingered hands in her lap. "I thought you didn't believe in mysticism."

"You changed my mind," Jason replied. Alicia Lysander had told him things no one could possibly know, specifically the heart-wrenching details of his parents' final moments.

"Now you're just humoring me, my lord."

"Mrs. Lysander, I don't know what I believe, and that's the truth, but I am in desperate need of help. When I realized you were back in London…" Jason's voice trailed off as he tried to gauge Mrs. Lysander's willingness to hear him out.

"You thought you'd enlist my help."

"I will pay whatever you ask."

"It's not about the money," Alicia Lysander replied, waving a hand dismissively. "This is quite personal for you, isn't it? Whom do you need to contact, my lord? Have you suffered a bereavement since we last met?"

Jason explained the situation. "I need to find Charlotte."

"You do realize she might have already passed."

"If she has, then I need to retrieve her remains. The not knowing will destroy Daniel."

She nodded. "I will help you, but you must understand that I can offer no guarantees. The spirits are unpredictable and don't always wish to make contact, especially so soon after their passing. There's a period of adjustment."

"I understand, but I would still like to try."

Alicia Lysander nodded, her expression thoughtful. "I will ask you not to invite Daniel Haze. I think we will fare better without him. An emotional outburst might drive the spirit away. However, I find that the séances work best when there are at least four people. Can you produce two more people who knew both Rebecca Grainger and Charlotte?"

"Yes."

"Good. I should be finished here no later than nine. Then I will come to you."

"Is there anything you require?"

"A small, dark room with a round table, where we will not be disturbed. It's best if you dismiss the servants."

"All will be ready for you."

"Does your lady wife know she's about to host a séance?" Mrs. Lysander asked as she rose gracefully to her feet.

"My wife loves Charlotte and will do anything to help me find her."

"Is your wife a spiritual woman, my lord?"

"She's more spiritual than I am."

"Well, that's something, I suppose," Alicia Lysander said, and turned toward the door, indicating that their interview was at an end. "I will see you tonight. Now, if you will excuse me, I must prepare for Lady Cosgrove's séance."

"Thank you, Mrs. Lysander," Jason said. "I appreciate your willingness to help me."

"Don't thank me yet," she said, her gaze growing serious. "Let's see what we can discover."

Jason handed Alicia Lysander his card, bowed from the neck, and let himself out of the room.

Lady Cosgrove was hovering in the corridor and looked at him anxiously, but once she saw that he was ready to leave, her anxiety seemed to evaporate.

"Thank you, my lady. And again, I apologize for the intrusion."

"Not at all, my lord. Did you get what you came for?" she asked carefully.

"I've yet to find out," Jason replied, and walked through the door and into the street.

Chapter 28

Jason was glad Alicia Lysander had instructed him not to invite Daniel since he would have felt a nagging sense of guilt had the choice been his. He did think it was best if Daniel didn't know. If Jason was able to find out anything that might help, then he'd share the news, but if he didn't learn anything useful, then he'd spare Daniel false hope and a possible confirmation that Charlotte was already gone.

As the hansom pulled up to Jason's townhouse, he made another decision. He was going to dine with his family and allow himself a brief respite from the case until Mrs. Lysander arrived. He needed to clear his mind and hoped that he could put Katherine and Micah at ease before informing them about the upcoming séance. But that was not to be.

"Jason, is there any word?" Katherine exclaimed as soon as Dodson let Jason in. She was halfway down the stairs but hurried down the last few steps and wrapped her arms around Jason's neck. "I haven't been able to think of anything else all day. And then Micah said you saw something in the newspaper and hurried off. Where on earth did you go?"

"Belgravia Square."

"Why?"

"To see Mrs. Lysander."

"The psychic?" Katherine's brow creased with obvious disapproval. "Why?"

"Because I'm desperate, Katie. Every avenue of inquiry has proved to be a dead end. Time is running out for Charlotte, if it hasn't already."

"And you think Mrs. Lysander can help?" Katherine's look of consternation made Jason wonder if he'd made a terrible miscalculation.

"If she can contact Rebecca—"

"Contact Rebecca?" Katherine echoed.

"Cor, Captain, you really are desperate," Micah said as he came out of the drawing room and joined them in the foyer. "I've never known you to believe in that tripe."

"I can't afford to allow my prejudices to prevent me from seeking help. I know it's unorthodox, but if there's anything Mrs. Lysander can tell me, I'm willing to listen. She has requested that two people who knew Rebecca Grainger also participate."

No matter how much Jason needed their assistance, he wasn't going to strongarm either Katherine or Micah. They had both lost those dear to them, and the prospect of a séance might be unsettling. If they were unwilling to participate, he would have to ask Mrs. Dodson and his valet, Henley, who'd briefly thought he might have a chance with Rebecca when she and Charlotte had come to visit. Mrs. Dodson and Henley were not ideal, but they would have to do.

Katherine reached out and took hold of Jason's hand, then looked up at him and smiled reassuringly. "If there's even the slightest chance that the séance will help, then I will gladly take part."

"You don't have to, Katie," Jason said. "I can ask Mrs. Dodson. I wouldn't want you to go against your beliefs."

"No, I want to. It's the least I can do."

"I'll do it," Micah said. "What's the worst that can happen?" he added with an insouciant shrug.

"We will do whatever is necessary, Jason," Katherine said, her eyes shining with love and support.

"Thank you, both," Jason said. "I can't do this without you."

"You won't have to," Katherine said, visibly pushing her misgivings aside in her desire to support him. "Just tell me what Mrs. Lysander will need."

"She doesn't require anything out of the ordinary. We can use the morning room. It has a round table for four."

"Morning room it is, then."

"We can't have any interruptions," Jason added.

"I will speak to Dodson and ensure that no one goes near the morning room while Mrs. Lysander is here. Now, we have some time until she gets here. Shall we go in to dinner?" Katherine asked, laying a hand on Jason's forearm. "You look tired, Jason."

"It's been a trying day." That was the understatement of the year, and the day wasn't over yet.

Chapter 29

Alicia Lysander arrived just after nine. Alone. Jason thought it was remiss of Mr. Moore to allow her to travel on her own after dark, but their arrangement was none of Jason's affair, so he made no comment. He waited for Dodson to take Mrs. Lysander's silk cape and matching hat, then led her into the drawing room, where Katherine and Micah were anxiously awaiting her arrival.

"Good evening, Mrs. Lysander," Katherine said as she came forward to greet the medium.

"Lady Redmond," Mrs. Lysander replied coolly. "And is this our fourth?" she asked, her dark gaze settling on Micah.

"May I present Micah Donovan, our ward?" Katherine replied. "He is, indeed, our fourth."

"It's good to meet you, Micah," Mrs. Lysander said.

"Likewise, ma'am," Micah said. He looked nervous and probably wished he could escape to his room.

"Please, make yourself comfortable. Would you care for a drink before we get started?" Katherine asked solicitously.

"No, my lady. I would prefer to begin. Do you have the room set up?"

"Everything is in readiness," Jason replied. "Shall we?"

"There are some things I would like to explain before we begin," she said, her eyes moving to each of them in turn.

"Of course," Jason said, giving her the floor.

"I don't do private sessions," Mrs. Lysander said, fixing Jason with a stern look. "Mostly because there's no way to ensure that the dearly departed of the individual paying me will make an appearance, and I have no wish to deceive them by putting on an act and profiting from their grief. When summoning a particular person, there's no telling what will happen, especially when that person is very recently deceased. Newly passed souls are often confused and overly emotional, still trying to adjust to the loss of their corporeal form and in the process of accepting their new state. At times, a different, stronger spirit may appear and take advantage of the chance to pass a message to those they'd left behind."

Mrs. Lysander paused, letting that sink in. "The best way to ensure the right spirit comes through is to focus on a particular memory of them instead of allowing your mind to wander. That's why I requested that only the people who knew Miss Grainger and Charlotte be present. I will ask you not to call out during the séance or break physical contact with the person next to you until the spirit leaves of their own accord. Are we ready?"

The three of them nodded, and Mrs. Lysander turned to Jason once more. "Lead the way, my lord."

The morning room faced east and was normally airy and bright, a place to eat a light breakfast or enjoy a cup of coffee or tea if one had no wish to sit in the dining room or the drawing room. Tonight, it was almost completely dark, the only light coming in through the door open to the gaslit corridor. The curtains were drawn against the night, and the pale pink flowers on the wallpaper were lost in shadow. The white tablecloth had been replaced by one of fringed green velvet, and a single silver candleholder stood in the center of the table, the candle yet to be lit. Alicia Lysander walked into the room first, set her reticule on the walnut sideboard, and settled in one of the chairs, her back to the window. She instructed Jason to sit across from her, with Katherine and Micah on either side.

The atmosphere in the room felt dense, the darkness otherworldly and viscous once the door was closed to shut out the light. The corridor beyond was silent, Mrs. Dodson, Fanny, Kitty, and Henley in their respective rooms, getting ready for bed. Only Dodson was still about and would retire once Mrs. Lysander left and he locked up for the night.

Mrs. Lysander lit the candle, and the participants' faces swam into view, pale and tense.

"Please, join hands and do not let go, no matter what you hear. I will ask you to close your eyes and bring forth a memory of Rebecca Grainger. Allow the memory to play out in your mind, then focus on Rebecca and silently call to her spirit. Keep your eyes shut until I tell you to open them. Can you do that?"

They all nodded like marionettes, their gazes fixed on Mrs. Lysander, who looked entirely too businesslike for a woman who was about to commune with the dead. Jason held out his hands to Katherine and Micah. Alicia Lysander did the same. Katherine's fingers were cool and dry, but Micah's hand was clammy and way too warm. Jason briefly wondered what Mrs. Lysander's hand felt like. Was she nervous, excited, afraid? Jason tried to pull up a memory of Rebecca Grainger, but his mind wouldn't comply. Instead, what he saw was a battlefield, the scene shrouded in billowing smoke.

Men were running toward each other, their screams amplified by gunfire. The terror of horses and the explosions plunged the landscape into an apocalyptic chaos as the cannonballs gouged out chunks of earth and tossed able-bodied men aside as if they were nothing more than rag dolls. Their severed limbs landed feet away from their bodies, their eyes rolling with pain and shock as they either succumbed to their wounds or screamed for help, largely ignored by their friends until the heat of battle was over. For a brief moment, Jason saw Elias Garfield. He stood stock still, his gaze fixed on something just beyond the battlefield, the dark blue wool of his uniform pristinely clean.

Dragging his mind away from the unwelcome image, Jason scrambled to find a memory of Rebecca. When he finally did, he saw her sitting in the wingchair by the hearth in Daniel's small parlor, a book in her hand. She wore a prim gown of dove gray wool, but neither the severe cut nor the unflattering color did anything to detract from her loveliness. She looked up and smiled, her pleasure at seeing him again evident. Rebecca's fair curls danced around her face, and her dimples deepened as she smiled up at him, the look in her blue eyes entirely too playful for a nursemaid.

Rebecca, Jason thought, and for the first time since looking down at Rebecca's remains, he felt a deep sadness rather than anger, frustration, and a need to get justice for the young woman whose life had been so suddenly snuffed out. *Rebecca*, he thought again, and focused on Mrs. Lysander's soft voice.

"O, Spirit," Mrs. Lysander moaned. "We beseech you, make yourself known to us. We seek your guidance and light. You are safe here with us."

For a while nothing happened, and Jason cursed himself for a fool for believing this could help in any way, but then Mrs. Lysander tried again. "O, Spirit, we summon you here tonight because we seek your guiding light. Help us and show us a way forward."

Mrs. Lysander stopped speaking, and Jason heard the barely audible breathing of those present. Katherine was squeezing his fingers tightly, while Micah's grip had slackened. Suddenly, Mrs. Lysander's voice took on a different cadence. "I feel your presence," she whispered urgently. "Thank you for joining us. Can you tell us your name?"

Despite his better judgment, Jason allowed himself a peek at Mrs. Lysander. She sat quite still, her face a pale oval in the glow of the candle. Her eyes appeared to be moving rapidly beneath her closed eyelids, as if she were watching something play out, and her back was ramrod straight, her body utterly rigid.

"I feel your presence, O Spirit. Can you tell us your name?" Mrs. Lysander moaned again, and then Jason saw something that made the breath catch in his throat.

The air behind Alicia Lysander's right shoulder seemed to shimmer, the ethereal shape taking on a translucent outline that couldn't be mistaken for anything other than a woman. It was impossible to make out the wraith's age or features, but there was definitely a presence that couldn't be fabricated using some well-practiced parlor trick. The glowing shape hovered there for a moment, as if unsure if it wished to remain. Afraid to do anything that might drive it away, Jason shut his eyes and kept them closed as he had been instructed. There was a momentary silence, and then Jason's heart thundered with shock as he recognized Mary's voice, her Irish lilt unmistakable.

"Micah, *a stór*," Mary whispered. "Oh, my greatest treasure. I'm so sorry for leaving ye."

Jason found that he was holding his breath. He didn't know what *stór* meant but thought it was a Gaelic endearment. A jolt passed through Jason's entire being as the full impact of the words settled on him. If Mary was calling out to Micah, that meant she was dead, and Micah now knew it.

Micah's hand vibrated in Jason's, his breath coming in raspy gasps. Jason gripped his hand tightly, but Micah was squirming in his seat, unable to contain his emotion.

"Mammy," Micah cried, despite being asked to remain silent. "Mammy, I miss you so."

Jason breathed a sigh of relief. He'd assumed the spirit was Mary, but he'd never met Micah's mother. She had come through to her younger child, desperate to tell him she loved him. Perhaps this would bring Micah comfort once he got over the shock of hearing his mother's voice.

"My brave boy," Mrs. Donovan whispered. "Ye must get Liam. Mary is…" The last word was hardly more than an exhalation, but to Jason, who peeked through his lashes despite his better judgment, it sounded like *gone*. And then the apparition dissolved, leaving behind a great, dark void.

"Mammy," Micah cried. "Please don't go. Mary is what? Mammy, please." But there was no answer.

Jason heard Micah's stifled sobs and felt Katherine's nails as they dug into his skin. She was frightened and overcome with emotion, but they couldn't stop now, and Micah had to remain in order to continue. Micah seemed to sense Jason's thoughts and quieted down, his hand stiff in Jason's and his breathing ragged as he tried to regain control of his emotions.

"O Spirit of Rebecca Grainger, please come to us," Mrs. Lysander intoned. "Tell us who hurt you."

Jason highly doubted that Rebecca would appear on cue, but Mrs. Lysander kept trying and calling out to her. "Rebecca Grainger," she moaned softly. "I know how frightened and confused you must be, but those left behind love you and miss you, and want to see justice done. Come to us, Rebecca."

Mrs. Lysander stopped speaking, and there was a dense silence. Jason thought she might try again, but she remained quiet. The moments ticked by with painful slowness. Normally, Jason could sit still for hours if he needed to, but the tension inside him begged to be released, and he desperately wanted to get out of this room. There was nothing holding him back except the hands of Micah and Katherine, but he felt as if steel cables bound him to the chair and he couldn't get up even if he wanted to. His chest tightened with anxiety, and he sucked in a deep breath, willing himself to calm down. Unable to keep his eyes shut for so long, he opened them for just a second, and there it was, that shimmer. He forced his eyes shut, fearful he'd driven Mrs. Donovan away.

"Ah," Mrs. Lysander suddenly breathed out. "She is here. Speak to us," she implored.

"Daniel," the apparition moaned. "Daniel, please help me."

Even though the voice was feeble, it sounded just like Rebecca's, and Jason fought the desperate need to call out and ask her questions.

"How can Daniel help you?" Alicia Lysander asked softly.

"Daniel, don't let him hurt me," Rebecca's voice pleaded. "Please."

"Who wishes to hurt you?" Jason asked, and instantly regretted his outburst.

"There's blood dripping from his mouth," Rebecca cried shrilly. Her terror was obvious. "The blood of the dead. And he wishes to revenge himself on me."

"Eternal Spirit, Spirit of truth, who's this man?" Alicia asked.

"A demon," Rebecca said on a sigh. "Come back from the dead."

The room suddenly grew warmer, and Jason felt a desperate need to loosen his collar. He felt like he couldn't breathe. Micah was sniffling softly next to him, and Katherine sat completely still, rigid with shock.

"She is gone," Mrs. Lysander said with resignation. "You may let go and open your eyes now. There will be no more visitations tonight."

Micah yanked his hand out of Jason's and exploded from the room, his footsteps pounding on the stairs. Jason met Alicia Lysander's gaze over the light of the candle. She looked demonic, her dark eyes reflecting the flame, her lips almost black against her unnaturally pale skin. *She must use rice powder to lighten her natural hue*, Jason thought, and realized just how ridiculous it was that he was questioning the pallor of her skin when what he had just experienced defied all reason. He was a logical man, someone who believed in learning and science, but he couldn't deny that something otherworldly had just taken place and he had been a part of it.

Had the séance taken place someplace else, he would have instantly assumed that Alicia Lysander and Constantine Moore had devised some kind of a trick that would project a floating image into the darkness, but this was his house, and no one had been inside the morning room this evening save himself and Dodson. There was no one hiding behind the drawn curtains, and there was no mirror or any conceivable way to project the image into thin air.

198

It had been real, and no matter how much he wanted to dispute the fact, deep inside, he knew it.

For one brief moment, he considered asking Alicia Lysander to summon his parents, but he instantly dismissed the urge. He wasn't going to become one of those people who chased a medium all over the country in the hope that she would bring forth their lost loved ones. Jason's parents were gone, and he had to allow them to rest. There was nothing he urgently needed to know. They had loved him and would be proud of him. That was enough.

Tearing his thoughts away from what had just occurred, he turned his attention to Alicia Lysander, who was patiently waiting for him to compose himself.

"I'm sorry," she said, a small smile of triumph tugging at her lips. "I don't have any influence over who comes through or how long they remain. Was any of what took place useful?"

Jason considered the question. "I don't know what it means. Any of it. Do you?"

"I'm only a messenger, a mouthpiece, if you will."

"Why would Rebecca call out to Daniel? What can he do for her in the afterlife?" Katherine asked. Her face was set in tense lines, and she was clearly trying to make sense of what she had just heard and apply it to the principles she had held all her life.

"As I have mentioned before, Lady Redmond, newly departed souls are frequently confused since they are still caught between the two realms. I believe Rebecca's spirit called out to a person she trusted."

"What if we do it again?" Katherine asked, looking from Jason to Mrs. Lysander. "Perhaps the spirit would be able to tell us more."

Alicia Lysander shook her head. "It doesn't work like that, my lady. Summoning the spirits again and again doesn't mean they will return or that they will tell us anything different."

"In that case, please excuse me. I must see to Micah," Katherine said, and left the room. Jason knew she was shaken, but Katherine and Micah would have to wait.

"Mrs. Lysander. Alicia, please help me to understand," Jason pleaded. "I have to find Daniel's little girl."

"I did not sense a child's presence, Lord Redmond," Alicia Lysander said as she reached out and placed her cool hand over Jason's. "But I did see an image of a ship. A floundering ship."

"Can't you tell me something more?" Jason pleaded.

"I can only relay what the dead want you to know when they make themselves known to me. I'm sorry."

"What about Mrs. Donovan?" Jason cried. He suddenly realized that he didn't even know her Christian name.

Alicia Lysander shook her head sadly. "I felt the warmth of her love and her worry for her children, but I can't tell you anything more." She rose gracefully to her feet and reached for her reticule. "I must go. I'm very tired."

"Allow me to find you a cab," Jason said as he staggered to his feet, his mind still on what he had heard.

"No need. Constantine will be waiting for me." Alicia Lysander looked at Jason, her gaze anxious. "I'm sorry to have caused your boy pain. I'm afraid he was taken unawares."

"Is Mary dead?" Jason asked, his voice breaking on the last word.

Mrs. Lysander shook her head. "I really couldn't say, but I did feel the presence of a young woman."

"Thank you for trying to help."

"I hope you find Charlotte, my lord. I really do think she's still alive."

"I pray that she is."

Chapter 30

Jason found Micah and Katherine in Micah's room. Micah was lying on his bed, his face pressed against the pillow. Katherine sat on the edge of the bed, her hand on Micah's back, but it was obvious Micah didn't want her there. He wasn't crying, but his lips were trembling, and his eyes were firmly shut.

"Give us a minute, will you, Katie," Jason said softly.

Katherine nodded and left the room, leaving Jason and Micah alone. As soon as she was gone, Micah sat up and threw himself into Jason's waiting arms, using Jason's shoulder to stifle his sobs.

"She's dead, Captain," he mumbled into Jason's chest. "Mary's dead."

"Micah, we don't know that for certain."

"If Mam came through to warn me, then Mary's gone," Micah cried, raising his tear-stained face to look at Jason.

He wanted Jason to say it wasn't true and it was all some sort of confidence trick, but Jason couldn't lie to him. Mrs. Lysander might have known of Micah's existence before she had arrived at the house, but she certainly hadn't known he was going to be at the séance tonight, nor had she known about Mary or Mrs. Donovan, who'd died years before in Maryland. She would have known that Micah was an orphan, Micah being Jason's ward, and, of course, she had known he was Irish as soon as he'd spoken to her, but why would she torment the boy? Could she have somehow used what she knew of Micah to build trust before bringing forth Rebecca? But to what end? Jason had come to her and was willing to pay her for any information she was able to provide. There was no need to cause the boy such pain.

More than anything, Jason wanted to believe that the séance was a hoax, a scam perfected over time by Alicia Lysander and her faithful sidekick, but he couldn't. He knew what he had seen and heard, and he still trusted his senses. Jason believed that something had happened to Mary to warrant her worried mother's appearance, and if something had befallen Mary, then he needed to discover what had happened to Liam and the child Mary had been expecting with her new husband.

"Captain, we need to go to Boston," Micah exclaimed. "We need to find Mary. And Liam. If Mary is dead, then Liam is all alone." Micah seemed to forget about the new baby. Or maybe he assumed that Mary had died in childbirth.

"Micah, we can't simply drop everything and go to Boston on the word of a psychic."

"But you invited her here. You trust her."

"I wouldn't go that far." Despite what he'd witnessed, Jason still couldn't bring himself to say that he trusted Alicia Lysander. He needed more time to process what he'd seen and heard and figure out if there was any truth in what Mrs. Lysander had said about Rebecca.

Micah fixed Jason with a sorrowful stare. "I need to know, Captain. I need to know what happened to Mary."

"I will wire Mr. Hartley first thing tomorrow. He's a competent investigator and was able to find Mary before, when others, including me, had failed. It will take him all of a day to travel to Boston from New York, but it will take us weeks."

Micah sniffled loudly and nodded. "All right. But if he can't find out what happened, I'm going."

"Micah, whatever happens, you have my support," Jason said. "Always."

"So, you'll come with me?"

"If the situation calls for it, yes."

"Thank you," Micah said softly. "I love you, Captain."

"I love you too, and I will always look after you and yours. You have my word."

"I'd like to go to bed now," Micah said.

"Of course."

"Captain, can you take me to Mass on Sunday? I'd like to pray for Mary and Liam."

"Certainly," Jason said. He kissed Micah on the forehead and left him to wrestle with his feelings on his own.

Chapter 31

Once Jason returned downstairs, he poured himself a very large whisky and settled in the drawing room, pulling the armchair as close to the fire as possible without setting himself aflame. He was cold from the inside out and could hardly feel the warmth emanating from the hearth.

"Are you quite all right?" Katherine asked as she came to join him.

"Not really," Jason replied. "I can't begin to imagine what happened to Mary, but I do believe something has."

"Mrs. Lysander did sound like Rebecca and Mrs. Donovan, or a woman with an Irish accent," Katherine added thoughtfully. "It was all very spooky, but I'm not convinced any of it was real. Are you?"

Now, sitting in a brightly lit drawing room with a warm fire and a drink in his hand, he was no longer sure what he had experienced. Alicia Lysander had no reason to deceive him, but she did have a reputation to maintain, and he had wounded her pride when they had last met, so perhaps she'd also had a point to prove.

She had sounded like Rebecca and Mrs. Donovan when she had channeled the apparitions, but one could also argue that she had sounded like any Englishwoman and Irishwoman. Perhaps he was so worn out, desperate, and disheartened by the events of the past few days that he had imagined the ethereal shape he'd seen. Fatigue could play tricks on the mind, and he was tired, and terrified to fail Charlotte and Daniel.

Jason supposed it would be easy enough to discover if Alicia Lysander was right about Mary. Mr. Hartley was like a bloodhound when he was on a case, and Jason would contact him first thing tomorrow, as he had promised Micah. With any luck, they would have an answer within two days.

What Alicia Lysander had said about the demon coming back from the dead and the floundering ship was more difficult to verify. Jason replayed her words in his mind and tried to unpick their meaning. The fragments could fit into what he knew of Malcolm Briggs' untimely death, or he could take the words at face value. Countless ships sank, taking the crew and the passengers with them to the bottom of the sea. A person might think someone had died, but they might have survived and eventually found their way back. The so-called demon had the blood of the dead on his lips. Didn't they all have the blood of the dead on their lips every time they consumed meat? Had Alicia Lysander been implying that Malcolm Briggs had survived the wreck and returned to England, or was her implication a clever fabrication? Unless Jason solved the case, he'd never know and would have no proof to say whether Alicia Lysander had actually seen something or had been making it up as she went along. Despite what he'd seen, he wasn't given to flights of fancy and needed factual evidence to admit that he believed Alicia Lysander was the real thing and he hadn't been cleverly duped.

"No, I'm not convinced," Jason replied when he realized that Katherine was still waiting for him to respond.

She smiled in a way that made him believe he had just given her the correct answer. "So, what do you mean to do?"

"I mean to wire Mr. Hartley, who found Mary the last time, and ask him to travel to Boston to see if he can verify what Mrs. Lysander has said. And I will see if I can find out anything more pertaining to the sinking of the *Verity*."

"Let us say that Rebecca's intended survived the sinking of the ship. Why would he wish to kill her?"

"She was about to marry another man."

"But surely, if Rebecca loved him and had suddenly discovered that he was still alive, she would have reconsidered the marriage to Leon Stanley."

"Maybe not. It's been years, Katie. Rebecca was practically a child when she became involved with Malcolm Briggs. As a woman, she may not have wished to go back to that life, or to him."

Jason didn't say anything about the abortion and hoped his explanation was enough to satisfy his clever wife.

"Yes, that does make sense," Katherine agreed. "I always took Rebecca for a sensible woman. I can't see her wishing to go back to a life of crime. So you think Malcolm Briggs returned from the dead, so to speak, and killed her in a fit of rage?"

"I think I need to find out if there were any survivors," Jason replied, and drained his glass. "Let's go to bed. I think this day has lasted quite long enough."

Chapter 32

Tuesday, March 9

Jason's first stop was the telegraph office, where he sent a cable to Mr. Hartley. Having done that, he headed to St. John's Wood to collect Daniel. As the brougham stopped before Daniel's modest house, Jason was surprised to note that the curtains were still drawn in both the upstairs and downstairs windows. When Grace answered the door, she looked pale and tired, and relieved to see Jason.

"Grace, has something happened?" Jason asked, his chest tightening with foreboding.

Grace shook her head. "There's been no news, my lord, but Inspector Haze was poorly last night."

Jason took the stairs two at a time. The door to Daniel's bedroom was closed, so Jason knocked and walked in without waiting for an answer. Daniel was still abed, his skin pallid and sweaty, his pupils dilated. Jason pulled up a chair and sat down.

"Daniel, tell me what happened."

Daniel seemed to have difficulty focusing on Jason. His lips were dry and nearly colorless, and he was visibly agitated.

"Grace, please bring Inspector Haze a glass of water," Jason said, his gaze never leaving Daniel's face. He took hold of Daniel's wrist and took his pulse. It was elevated. "Daniel, what are you feeling?"

"I woke in the middle of the night. I couldn't breathe," Daniel said at last. "There was a tightness in my chest, a terrible pressure." Daniel's hand went to his chest as if he could still feel the constriction. "I was gasping for breath, my heart was racing, and I thought I was going to die." He was searching Jason's face for confirmation that he had indeed been near death.

"Drink this," Jason said once Grace brought the water.

Daniel obediently drank and set the glass down on the bedside table. "I must get dressed," he said as he made to rise. "We need to go. Charlotte will be waiting."

"You're not going anywhere," Jason said, and gently pushed Daniel back down onto the pillows.

"Am I really in danger of dying, then?"

"You're not dying, Daniel. What you're experiencing is a physical response to extreme emotional stress. I've seen this before. You require a period of rest."

"I can't afford to rest," Daniel cried. "My daughter is out there."

Jason laid a hand on Daniel's wrist. "I will not give up until we find Charlotte, but today, I will continue my inquiries without you."

Daniel sank deeper into the pillows. He looked both guilty and relieved. Jason didn't think he had the strength to get to the front door, much less spend the day pursuing whatever clues they could find.

"I'm so tired, Jason. And so sad. I'm never going to see her again, am I?"

Jason couldn't bring himself to reply honestly. "Daniel, you must not lose hope. There's still a chance."

"You needn't lie to me, Jason. I'm a grown man."

"You are a father, and as a father, you owe it to Charlotte to keep believing."

Daniel nodded miserably. "What will you do today?"

"First, I will stop by Scotland Yard. I need to speak to Superintendent Ransome. And then, I will continue with my inquiries."

"Do you have any leads?"

"Daniel, I will return later today, not only to check on you but to apprise you of every single detail of my day. Until then, I want you to get some sleep."

"I won't be able to sleep," Daniel grumbled.

"You will. You are depleted, and sleep is the best remedy. I would really prefer not to douse you with any more laudanum."

"I won't take it," Daniel said gruffly. "Never again."

"I understand." Jason stood. "I must go."

"I'll be waiting for you."

Jason nodded and left.

Chapter 33

John Ransome always arrived at work well before the others, so he was already in his office when Jason knocked on the door jamb. Ransome looked up in surprise and set down the cup of tea he'd been drinking.

"Good morning, Lord Redmond. Please." Ransome gestured toward the guest chair.

"Who insured the *Verity*?" Jason asked as he took a seat across from the superintendent.

"What?" Ransome asked, staring at him as if Jason had taken leave of his senses.

"Who insured the *Verity*?" Jason repeated.

"I don't recall. Why do you ask?"

"I think there may have been survivors."

"And what makes you say that?" Ransome fixed Jason with an appraising stare. "What are you not telling me?"

"Has the number of safe breaks increased recently?" Jason asked.

"Not that I'm aware of. Are you seriously suggesting that Malcolm Briggs has returned from the dead?"

"Is there absolutely no possibility that he could have survived?"

"The ship sank. All souls were lost. A settlement was paid out to the proprietors of the vessel. Besides, if Malcolm Briggs did indeed survive, where's he been these four years?"

"Anywhere," Jason replied.

John Ransome sighed heavily. "If you believe Malcolm Briggs might be alive, then I give you leave to find him, my lord. But to be perfectly honest, I don't have the resources to search for a phantom when I have a living, breathing monster on the loose. Another prostitute was murdered, her corpse left to be discovered."

"Where?"

"Whitechapel. And the newspapers got hold of the story. I've no doubt that every clergyman will preach sin and retribution come Sunday and insinuate that these women had brought this on themselves, but they were human beings who were murdered for sport. And what will our esteemed vicars say if a parliamentarian's daughter or a minister's wife is Edward Marsh's next victim? We must apprehend Edward Marsh before he kills again," Ransome said forcefully.

"Charlotte Haze is still missing, sir," Jason reminded him.

"You and I both know that the likelihood of finding Charlotte Haze alive is virtually nonexistent. That child is either buried in a shallow grave somewhere or has been tossed into the river, her pockets filled with stones. I have every constable on the lookout, and I have personally visited every deadhouse and the City Morgue to check for the child's remains, but I haven't found her, my lord. I think it's time you prepared Daniel Haze for the inevitable outcome of this investigation."

"Not yet," Jason said. "Who insured the *Verity*?" he asked again.

"Let's find out."

Jason followed Ransome to a room he had not visited previously. It contained nothing but cheaply made wooden cabinets, each with multiple drawers. Each drawer was labeled. John Ransome found the one he was searching for and pulled it open, rifling through the files within until he found the right one. He handed it to Jason. It was the file on Malcolm Briggs.

"That information should be in here." He handed the file to Jason. "Please return the file to me once you have finished."

Jason found an empty desk, which wasn't difficult at that time of the morning, and settled in to read. The documents within didn't reveal anything he didn't already know, including the outcome of the voyage to Australia. The insurer of the *Verity* was briefly mentioned on the last page, and Jason made a note of the name and address. What did give him pause was the photograph of Malcolm Briggs. Jason removed it from the file and held it up for closer inspection. Malcolm was a man of perhaps twenty-five with thick dark hair that was brushed back from a high forehead. His eyes were very dark, his eyebrows like the wings of a seagull in flight, his expression one of defiance, his mouth twisted into a sneer.

It was impossible to tell how tall he was, since the photograph was only of the upper body, but although thin, he appeared to be wiry and strong, his arms ropy with muscle beneath the fabric of his shirt. The man in the photograph wasn't wearing a coat, but his shirt didn't look homemade, and his waistcoat was a thing of beauty, silk or satin and embroidered with an intricate pattern of branches and hummingbirds. A watchchain extended from the button of the waistcoat toward the pocket where the timepiece was kept, and although it was impossible to be certain, Jason thought it might be solid gold.

This was a man who'd taken pride in his appearance and had enjoyed showing off his finery. In fact, he'd done so well for himself that he'd felt the need to keep his address secret from those who knew him. What had happened on the night he was caught? Had he made a careless mistake? There was no mention of a tip-off from a source, and nothing in the file to suggest that the arrest had been anything but the result of an ongoing investigation. Malcolm Briggs was the only perpetrator arrested that night in connection with the break-in. What had happened to his associates? Had they simply run for it once they realized that Malcolm had been nabbed?

Jason continued to study the photograph. There was something about Malcolm Briggs that bothered him, but he couldn't put his finger on it. Jason barely looked up when Constable Napier entered the office and wished him a good morning. He glanced at the photograph in Jason's hand as he passed by to get to the cabinet in the corner.

"Is that Inspector Haze in his younger days?" Constable Napier joked. "Never took him for a dandy."

Jason looked up at Constable Napier, amazed that the young man had so quickly spotted what had eluded Jason. Malcolm Briggs did resemble Daniel. He could have passed for Daniel's younger brother—a more dashing, more troublesome brother. Perhaps that was what had attracted Rebecca to Daniel. He bore a resemblance to the man she had loved. And ultimately, that must have been what had driven her away as well. She knew all too well what it meant to lose a lover. Criminal or policeman, they were sides of the same coin and often met the same fate, as the attack on Daniel that had almost cost him his life last year had demonstrated all too clearly.

Jason returned the photograph to the file, handed it to Constable Napier with instructions to bring it back to Superintendent Ransome, and headed for the door. He was on his way to the offices of the Atlantic Maritime Insurance Company.

Chapter 34

The premises were located on Broad Street in Moorgate and occupied two rooms on the ground floor. The clerk who received him was as shabby as the room he inhabited and exhibited little interest in helping with Jason's inquiry. He asked Jason to wait and went to consult with his employer, who, despite the lack of an appointment, had agreed to see Jason as a gesture of goodwill toward the police service.

Mr. Patton was a man of about sixty with shrewd blue eyes and a circlet of graying hair shaped much like Caesar's laurels. He had a short neck, meaty shoulders, and a belly that strained against a waistcoat soiled with what looked like red wine or possibly even blood. He didn't bother to stand when Jason entered and gestured toward the guest chair with tobacco-stained fingers.

"How can I help you, my lord?" he asked, not bothering to disguise his curiosity about Jason and his association with Scotland Yard.

"I would like to ask you about the *Verity*. The ship sailed out to Australia in 1865."

"You're American," Mr. Patton said with obvious surprise.

"I am."

Mr. Patton shook his head in wonder but didn't question Jason further on the subject. "Why do you wish to know about the *Verity*?"

"Because the fate of the ship has bearing on a case I'm investigating."

"All right," Mr. Patton said. He seemed reluctant to speak of the shipwreck, perhaps because he'd had to pay out a substantial sum to the owners. "The *Verity* went down approximately six weeks after leaving Southampton. The vessel encountered a bad storm off the coast of Mauritania."

"How do you know?" Jason asked.

"How do I know?" Mr. Patton echoed.

"Yes. How do you know?"

"The debris washed up in Dakar. That's in Senegal," he added smugly.

"How can you be sure there were no survivors?"

"None washed up."

"But that doesn't mean no one survived," Jason countered. "Might someone not have been carried further along the coast?"

Mr. Patton considered this, cocking his head to the side like a rather large owl. "As an insurer of the vessel, I'm not really concerned with the individuals aboard. I know for a fact that the *Verity* sank, and I have paid out the insurance to the proprietors of the vessel. That's the end of my involvement, as it were. Unfeeling as it might sound, Lord Redmond, the loss of the crew, the soldiers, and the convicts bound for Fremantle are of no interest to me personally."

"But could someone have survived?" Jason persisted.

"If you're asking me if it's possible, the answer is yes. Is it likely? No. Have you ever visited that part of the world, my lord?"

"I haven't had the pleasure."

"It's hardly a pleasure, believe me. It's barren land, populated by primitive inhabitants who live no better than the apes Mr. Darwin is so fond of saying turned into civilized men." Mr. Patton's disgust with the theory of evolution was obvious, as was his attitude toward the man who'd put it forth.

"Have *you* been there, Mr. Patton?" Jason asked, not bothering to hide his distaste with the man's description of the natives.

"No, I haven't. But I've heard tales that will raise the hair on the back of your neck."

"No doubt you have," Jason said. "But I can't imagine that the locals would refuse to help someone in need."

"I wouldn't count on their mercy. They'd as soon eat the poor fellow as help him."

"Do many of the ships you insure go down?"

"A goodly number, but it's still a profitable enterprise," Mr. Patton replied with a self-satisfied smile. "Like printing your own banknotes."

Jason didn't know anything about the insurance business, but he supposed it was in Mr. Patton's best interests to prove that a ship was not lost in order to avoid paying out a settlement. If he was freely admitting that the *Verity* had gone down in a storm, then it must have. But since the ship had sunk so far from English shores, anything could have happened to those on board. And it was possible that someone had survived—someone like Malcolm Briggs.

"Thank you, Mr. Patton," Jason said as he pushed to his feet.

"Sorry I couldn't be more help, but that's just the way of it. Ships sink, people drown, life goes on."

Jason didn't bother to say goodbye when he walked out. Once back in the street, he glanced up at the pale blue sky. The city around him was awash with golden light, a pleasant breeze caressing his face, but Jason hardly noticed the spring weather. He was deep in thought. If, indeed, Malcolm Briggs had survived the sinking of the *Verity* and found his way back to England, he was sure to have returned to his family. Perhaps not permanently, not if he didn't wish to be arrested again, but at least long enough to let them know he was alive.

Sally Malvers had known the family; she had said as much. Having come to a decision, Jason instructed Joe to take him to Seven Dials and climbed into the carriage. He only hoped he'd find Sally at home.

Chapter 35

Jason found Sally asleep. She was curled up on her mattress, her arm flung over her face to block out the light that penetrated the worn curtains. Sally was still dressed, her gown soiled and foul-smelling. There was only one other woman in the room. She was dressed in a dark blue skirt and was in the process of buttoning a patterned shirtwaist blouse. It was too early in the day to solicit customers, and she obviously saved her only gown, which was carefully folded on the chair by her mattress, for when she was working.

"Sally came in late last night," the woman said, eyeing Jason suspiciously. "Dead to the world."

"I need to speak to her," Jason explained.

"Oh, is that what we're calling it these days?" the woman scoffed.

"I'm not a client," Jason snapped.

"Nah, ye look like ye can afford summat better than our Sal."

Jason turned away from the woman and gently shook Sally by the shoulder.

"Wha'?" she muttered.

"Sally, it's Dr. Redmond."

Sally opened one eye and peered at him from beneath greasy hair. The other eye opened, and she sat up and stared at him. She reeked of gin, and Jason noticed that she wore a locket that hadn't been there when he'd seen her a few days ago.

"Sally, are you taking customers so soon after giving birth?" Jason demanded. Sally needed at least a few weeks to recover.

"I can't afford not to," Sally replied, fixing him with a defiant stare.

"You can cause yourself irreparable harm," Jason said.

Sally shook her head. "There's more than one way to please a client, Doctor. My arse is mighty sore, though, and my belly is full of—"

"I get it," Jason interrupted.

Sally smiled at him playfully. "If it's payment ye've come for, I'll be happy to oblige. For once, it will be my pleasure." She fixed her gaze on Jason's groin and licked her lips suggestively. "I bet ye're a mouthful."

"Sally, I didn't come here for that. I have something to ask you."

Sally's expression became dour. "Did ye find that little girl?"

"No, not yet."

"It's too late for her, Doctor. Surely ye know that."

"Sally, you said Malcolm Briggs had a mother."

"What of it?"

"Where does she live?"

Sally tilted her head to the side and exhaled loudly. Her breath was sour, and wet patches had appeared on her bodice, her breasts leaking milk even though there was no child to suckle. Jason had instructed Sally to bind her breasts, but she had obviously ignored his advice.

"Used to live 'ere in Seven Dials, but they're long gone," Sally said at last. "Told ye that the last time."

"They?"

"Ma Briggs and Michael."

"Who's Michael?"

"Malcolm's younger brother."

Jason made a mental note of the fact that Malcolm Briggs had a brother, but he was more interested in where he could find the family.

"I think you know where they've gone, Sally." Jason took out a half-crown coin and held it up. Sally's eyes lit on the coin, and she licked her lips again, tempted by the glint of silver. "I wager Rebecca told you, since you were such good friends."

Jason watched Sally squirm. He was certain she knew but was afraid to tell him. Sally casually looked at the other woman, who was now pinning up her hair.

"I can't tell ye where they live 'cause I don't rightly know," Sally said at last, "but I do know who Michael works for. I seen 'im recently," Sally admitted with obvious reluctance.

"Is he a client of yours?"

"Nah," she said with a dismissive gesture. "I bumped into 'im at the market. 'E were buying grapes for Mr. Carmichael."

"Michael Briggs works for Tristan Carmichael?" Jason exclaimed.

"Ye know 'im, then?"

"I do. What does Michael Briggs do for Mr. Carmichael besides shop for produce?"

"Damned if I know," Sally muttered. Her gaze followed her mate as the woman left the room and shut the door behind her.

Jason waited until the woman's footsteps receded. "Where can I find Malcolm Briggs' family, Sally?" he asked again. He lifted the coin so that Sally had no choice but to stare directly at it.

Now that the other woman was gone, Jason thought Sally might be more cooperative. She looked conflicted, but the need to get the money won out.

"St. John's Wood. Near the old burial ground. Elm Tree Road. Number five, I think," she added hastily, and snatched the coin from Jason's hand. "Ye never 'eard that from me, ye understand?"

Jason felt as if the floor had just tilted beneath his feet. Malcolm Briggs' mother and brother lived a short distance from Daniel and within a few minutes of the burial ground where Rebecca had been murdered.

"Thanks," Jason said, and walked out. There was nothing more he needed from Sally since she had just told him everything he needed to know.

Jason reached inside his coat and fingered the smooth handle of the Colt he'd strapped on that morning. At the time, he hadn't been sure why he'd felt the need to take the firearm but realized he had Alicia Lysander to thank for the forethought. She had told him enough to point him in the right direction, and some part of him expected to come face to face with Malcolm Briggs.

Jason couldn't be certain that the man had survived the shipwreck and returned to London, but the fact that his nearest and dearest lived within walking distance of both Daniel and the burial ground where Rebecca's remains had been discovered couldn't be mere coincidence. And Michael Briggs was employed by none other than Tristan Carmichael. Perhaps Daniel hadn't been so far off the mark when he'd suggested that Rebecca's murder and Charlotte's kidnapping were all part of an elaborate plot to get revenge on the policeman who'd dared to interfere with Carmichael's criminal enterprise.

Jason had yet to piece together all the facts, but he was certain that Briggs was responsible for Rebecca's death.

"Elm Tree Road, Joe. It's in St. John's Wood," Jason said as he approached the carriage.

"I know it, sir. What number?"

"Five, but stop at the corner. I'll walk the rest of the way."

"Very good, sir."

Chapter 36

Elm Tree Road was a far cry from Seven Dials. Although the houses were not stately or particularly attractive, they appeared to be well constructed and in good repair, the homes of middle-class Londoners who'd made their money by earning it and had settled in St. John's Wood, which was not fashionable but sufficiently genteel to give one a respectable address.

Jason walked down the street, looking for the correct number and wondering what he was going to say to Mrs. Briggs. How did one tell a woman who'd lost her son that he suspected said son of murder and abduction? If Malcolm had survived the shipwreck and she knew the truth, Mrs. Briggs would try to cover for her son and deny his very existence, which wouldn't help Jason to locate him. If he hadn't survived and Jason suggested that he had, she'd be reminded of her grief and refuse to help Jason all the same. And what if Michael Briggs happened to be at home? If he worked for Tristan Carmichael, chances were he was at one of Carmichael's many brothels or warehouses, but the possibility couldn't be discounted.

Jason was man enough to admit that this was an ill-conceived plan and he was about to make a dreadful mistake that could cost him dearly. He couldn't afford to go charging into the Briggs' residence without backup, even if he was armed, since he had no idea what sort of situation he would encounter. He could come face to face with Malcolm Briggs, his brother, or both. The best thing to do was to walk past the house, return to the carriage, and head to Scotland Yard to beg reinforcements.

Jason decided to do just that but couldn't help casting a swift glance at the façade of number five as he passed. A movement in an upstairs window caught his eye. He couldn't afford to stop for fear of drawing attention to himself, but he was sure he'd seen someone looking down into the street. Jason lowered his head so that the person at the window would only see the top of his hat, then crossed the road and walked along the other side, looking at house numbers until he selected one at random and knocked on the door.

He made sure to speak to the maidservant for a few moments, apologizing for his mistake, before tipping his hat and walking away. If someone inside the Briggs' house was watching, then they'd assume he was simply someone who'd been looking for a particular address and had completed his errand. Unless they had been forewarned by Tristan Carmichael that he was on the case. Still, they couldn't be sure of his identity, since they'd never met him, which gave Jason a slight advantage.

"No luck?" Joe asked.

"Take me back to Scotland Yard, Joe. Hurry!"

If Joe was surprised to be directed to the same address for the second time that day, he made no mention of it. Instead, he snapped the reins, and the carriage lurched as it pulled away from the curb and merged with the traffic on Grove End Road.

Jason was out of the carriage before it came to a complete stop, running up the steps and practically exploding into John Ransome's office.

"My lord?" Ransome asked, his brows lifting in astonishment.

"Elm Tree Road. Now. I must have at least two constables."

John Ransome didn't bother to ask questions that would lead to wasting precious time. He was too intuitive a copper not to understand the urgency behind Jason's request. Instead, he erupted out of his chair.

"I'm coming with you," he said as he grabbed his coat and hat. "Napier, Collins, Putney, with me!" he cried. "Napier and Collins, take my carriage. Putney, bring the police wagon to number five, Elm Tree Road. And cuffs," Ransome reminded him as he followed Jason toward the brougham. The two constables would follow in Ransome's carriage since there was no room for four men inside Jason's sleek conveyance.

By the time Jason and John Ransome arrived at Elm Tree Road, a plan had been worked out, and all that the inhabitants of the street saw was a stately carriage making its way toward number five. There was no sign of the constables or the police wagon that waited around the corner. Jason touched his Colt for good luck and said a prayer to a God he didn't really believe in as the brougham approached the Briggs' house.

It wasn't yet four o'clock, but the sun had vanished behind thick, ominous clouds that leached the remaining daylight, replacing it with sullen gloom. Several windows glowed with soft gaslight, while others were still dark, including the one where Jason had seen the face only an hour before. He and Ransome walked up to the front door and stood side by side, while the constables, too conspicuous in their uniforms, were positioned behind the house and hidden from view by thick shrubbery.

Jason knocked and then exhaled sharply when he realized he was holding his breath. A maidservant opened the door and stared at them in surprise. Perhaps her employers didn't get many visitors.

"How can I help ye, sirs?" she asked when neither man stated their business. She was no older than sixteen, but there was an assurance about her that Jason would have found amusing had he not been focused on getting inside the house. The maidservant glared at them, and Jason thought she might slam the door in their faces.

"Dr. Redmond to see Mrs. Briggs," he hurried to explain. "And this is my assistant."

"Mrs. Briggs didn't summon no doctor," the girl replied. She was growing suspicious, her gaze scanning the road behind them.

"I was sent by Mr. Carmichael," Jason replied, and smiled. He had no wish to alarm the poor girl.

"And why would Mr. Carmichael send a doctor when one ain't needed?" The maidservant had her hands on her hips now, her gaze openly hostile. She might be young, but she was no fool and knew that something wasn't right.

Jason was considerably taller than the maidservant and was able to see over her head into the foyer and the corridor beyond. The ground floor appeared empty, but Jason was in no doubt that someone was inside one of the rooms, listening and assessing the situation. The time for pretense was gone, and if he and Ransome took any longer to explain their presence, whatever element of surprise they still had would pass them by.

Having come to a decision, Jason pushed past the girl, mumbling an apology when she cried out in protest. The moment Jason and John Ransome were inside, blows from a sturdy cane rained on Jason's shoulders, while Ransome was tackled by an angry dark-haired man. Jason had only caught a glimpse of him, but he thought they had found Malcolm Briggs.

"Ye think ye can force yer way in?" Mrs. Briggs hollered as she tried to clobber Jason over the head. "Think ye can just take my boy? Over my dead body." She glared at Jason and bared her teeth as she raised the cane yet again. Jason managed to block the blow, but Mrs. Briggs was far from done with him. She kicked his shin as she called out, "I'll hold 'em off, son. Ye go. And ye stay gone."

She wasn't a large woman, but she had all the ferocity of a rabid racoon and would fight until she either collapsed or Jason managed to subdue her. Jason noted in an absentminded way that the maidservant had disappeared. She was probably hiding in the kitchen, too afraid to get hurt in the melee.

"Run, ye daft fool!" Mrs. Briggs yelled at her son.

Malcolm Briggs, who'd backed John Ransome against the wall and punched him in the stomach, seemed reluctant to let go. He looked furious but also shocked, clearly having realized who his opponent was. He would remember John Ransome from four years ago, when Ransome had made the arrest.

Having decided it was worth it to get his revenge, Briggs knocked John Ransome to the floor and kicked him viciously in the ribs before sprinting for the back door. His nose was bloodied and his lip busted. At least Ransome had got in a few good punches before Briggs overpowered him.

John Ransome was curled into a ball, moaning pitifully as he wrapped his arms around his battered stomach and ribs. Jason would have rushed to help him had he not had an old woman with a cane to subdue. He didn't want to hurt her, but given the relentlessness of her attack, he had little choice but to use force. Jason yanked the cane out of her hand and tossed it aside, then pushed Mrs. Briggs against the wall and pinned her arms to her side.

Mrs. Briggs snarled at him, and Jason thought she might spit in his face, but instead, she tried to kick him in the groin. Jason dodged her bony knee, but it struck his thigh, and he yelped with pain, then swiveled out of the way just as the old woman tried to bring her booted heel onto his foot. He had to give her credit; she was a fighter, and this clearly wasn't her first altercation with a grown man. She knew what she was about and went for weak, unprotected areas.

"Stop fighting or I will be forced to hurt you," Jason warned.

"And ye a gentleman," Mrs. Briggs taunted him. "Threatening to hurt a woman old enough to be yer mother."

"I'm a gentleman when it suits me," Jason replied, and grabbed her arm, twisting it so that she spun around, face to the wall. Jason pinned her against the wall, her arm between them.

"Let me go, ye fecking whoreson," Mrs. Briggs screamed, but Jason held her fast.

"Don't make me tie you up," he panted, still catching his breath from the exertion of trying to evade Mrs. Briggs' blows.

Jason was certain Mrs. Briggs was desperately trying to figure out how to best him when he heard the scuffle at the back door. The constables had apprehended their man as soon as he opened the door. They had taken him down and cuffed him. Malcolm Briggs lay on his stomach, his cheek pressed to the threshold, his curses reverberating through the house.

Mrs. Briggs stopped struggling as soon as she saw her son on the ground, her body sagging against Jason as if all the strength had suddenly seeped out of her, leaving nothing but a sack of flesh and bones. Jason loosened his hold on the woman and allowed her to turn around. She just stood there, her face the color of curdled milk.

"No," she moaned softly. "Please, God, no."

Malcolm's gaze was fixed on his mother, whose eyes were filled with tears. They seemed to be silently saying goodbye, and with good reason. Malcolm Briggs wasn't going to evade the death penalty again. He'd killed two people and kidnapped a child.

"Go inside the drawing room and sit down, Mrs. Briggs," Jason ordered.

The woman appeared on the verge of collapse now that all the fight had gone out of her. She nodded and hobbled toward the room on the right, while Jason turned his attention to John Ransome, who had managed to get up and stood leaning against the wall, his arm wrapped protectively around his middle.

"Are you badly hurt?" Jason asked.

Ransome shook his head. "Just bruised, I think. Go on."

Jason took the stairs two at a time and stopped before the door he believed led to the room that faced the street below. He took a deep breath and opened it softly, so not to alarm the room's occupant.

Charlotte sat on the cot pushed up against the wall, her eyes huge with fear, her little hands clutching the flowery coverlet for protection. Her cheeks were wet with tears, but when she saw Jason, she dropped the coverlet and reached out, her mouth opening in a silent cry. Jason scooped her up and held her close, whispering words of love and reassurance until they both calmed down.

"I want my papa," Charlotte whimpered. "Please."

Charlotte didn't appear hurt, only frightened by the screams she'd heard from the ground floor. Jason didn't want to delay taking her home for even a moment.

"I'll take you to your papa right now," he promised.

He carried Charlotte downstairs and felt her little body tense and shrink against him when she saw Mrs. Briggs and John Ransome through the open door of the drawing room.

"Ye leave my granddaughter be," Mrs. Briggs hollered. "It's all right, sweetheart. Don't be scared. Granny will see ye right."

Jason stared at the woman but saw no evidence of deceit. She seemed to genuinely believe that Charlotte was her granddaughter. Jason exchanged looks with John Ransome, who shrugged and immediately winced with pain. He'd taken quite a pummeling at the hands of Malcolm Briggs, and Jason was sure Briggs would pay for every blow he'd inflicted with interest.

"I'll see you at Scotland Yard," Jason said to Ransome, and walked outside.

Joe was waiting with the carriage, and Jason gently settled Charlotte on the seat before getting in next to her. He needed to remain calm for the child, but his heart was racing, and he felt an overwhelming urge to cry. Charlotte reached out and grasped his hand, then pressed her head to Jason's arm, needing to remain close. After a moment, Jason lifted her into his lap, and they sat like that until Joe pulled up before Daniel's home.

"Oh, my sweet darling," Grace whispered when she opened the door and reached out for Charlotte, but Jason wouldn't give her over.

He looked at Grace, asking a silent question, and she jutted her chin toward the parlor. "He couldn't rest," she said. "Too distraught, the poor man."

Jason knocked on the door and waited for Daniel to invite him to come in. Despite being fully dressed, Daniel still looked as ill as he had that morning, his skin ashen, his eyes glazed with misery. His gaze traveled over Jason, but he didn't seem to notice the child in Jason's arms, since Charlotte was wearing a dark-colored smock and had rested her head on Jason's shoulder.

"Papa!" she cried when she spotted Daniel.

Had Jason not been holding on tight, she would have flipped right out of his arms as she leaned toward Daniel with her entire body.

"Oh!" Daniel cried, exploding out of the chair. "Oh, my sweet girl!"

He was laughing and crying and holding on to Charlotte so tightly, the child started to squirm. "Are you all right?" Daniel kept asking. "Is she hurt, Jason?"

"She's absolutely fine. Just a little confused by what's happening." Daniel looked questioningly at Jason over Charlotte's dark curls, but Jason shook his head. "I'll explain later," he said. "I will return in a few hours. You need some time together, and I need to get some answers."

Daniel nodded. "Jason, I don't know how to thank you."

"No thanks necessary. But you might wish to thank Alicia Lysander."

Daniel's mouth opened in incomprehension, but Jason just grinned and left the father and daughter to their tender reunion.

Now that Charlotte was back, the urgency had gone out of him, but he still wanted to understand why Mrs. Briggs thought Charlotte was her granddaughter.

Chapter 37

When Jason returned to Scotland Yard, he found John Ransome in his office, enjoying a restorative glass of brandy. He looked a bit worse for wear but claimed to be otherwise unharmed and refused to allow Jason to examine him.

"I'm fine, Lord Redmond. The only thing bruised worse than my ribs is my ego," he said with a shaky smile. "Wish I could have witnessed the reunion," John Ransome said wistfully. "It's not often that we have a positive outcome." His moment of paternal sympathy passed as quickly as it had come upon him. "I waited for you to interview the suspects. Thought they might need time to calm down. I know I did."

"And have they?"

"Let's find out. Which one would you like to speak to first? It's your case."

Jason appreciated that John Ransome wasn't taking over the investigation and was allowing Jason to see it to its bitter conclusion. Jason would most likely be sending one or both Briggses to the gallows, but he felt no pity for them, not after what Daniel had been through these past few days.

"Mrs. Briggs," Jason decided.

When Constable Napier brought Mrs. Briggs to the interview room, she looked shrunken and subdued. There seemed little point in cuffing her to the table. She wasn't going anywhere, not with three men to stop her. She looked balefully from John Ransome to Jason, squeezing her lips until they were barely visible.

"Well, go on, then," she snapped, clearly eager to get the ordeal over with.

"Although we have already met, we haven't been properly introduced," Jason said. "I am Dr. Redmond, and this is Superintendent Ransome."

"As if it makes any difference," Mrs. Briggs scoffed. "Who cares who ye are."

Jason ignored the jibe and began. "Why do you think the child I took from your house is your granddaughter?"

"Because she is."

"And who do you think her mother is?" Jason asked.

"That whore as was going to take 'er to Argentina."

"Are you referring to Rebecca Grainger?"

"Levinson, as I knew 'er. She ran away after Malcolm were charged, changed 'er name, and kept Lottie away from us," Mrs. Briggs said angrily.

"Did Malcolm come across Rebecca Grainger by accident?" John Ransome asked.

Mrs. Briggs stared at him, uncomprehending. "What ye mean, Malcolm?"

"Your son murdered Rebecca Grainger and took the child he believed to be his," Ransome replied.

Mrs. Briggs continued to stare at him, and then her mouth twisted into an ugly grin. "That's not Malcolm, ye fool. That's Michael."

John Ransome and Jason exchanged glances. They had both seen the photograph of Malcolm Briggs in the file kept at Scotland Yard and would both swear that the man down in the cells was the same man.

Mrs. Briggs shook her head. "They was identical twins, Malcolm and Michael."

"I was told Michael was Malcolm's younger brother," Jason said, but he suspected he already knew what Mrs. Briggs would say.

"Younger by twenty minutes," she replied.

"So Michael came across Rebecca Grainger, saw the child, and believed her to be his brother's daughter?" John Ransome asked.

"Ye got it in one." Mrs. Briggs teared up. "Lottie looks just like 'im, the sweet little lamb."

"Mrs. Briggs, I delivered the child I took from your home. She was born to Sarah and Daniel Haze, and her name is Charlotte Haze. She is not your granddaughter," Jason said.

That took Mrs. Briggs by surprise. She gaped at Jason, obviously thinking he was lying to her, but she must have seen the truth of his words in his face.

"Then where's Malcolm's babe?" she asked in a quavering voice.

"Rebecca Grainger never bore a living child, Mrs. Briggs." Jason decided not to tell her that Rebecca Levinson/Grainger had aborted her son's child after he was sent down.

Mrs. Briggs began to cry, first softly, but then great sobs escaped from her chest. "I'm sorry," she moaned. "I never meant to hurt no one. I thought she were our girl. Malcolm's girl. I just wanted a piece of my boy back."

"Did you know your son murdered Rebecca Grainger?"

Mrs. Briggs refused to answer, covering her eyes with her hands as she continued to cry softly.

"Take her to the cells," John Ransome said to Constable Napier, who was standing by the door in case the suspect became violent.

"Come now, Mrs. Briggs," Constable Napier said as he helped her to her feet. "I'll bring you a nice cup of tea."

Ma Briggs shuffled ahead of him, her gaze fixed on the floor, and then the door closed behind her.

Chapter 38

Michael Briggs wasn't nearly as distraught as his mother. When led into the room, he stared at Jason and John Ransome defiantly, his eyes blazing with hatred. He rattled the restraints when Constable Napier chained him to the table, even though it would take considerable strength to yank the ring out of the table. Jason thought he just might try to do it, but Michael Briggs seemed to change his mind and quieted down.

"Why did you kill Rebecca Grainger?"

Michael Briggs didn't bother to deny the charge but simply stared ahead, the pain in his eyes taking Jason by surprise.

"I never meant to hurt her," he said at last. "I loved Rebecca all the days of my life. She was a saucy little minx even when she was a girl, but once she blossomed into a woman, I couldn't help myself. She was like one of those sirens that sang to the men from the rocks and made them lose their minds with desire. I could never see anyone but her."

Michael Briggs' speech was not that of a man raised in Seven Dials. Perhaps spending time with Tristan Carmichael had left its mark. Or maybe he was a reading man, if his reference to the sirens was anything to go by. In either case, he wasn't at all what Jason had expected.

"Did this siren reject you?" Ransome asked snidely.

Michael Briggs exhaled deeply. "She did, but it was the one time she didn't that changed everything."

All belligerence had gone out of him, and he seemed resigned to his fate. It seemed to Jason that what he really wanted was to talk about Rebecca to someone who'd listen.

"What happened?" Jason asked softly, and hoped John Ransome wouldn't interrupt.

"Malcolm met her first when he went to see Mr. Levinson. She was no more than twelve then, but already she was a beauty. And she had this way about her," Michael reminisced. "Carried herself like a lady."

Both Jason and John Ransome remained silent, letting Michael go on.

"Mr. Levinson didn't approve of the match, but he understood. His own wife had come down in the world to be with him, and he knew love when he saw it. He would have given his blessing had he not died. As it was, Rebecca came to live with us. She was seventeen then. Old enough to wed. They were making plans, her and Malcolm, but then Malcolm was taken up."

"What happened that night?" Ransome asked, unable to remain quiet when his own case came up.

"Malcolm was betrayed. Someone tipped off the rozzers, told them that Malcolm was going to hit that house."

"Do you know who had supplied the information?" Ransome asked.

"I didn't then, but I do now. Mr. Carmichael told me. He knows things. Talks to people."

"So who betrayed your brother?"

"Leon Stanley, just as he had betrayed Edgar Levinson. How do you think he got the money to go to Argentina and buy a hundred-acre ranch? And he didn't just go there for a peaceful life. He ran to protect his worthless skin, because he would have died a slow and torturous death had any of his victims or their kin got their hands on him. Leon Stanley sold out his associates, and he profited very nicely, indeed."

"So what happened with Rebecca?" Ransome asked. He'd taken over the interview, but Jason was happy to let him. He had already figured out what had happened, and now he simply needed confirmation, which Michael Briggs was ready to offer.

"After Malcolm was sentenced to life in Australia, Rebecca was broken. She just couldn't believe she'd lost him so suddenly."

"And you stepped in to comfort her," Ransome said.

Michael nodded. "I did. God forgive me, but I was happy Malcolm had been arrested. I thought this was my chance. I could have the riches we'd accumulated, the house, and the girl. There was enough coin put by to allow us to live comfortably for the rest of our days. I wouldn't have to risk my neck the way Malcolm had."

"But Rebecca didn't want to be with you and ran off," Ransome deduced. "She sought refuge with her grandfather."

"Yes. She felt guilty for betraying Malcolm and wanted nothing to do with me."

"But you hounded her, so she disappeared," Jason interjected.

"I could have tracked her down, but I let her go," Michael said. "I thought she'd come around in time, once she'd had time to grieve."

"But she didn't," Ransome said forcefully.

"No, she didn't. I knew I'd lost her."

"Until the day you found her again," Ransome cut in.

Michael nodded. "I saw her walking down the street with the child, and I knew as soon as I saw Lottie that she was mine. The age was right, and she looked like me. God, when Rebecca first saw me, the fear in her eyes. For a moment there, she thought I was Malcolm, come back from the dead, but as soon as I called out to her, she realized her mistake."

"Could the child not have been your brother's?" Jason asked.

Michael shook his head. "Rebecca and Malcolm never…" His voice trailed off, but his meaning was clear. "They wanted to wait until they were married."

"So you took a grieving woman's virginity and got her with child, and then when you met her years later, you murdered her and took the child. You're quite the big man, aren't you?" Ransome taunted him.

"I never meant to hurt her," Michael cried. "I only wanted to talk to her, to tell her that I still loved her, and I would take care of them both. We could be a family. I thought that maybe she'd let go of Malcolm by that time and I had a chance. But she laughed at me. Told me I was pathetic, always desperate to have what my big brother had. She said she was getting married to Leon Stanley."

"Did you tell her that he had betrayed both her father and her intended?" Jason asked.

"Of course I did, but she didn't believe me. She said I was making it up just to hurt her. She said he was ten times the man I was and that she loved him."

"Did you lose your temper then?"

"Yes. I went for her and grabbed her by the throat. I only meant to frighten her, but I was so angry, I'd throttled her in my rage. Rebecca was gone, and the child was just standing there, terrified. So I picked her up, asked her name, comforted her, and took her home to meet Ma. I told her Lottie was Malcolm's. I couldn't bring myself to tell her that I'd lain with my brother's betrothed and got her with child. Ma would never forgive me for betraying Malcolm in that way."

"Rebecca Grainger aborted your child," Ransome said. "Killed it in the womb."

Michael's eyes widened with shock, and he shook his head in denial. "No, Lottie is mine."

"Her name is Charlotte Haze, and she's the daughter of Inspector Haze. She is not yours," Ransome snapped. "And a good thing it is too because you're going to hang for the murders of Rebecca Grainger and Leon Stanley."

"Leon Stanley deserved it. He was a lowlife prick."

"Is that why you severed his genitals?" Jason asked. "Because he was a prick?"

"He died too fast," Michael said angrily. "I wanted him to suffer."

"So you mutilated him to satisfy your bloodlust?"

Michael nodded.

"How did you get into his room?" Ransome asked.

"I knew he was staying at the hotel. Rebecca said as much. So I sent a note to reserve a room and checked in as a guest. It wasn't difficult to find out what room he was in. Just as it wasn't difficult to pick the lock. He was sleeping when I came in. I woke him, told him this was a reckoning for what he'd done to Edgar and Malcolm, and slit his throat. Then I sliced off his cock and bollocks, tossed them into the piss pot, and tucked him in, all nice and cozy. I washed my hands, let myself out, and went to my room, where I slept like a baby. The next day I had breakfast in the restaurant and waited to see how long it would take for someone to discover the body. It didn't take long. I saw you," Michael said to Jason. "You were talking to the manager. So I asked for a cab to the British Museum and made myself scarce."

"Thank you for clearing things up," Ransome said. "But I'm afraid your day of reckoning has come as well. You are hereby charged with two counts of murder, and since you have confessed to both, you will hang."

Michael Briggs fixed John Ransome with his dark gaze. "I don't fear death, Superintendent. The only thing I'm afraid of is meeting my brother in hell."

"Think Malcolm is in hell, do you?" Ransome asked.

"I know he is after what he did."

"What did he do?" Jason asked. He didn't think Michael was referring to Malcolm's thieving.

For the first time since entering the room, Michael looked frightened. "I knew Malcolm had died long before we learned the *Verity* sank."

"How did you know?" Ransome demanded.

"Malcolm and I were identical twins. We shared a connection, a bond that couldn't be weakened by distance. I was sure Malcolm knew what I had done with his girl and hated me for it. He'd find his way back if it was the last thing he did, and then I'd have to face his fury." Michael sucked in a sharp breath. "And then the nightmares began."

"What did you see?" Jason inquired.

"I saw Malcolm, drifting in the sea and clinging to a wooden spar. There was another man with him, a boy really. Malcolm was so hungry and thirsty, I could feel it in my gut. It was a gnawing hunger that wouldn't abate no matter how much I ate. And then it passed."

"Why?" Jason asked.

"Because Malcolm wasn't hungry anymore."

"He died?" John Ransome asked.

Michael shook his head. He looked stricken. "Malcolm strangled the boy, then ate his flesh and drank his blood to stay alive. I kept seeing his face in my dreams, his lips dripping with blood, and the boy next to him, his face angelic in death, his arm still bearing the marks of Malcolm's teeth. It was horrible."

"How does one strangle someone when hanging on to a spar?" Ransome inquired.

"Easy," Michael replied. "Hang on with one arm and get the other man in a headlock with the other. Choke the life out of him. It wouldn't take much."

"Right," Ransome said as his hand went to his own neck, and he adjusted the starched collar that seemed to be strangling him.

"In your dreams, did Malcolm survive?" Jason asked.

"Malcolm is dead. I know it as surely as I know that I will be dead soon."

"Did he die of exposure?"

Michael chuckled bitterly. "God has an odd sense of humor. Malcolm was eaten by a shark. It smelled the boy's blood and came to find the body. It found Malcolm instead."

Jason winced, his mind putting forth a very unpleasant image that refused to leave.

John Ransome stood and faced Michael Briggs. "Mr. Briggs, you are hereby charged with two counts of murder and one count of abduction and unlawful imprisonment. You will be provided with a written confession to sign and then transported to prison."

"Will I stand trial?" Michael Briggs asked.

"Since you have already confessed, I expect you will face the judge just long enough to be sentenced."

"And Ma?"

"Mrs. Briggs will be charged with unlawful imprisonment, harboring a murderer, and assault."

"She believed Lottie was Malcolm's, and she didn't want to lose her only surviving son," Michael cried. "Please, Superintendent, let her go. She'll die in prison."

"I'll think about it," Ransome said grudgingly. "Constable, take him away."

"Wait," Jason interrupted. "Did Tristan Carmichael know you murdered Rebecca Grainger and took the child?"

Michael looked genuinely surprised by the question. "No. How would he know? I never told him, and we kept Lottie in the house, in case anyone was looking for her."

Jason breathed out a sigh of relief. At least Tristan Carmichael wasn't involved and hadn't been seeking retribution for Daniel's interference in his affairs.

After Michael Briggs was taken back to the cells, John Ransome turned to Jason. "Should I charge the mother with unlawful imprisonment?"

"I don't think she would have kept Charlotte had she known the truth," Jason said. "She believed Charlotte was her granddaughter."

"She knew her son killed who she believed was the child's mother."

"She did," Jason agreed. "She was most definitely an accomplice."

John Ransome had opened his mouth to reply when the door flew open, a pale-faced Sergeant Meadows standing in the doorway.

"What's happened, Sergeant?" John Ransome asked.

"There was a break-in at the Pine Grove Asylum. Two porters were hurt, and the director, Dr. Garfield, is dead."

"Was the intruder apprehended?" Ransome cried, already on his feet.

"They got him, sir. It was Edward Marsh. One of the orderlies hit him over the head with a marble ashtray."

"Is he dead?"

"No, sir. But he is locked up securely. I don't think he's going anywhere."

"Dear God in Heaven," Ransome said as the urgency left him. "What a shambles. Any idea why he returned to the asylum, Sergeant Meadows?"

"I suppose he must have held a grudge against Dr. Garfield," Sergeant Meadows replied.

"Perhaps Dr. Garfield wasn't as humane as he purported to be," Ransome said. "In any case, Marsh is stark raving mad, so Lord only knows what went on in that head of his. For all we know, he might have painted Dr. Garfield as the devil himself or was finished with his killing spree and wanted to go back inside." Ransome turned to Jason, who sat with his head bowed as he tried to process the unexpected news. "Dr. Garfield was known to you, was he not, Lord Redmond?"

"He was."

"I'm sorry for your loss, then," Ransome said softly.

"Will Edward Marsh be tried for the murders?"

"That depends on how much influence his family has. I expect he'll spend the rest of his days in that institution, chained to a wall, which, in my opinion, is a fate worse than death."

Jason thought the man deserved to be tried and executed for the lives he'd taken, but it wasn't his case, and he had no wish to confront Edward Marsh, even if the man was handcuffed. John Ransome would see that justice was served.

"God rest your troubled soul, Elias," Jason said softly once John Ransome had left the room.

Jason was no longer needed, and there was not only Daniel and Charlotte to see to but Micah as well. Now that he had heard Michael Briggs' account, he was certain that Mary was in some sort of trouble, just as Alicia Lysander had said. The messages from beyond didn't necessarily make perfect sense, nor was there a logical explanation for what he had seen, but there was enough truth in them for Jason to acknowledge that Alicia Lysander did, indeed, commune with the dead, and that in itself was enough to make him question everything he believed about life and death.

Jason wished he could go home, hole up in the library, and drink a bottle of something alcoholic in one go, but oblivion would have to wait. He had people who counted on him, and his own needs had to come last. When he left Scotland Yard and the carriage drove past a newsboy, he barely registered the headline of the evening edition of the *Daily Telegraph* that screamed:

MURDER AT CHARING CROSS HOTEL

Either reporters had got wind of the story or Bridget Connelly had gone to the press and now had sufficient funds to begin her married life. It no longer mattered since tomorrow's headline would assure the public that the murderer was no longer at large. Both murderers, actually. Jason fervently hoped that he'd never hear the name Edward Marsh again. He leaned back against the seat and shut his eyes, needing a moment of peace before he arrived at Daniel's house.

Epilogue

March 1869

Jason held the unopened telegram in his hands, his heart heavy with foreboding. He'd been able to convince Micah to return to school with the promise that Jason would deliver the results of Mr. Hartley's findings in person. Jason pinched the bridge of his nose, wishing he didn't have to do this, but he owed it to Micah, and to Mary and Liam, who would always be his family, even if they weren't related by blood.

Katherine walked into the room and sat down next to him, her eyes anxious behind the lenses of her spectacles. "Would you like me to read it?" she asked kindly, but Jason shook his head.

He tore open the missive and scanned the stark words before reading the message aloud.

Mary and Liam gone. Sailed on the Arcadia bound for London on February 27. Letter following.

H.

Jason and Katherine exchanged worried looks. "That was nearly three weeks ago," Jason stated unnecessarily.

"Was there anything in the newspapers?" Katherine asked.

"No. We have to operate on the assumption that the *Arcadia* has arrived safely."

"Then where are Mary and Liam, and why did they leave Boston so suddenly?"

"That's what we have to find out," Jason said, and pushed to his feet.

"Where are you going?" Katherine asked, rising as well.

"To the docks. I will try to discover as much as I can before I speak to Micah."

"Yes, that's a wise decision," Katherine agreed. "Oh, Jason, do you think they're dead?"

"No, but someone is," Jason said. He had no idea where the certainty came from, but he was sure there was something sinister behind Mary's abrupt departure. He grabbed his hat, gloves, and walking stick from Dodson and headed out into the glorious spring morning, but he didn't get very far Constable Putney was running toward him, his hand on his helmet to keep it from sliding forward and blinding him.

"I say, your lordship," he cried and came to an abrupt halt as soon Jason stopped walking, taking a moment to catch his breath. "I've been sent to fetch you. It's only that the horse lost a shoe—" Constable Putney didn't bother with the rest of the explanation since Jason could deduce what had happened easily enough.

"Where am I needed, Constable? Should I get my medical bag?"

Constable Putney chuckled, but immediately turned his amusement into an embarrassed cough. "Oh no, sir. No bag will be needed, on account of there's no body."

"I'm afraid I don't follow, Constable," Jason said, watching the emotions play across the young man's face. He seemed torn between giving in to speculation and performing his duty with dignity and respect for the dead, although Jason still wasn't sure someone actually was deceased.

"There's no body, sir, but there's a head. Left on the steps it was. Mr. Britteridge nearly tripped over it on his way inside."

"Who is Mr. Britteridge?

"He is the warden at Newgate, sir, and he was on his way in this morning when he came upon the head. Inspector Haze is awaiting your pleasure at the prison. Shall I find us a cab, sir?"

"We'll take my carriage, Constable. Just give me a moment."

Jason sighed with resignation and headed back inside. The trip to the docks would have to wait. There was a severed head awaiting him at Newgate Prison.

The End

Please turn the page for an excerpt from

Murder of a Hangman

A Redmond and Haze Mystery Book 13

An Excerpt from Murder of a Hangman
A Redmond and Haze Mystery Book 13

Prologue

Giles Britteridge drew a cleansing breath, enjoying the crisp freshness of the March morning. This was his favorite time of year, and the most pleasant part of his day. He enjoyed his morning walk and tried not to think of the business at hand, the myriad problems of running a prison the size of Newgate and the number of inmates and staff under his command. It was taxing and at times maddening, but he took pride in his work and greatly looked forward to his fast-approaching retirement. Another few years and he'd be free of the heap of human detritus he was charged with keeping in line. At least there were no executions or floggings scheduled for today. Even after all these years, watching someone brought so low gave him bouts of indigestion.

Giles approached the entrance he used to access his office and stopped. An innocuous-looking basket sat on the top step, the contents covered with a linen towel. Had someone forgotten it or left it there on purpose? Perhaps some grieving wife had brought a treat for her husband but realized the prison was not yet open for the day. But why would she leave such an offering by the door? Food was dear, and no wife of a common criminal would waste precious resources.

Too curious to simply walk past the basket, Giles bent down and pulled off the towel. A strangled scream tore from his chest, and for a moment he found that he couldn't move or draw breath. He'd seen many a gruesome spectacle in his life, but never had a gruesome spectacle glared back at him. The head was upright in the basket, the eyes open and staring, the hair neatly oiled and brushed. For one mad moment, Giles thought this had to be a sick joke, a theatrical prop left for him to find. He looked around, but no one seemed to be about to enjoy his shock. He reluctantly looked back at the offending object, and only now that he was marginally calmer did he realize that he recognized the face that stared back at him. And then he vomited the breakfast he had so enjoyed only an hour before and banged on the door, desperate to be admitted.

Chapter 1

Tuesday, March 23, 1869

Jason Redmond alighted from the carriage and looked up at the imposing walls of Newgate Prison. The structure was massive, the walls of the prison as high and thick as any castle fortification. Jason understood the need for such establishments, but everything inside him recoiled at the idea of keeping thousands of individuals behind bars and forcing them to live in unsanitary conditions and on starvation rations for years, sometimes decades. It was cruel and ineffective, and in most instances, the punishment was completely disproportionate to the crime they had been charged with. But until the world came up with a better solution for dealing with its criminal element, places like Newgate would continue to exist and take up valuable land in some of the world's greatest cities, a stark reminder of what happened when one broke the law and wasn't mentally agile enough to evade the authorities.

Jason's own imprisonment at a Confederate prison camp in Georgia at the end of the American Civil War had been a trial of mental and physical endurance that had left him emotionally shattered and physically broken. There were some things one never forgot or forgave, and there were certain fears that still lived inside one's soul and sprang to the forefront when entering an institution designed to reduce a human being to his or her most basic needs, and more often than not only kept them incarcerated until their appointment with the hangman. Jason had been lucky enough to survive, but most of the people currently housed behind the walls of Newgate would be leaving in a pine box to be buried in a pauper's grave with not even a marker to commemorate their existence.

Taking a calming breath, Jason followed Constable Putney to the warden's office at the end of a long stone-walled corridor punctuated by metal doors. The corridor was cold and dim, and

Jason felt something constrict inside his chest and wished he could go back outside and ask that the evidence be brought to him so he could examine it in the stark, white-tiled cellar mortuary of Scotland Yard. But he could hardly inform Constable Putney that he was suffering from a case of nerves. Jason drew back his shoulders, stiffened his spine, and followed the constable at a brisk clip until they reached the door. The constable knocked, then pushed it open.

Jason couldn't help but smile in relief when he saw Inspector Daniel Haze, whose pale countenance was illuminated by weak sunlight streaming through the barred window, the rays reflecting off the round lenses of his spectacles. Jason hadn't seen much of Daniel since the abduction of his daughter, Charlotte, and the death of her nursemaid, Rebecca Grainger. Daniel had needed time to grieve a woman he'd cared for deeply and forge a fragile peace with his own feelings of guilt. Rebecca's death had in no way been Daniel's fault, but he routinely resorted to self-flagellation when it came to the tragic decisions of others and blamed himself for his lack of foresight and his inability to prevent the inevitable. Daniel nodded to Jason, but any personal exchange would have to wait until they were alone.

A man of middle years, heavyset and bewhiskered, sat behind the massive desk, his jowls brushing the starched collar of his shirt, his face set in lines of displeasure. He eyed Jason with ill-concealed impatience, since it had taken Jason over an hour to present himself at the crime scene. He'd already left for the hospital when Constable Putney had come in search of him and had had to leave his surgical patients once the constable had tracked him down to answer Daniel's summons.

"Mr. Britteridge, may I present my associate, Lord Redmond," Daniel said as the warden rose laboriously to his feet and gave Jason a stiff bow.

The warden didn't bother to ask what a member of the nobility was doing in his prison or why Jason Redmond was the one to consult on this case instead of some third-rate surgeon who couldn't find gainful employment with one of London's many hospitals and was reduced to butchering corpses to earn his daily bread. He probably knew Jason by reputation, and at the moment, he appeared too shaken by whatever had happened to bother with the social niceties. After a brief greeting of "My lord," the warden launched into a succinct, if somewhat belligerent, explanation instead of allowing Daniel Haze to begin asking questions.

"I arrived at the prison at eight o'clock sharp, as I do every morning. The main entrance had not been unlocked, since the night shift had not left the premises and the day shift had yet to arrive. I discovered a basket, the contents covered with a linen towel. Naturally, I assumed that someone had left an offering of fresh bread or perhaps a ham, given the shape beneath, but when I pulled off the towel, what I saw was a severed head. I immediately sent a message to Superintendent Ransome. We're well acquainted," he added, giving Daniel a hard look meant to remind him that his performance would be harshly judged and discussed with his superior. "I had requested Inspector Yates, but it seems he's been assigned to another case, so Inspector Haze was sent in his stead. Superintendent Ransome assures me that the man is competent and can be trusted to conduct a thorough and well-thought-out investigation."

Daniel looked like he'd just swallowed a wasp but remained silent, allowing Jason to come to his own conclusions and formulate an appropriate response.

"Inspector Haze is not only competent and utterly trustworthy, but he's also a trusted colleague and dear friend, so I would thank you to treat him with the respect he deserves, Mr. Britteridge," Jason said coldly. "Now, if you would answer some basic questions, I will be happy to take the head off your hands."

The warden's fleshy cheeks turned a mottled red, and he inclined his head in acknowledgement of the rebuke. "My apologies, Inspector Haze. I have every confidence in your abilities. It was something of a shock, you see, since I was well acquainted with the victim."

Daniel pushed the spectacles further up his nose and pulled a small notebook and a pencil from his pocket. It would seem Daniel had been waiting for Jason to begin the interview. Given the obvious lack of evidence, Jason didn't think it'd take long. He settled in one of the hardback guest chairs and waited until Daniel took the other seat. Daniel did not look at him but focused his gaze on the warden.

In retrospect, Jason should have probably allowed Daniel to fight his own battles, but his response to the warden had been a result of his own discomfort at being inside the prison and the memories that crowded his mind despite the pressing issue at hand. A highhanded bureaucrat with no respect for a fellow law enforcement officer had galled him, and Jason had sprung to Daniel's defense without considering Daniel's fragile feelings.

"Mr. Britteridge," Jason began. "Do you frequently receive offerings of fresh bread or hams?"

The question clearly took the warden by surprise, and he faltered. "Well, no, but when one sees a covered basket, one immediately associates it with food."

"So this was highly unusual in itself," Jason summarized.

"Indeed, it was, your lordship."

"Can you describe the condition of the head when you first saw it?"

"It was just there, sitting in the basket, like a cabbage," the warden reiterated.

"Yes, you have mentioned that, but what I need to know is, was there any blood pooled beneath the severed head? Were the eyes open or closed? Was the head upright, face up, or face down?"

"Ah yes, I see. Of course," the warden muttered, probably a bit embarrassed by his lack of understanding. "The head was positioned upright, the stump of the neck resting on a bit of straw.

There was a smear of blood, but no pooling, as such. The eyes were open, and the hair was neatly brushed."

"Have you searched for the body?" Jason asked.

"Yes. I had my men scour the vicinity, but no body has been discovered as of yet."

"Did they find any traces of blood?"

"They did not."

"And who was this man?" Jason asked. "You said he was known to you."

"Yes. His name is Philip Hobart. He was one of the hangmen here at Newgate."

"May I see the remains?" Jason asked.

Mr. Britteridge rose from behind his desk, retrieved the basket from a tall wooden cabinet, and handed it to Jason.

"Couldn't bear to look at it," he explained as he resumed his seat behind the desk.

"Thank you," Jason said, and turned to Daniel, silently urging him to take up where he had left off while he studied the contents of the basket.

Jason lifted the plain white towel and studied the head before replacing the towel and setting the basket on the floor at his feet. This wasn't the first severed head he'd seen. After battle, the field was often strewn with limbs, the disconnected stumps resting on earth churned by prolonged cannon fire and soaked with blood. Few had their heads torn clean off, but there had been a few instances, the eyes still staring in horror at the sky they could no longer see. Philip Hobart's head did resemble a theatrical prop since the neck had been cleanly severed, the hair clean and brushed back from a high forehead, and the eyes wide open. The man had been in his forties and possessed of strong, angular features, his bullish expression not softened by death. It was difficult to draw

256

conclusions without the body, but Jason didn't see any signs of struggle or brutal violence. Aside from the fact that the head was no longer attached to the body, it looked remarkably undamaged.

"Can you think of any reason Mr. Hobart's head would be left on your doorstep, Mr. Britteridge?" Daniel asked.

"Well, I suppose someone wanted to make a point," Britteridge replied.

"What sort of point?" Jason asked.

The warden spread his hands in the universal gesture of having no inkling. "It could have been anything."

"Did Mr. Hobart have any known enemies, or had he received death threats?" Daniel asked.

"Not that I know of, Inspector."

"And did Mr. Hobart work with anyone closely?"

"He had recently taken on an apprentice. Clyde Barkley is his name."

"Is Mr. Barkley currently in the building?" Daniel continued.

"No. There are no executions scheduled for this morning."

"When was the last time you saw the victim and his apprentice?" Jason inquired.

"I saw them both yesterday. Mr. Hobart and Mr. Barkley left separately once their work was done."

"Do you have Mr. Barkley's address? And the address for Mr. Hobart?" Daniel asked, his pencil poised above the nearly clean page.

"Of course." Mr. Britteridge opened the top drawer of his desk and withdrew a thick ledger.

From what Jason could see, there was a section for prison employees and one for the inmates, which was considerably thicker. Mr. Britteridge withdrew a clean sheet of paper and copied out the two addresses before handing the page to Daniel.

"Mr. Britteridge, is there anything else you can tell us about Mr. Hobart or his final days?" Daniel inquired.

"Mr. Hobart was a very reticent sort of person. He never lingered after his work was done and did not mix with prison staff. I had invited him to take a drink with me on more than one occasion, but even though he accepted out of politeness, we never progressed beyond the mundane in our conversation. I knew virtually nothing of his life beyond these walls."

"And Mr. Barkley?" Daniel asked.

"Mr. Barkley took his cues from Mr. Hobart and kept his distance, although I do think he's a personable young man and would have benefited from the support seasoned guards could provide to a novice."

"And what will happen to Mr. Barkley now?" Jason asked.

"Well, I suppose he will become a principal executioner in his own right now that his mentor is gone. We have two executions scheduled for next week, and there isn't time to find a replacement on such short notice. Experienced hangmen are in high demand, and our official executioner, Mr. Calcraft, is often called away."

"Is Mr. Barkley ready to take on the role of the principal hangman?"

"I believe he is. I told him so only last week."

"Why?" Daniel asked. "What prompted the conversation?"

"Mr. Barkley had inquired whether he would remain Mr. Hobart's assistant until Mr. Hobart saw fit to retire, and I told him that if he felt he was ready, he could always seek a position as the principal hangman at another facility, perhaps one outside London.

That's when I assured him that I thought he was ready to take on the responsibility and that he should look beyond his duties here at Newgate."

"And did Mr. Barkley wish to seek another position?" Jason asked.

"He didn't say, but he appeared to consider my suggestion. I don't think it had occurred to him until then that he might be ready to strike out on his own."

"And why would you encourage Mr. Barkley to leave? Surely Mr. Hobart would still have been in need of an assistant."

"Mr. Hobart had many years of service left, Lord Redmond. He had no wish to relinquish his position as principal hangman, and he rarely required Mr. Barkley's assistance beyond what was needed in terms of preparation. I think Mr. Barkley was growing frustrated, so I merely pointed out that he had other options available to him. I know it's not the norm to encourage one's members of staff to move on, but Clyde is my son's age, and his father recently passed, so I thought I was doing him a service by speaking to him as a father would."

Daniel made a notation in his notebook, while Jason, satisfied that there was nothing more to say about Clyde Barkley, asked his next question. "Mr. Britteridge, why do you think someone would leave Mr. Hobart's head on the steps of the prison?"

"I imagine they wished to send a message," Mr. Britteridge said.

"To the prison authorities or to you personally?"

"I can't conceive of a scenario in which someone would want to send a message to me," Mr. Britteridge said. "Mr. Hobart did not answer to me, since I was not the one to pass sentence on the poor souls he executed. Perhaps to the prison governors. Or to our legal institutions, but then it would be more appropriate to leave the head for a High Court judge."

"And what message would someone wish to send to the legal institutions?" Daniel looked baffled by the possibility.

"As I'm sure you're aware, Inspector, public hangings have recently been outlawed. Seems the public has lost their taste for death, at least as a source of wholesome family entertainment," the warden said, his tone so sarcastic, it would be difficult to mistake his meaning. "There are those who believe the death penalty should be abolished altogether. It is a misguided and ill-conceived notion that has absolutely no merit within the guidelines of the law. Fear of death is the only thing that stands between a man or a woman and their criminal impulses. If the death penalty were abolished, the streets would no longer be safe for any of us. Anywhere. Anytime. We would be stripped of all we possess and likely murdered in our beds by those who feel we owe them a better life."

"Is there strong support for the abolition of the death penalty among any factions of Her Majesty's government?" Jason asked.

"Heavens, no. Every educated, rational man understands that to do away with this most basic capital punishment would only wreak havoc on the status quo. And no politician who prides himself on being a realist would sanction such folly, not if they hope to keep their seat and the support and respect of their constituents."

"I don't imagine they would," Jason agreed, also a tad sarcastically, but his true meaning seemed utterly lost on the warden.

"Mr. Britteridge, is there a list of individuals Mr. Hobart has executed?" Daniel asked.

"There is not, but if you think it will assist you in your inquiries, I would be happy to draw one up for you, Inspector Haze. It's easily enough accomplished."

"That would be most helpful," Daniel said. "And perhaps you can annotate it with any pertinent information that comes to mind."

"Such as?" the warden asked.

"Such as whether the family of the condemned might hold a grudge, or if the individual to be executed had continued to proclaim their innocence or admitted to the crime."

"And why would that matter?"

"If the family believed that an innocent man or woman was executed, they might wish to take retribution into their own hands," Daniel replied. "Whereas if the individual had confessed to the crime, the family would understand that justice had been done and accept their loss more readily."

"I'm not privy to the sentiments of the families, Inspector Haze, but I see no reason for them to hold a grudge against Mr. Hobart. He was only doing his job. If they felt their loved one was sentenced unfairly, they would have to take that up with the magistrate or the judge, as they are the instruments of the law. Besides, since the executions are no longer public, the families did not witness the hanging."

"Not those more recently sentenced, but surely there were many executions held before the new legislation," Jason commented.

"Yes, that's true, but do keep in mind, Lord Redmond, that Mr. Hobart sometimes took jobs outside the prison. Contrary to popular belief, we don't hold executions daily, so most executioners will travel for work in order to supplement their income."

"And did Mr. Hobart accept outside commissions often?" Daniel asked.

"I really couldn't say. Since his presence at Newgate wasn't required unless there was a hanging or a flogging on the day's agenda, his time was his own."

"Well, if you happen to remember anything pertinent, do send for me. And please, draw up that list and have it delivered to Scotland Yard as soon as possible," Daniel said as he pushed to his feet.

Jason followed suit, and they were back outside within a few minutes, Constable Putney trailing behind them, the covered basket containing the head of Mr. Hobart carried in his trembling hands.

"Constable, please take my carriage and deliver Mr. Hobart's remains to the mortuary," Jason said.

Constable Putney looked torn between relief at getting rid of the offending object and chagrin at being thus dismissed and missing out on the initial stages of the investigation. He was a clever young man who paid attention and hoped to make his way through the ranks sooner rather than later.

"Of course, sir. You can count on me," he said.

"Joe, you can return home after you leave Constable Putney at Scotland Yard," Jason told his driver.

"I'd be happy to come find you once I'm done, my lord," Joe Marin replied.

Jason suspected that Joe would much rather take part in the investigation by driving Jason and Daniel from place to place than take Katherine Redmond to one of her many charity meetings or wait for her outside a milliner's shop or her preferred modiste. Katherine wasn't one to spend her time chasing fashion, but since moving to London, she had taken a keener interest in looking the part of a lady and often consulted Jason on his opinion of her new acquisitions, which he was more than happy to offer. He liked to see her happy and finally settling into her position as Lady Redmond with confidence.

"Does Lady Redmond not have need of you today?" Jason asked.

"No, sir."

"All right," Jason agreed. "Daniel, where should Joe meet us?"

Daniel consulted his pocket watch, then the addresses Mr. Britteridge had provided. "Let's begin with the widow," he said. "The Hobart residence is not far from here." Daniel showed Joe the address. "Can you collect us at say, eleven?"

"Of course, Inspector. Your lordship," Joe said as he tipped the slouch hat that made him look like a highwayman.

Jason thanked Joe and turned to Daniel, who was ready to set off. "Did you not want to look at the head more closely?" Daniel asked.

"I have seen what I need to for now, and the rest will require more careful analysis. Even without the body, there's much a head can tell us."

"Can it?" Daniel asked, looking dubious.

"It can, which is why I would like to give it my full attention once I get to the mortuary."

"Is it possible to estimate the time of death based on the head alone?"

"I'd say that the victim died less than twelve hours before his head was deposited on the steps of the prison. That's as precise as I'm prepared to be based on a cursory examination."

"So, he would have been murdered sometime after eight o'clock?" Daniel asked.

"Give or take an hour or two, but yes. I would say he was murdered sometime last night rather than this morning."

"That's not much to go on," Daniel said sourly.

"Perhaps Mrs. Hobart can shed some light on her husband's final hours," Jason replied. "At the very least, she can help us narrow the window surrounding the time of death."

"I hope so," Daniel replied. "You heard the warden. He's a long-standing acquaintance of Superintendent Ransome, which means Ransome will be even more combative than usual."

"That he will be. You know how he loves a case that can garner him attention from the press."

"Oh, the press will be all over this one once they get a whiff of the details. Nothing sells newspapers like mindless savagery and a fascinating conundrum."

"I'm not so sure this was a mindless act," Jason replied. "In fact, I would say this looks to have been carefully planned and flawlessly executed."

"Executed being the operative word," Daniel replied.

Chapter 2

Had Jason not known Daniel as well as he did, he might have simply thought Daniel was anxious about the case and worried about disappointing his less-than-supportive superior, but Jason sensed there was something more behind Daniel's concern. Daniel Haze and John Ransome had had their differences in the past, but John Ransome was nothing if not intelligent and ambitious, and Daniel had solved enough high-profile cases to reflect well on the superintendent and earn himself a reputation for being diligent and fair when dealing with suspects. Jason saw no reason Ransome would wish to undermine Daniel, but perhaps Jason wasn't aware of some new development or power shift at Scotland Yard.

Sighing heavily, Daniel allowed his shoulders to relax and his step to slow. "Ransome let it be known that he would be appointing a new chief inspector by the end of the month. I threw my hat into the ring."

Jason suddenly realized that he'd never met the current chief inspector and wondered why that was since he was at Scotland Yard often enough to be acquainted with every detective and constable and know something of their experience and work ethic.

Sensing Jason's unspoken question, Daniel explained, "Chief Inspector Sandin was appointed by Commissioner Hawkins shortly before Ransome took up the post of superintendent. Sandin might have been a good copper in his day, but in recent years he's developed an unfortunate fondness for the opium pipe. He's become an embarrassment to Commissioner Hawkins and has been asked to quietly retire to avoid any unnecessary unpleasantness."

Daniel shook his head in disgust. "Sandin has not seen the inside of Scotland Yard for nearly as long as I've been in London and has not personally involved himself in any ongoing investigation for nearly as long. Commissioner Hawkins has asked

Ransome to choose a competent man, and Ransome is relishing the prospect of watching his inspectors vie for the privilege."

"How many men are in the running?" Jason asked.

"Four, not counting myself. Given their ambition and desire to replace Ransome when he makes commissioner, this is likely to be more of a gladiatorial match than a civilized selection process."

"I see," Jason said. "And you don't think Ransome would consider you for the position?"

"Ransome likes to play favorites," Daniel said. "But it would appear unprofessional to simply name a successor without impartially considering all the candidates. If I don't get a result in this case quickly enough, then I won't stand a chance."

"And does Commissioner Hawkins not have any say in who gets promoted?"

"Have you forgotten that Ransome is the commissioner's son-in-law? The Yard is Ransome's own personal fiefdom. Until he either moves up or retires, his word is law."

"Is this something you really want, Daniel?" Jason asked.

Daniel shrugged. "I don't know. I made my interest in the position known before I had given any real thought to the pros and cons of such an undertaking. To be perfectly frank, I won't be too disappointed if I'm not chosen. I am the youngest detective at the Yard and the most recent hire. It's Ransome's desire to always take me down a peg or two that rankles."

"Then don't let him," Jason said. "You have an admirable record and the qualifications and experience needed for the job. Ransome might like to play favorites, but he also likes to surround himself with men who make him look good. You are such a man, Daniel."

Daniel's smile lit up his gloomy countenance. "Thank you, Jason. I appreciate the vote of confidence."

"You don't need my vote. If this promotion will be awarded on merit, then you have a solid chance of getting the job."

Jason couldn't help but notice the renewed spring in Daniel's step as they turned the corner and stepped into the sunlight, the street beyond out of reach of the shadow of the prison.

"Do you have any preliminary thoughts on the case?" Daniel asked as he consulted the paper with the address once more.

"There are several things we know for certain. Since no body or evidence of the murder was found by the warden's men, we know that Philip Hobart was not murdered either near or inside the prison. He was killed elsewhere, his head left on the steps to make a point. We have yet to discover what that point is, but the head does offer a few clues."

Daniel looked surprised. "What sort of clues? I did not notice anything that might point us in the direction of the killer."

"The edges of the neck were not ragged, so the head was probably severed with one swift blow. This would require a sharp, straight-edged weapon, such as an axe or a machete. Had a knife been used, there would be evidence of hacking and sawing."

Daniel nodded, acknowledging Jason's point. "Anything else?"

"I saw no signs of a struggle, which would suggest that either Philip Hobart never saw the blow coming or had already been incapacitated at the time of the beheading."

"It would be helpful to find the body," Daniel said. "We'd be able to get a clearer picture of the attack."

"It would, but we know the probable cause of death and the fact that the murder most likely had something to do with Philip Hobart's chosen occupation."

"Probable cause of death?" Daniel asked, turning to look at Jason in surprise.

"It is possible that the victim was already dead by the time his head was severed."

"Would you be able to infer that from the appearance of the head?"

"I will check for bruising around the neck and for redness of the whites of the eyes, which would point to strangulation, and see if there's any odor coming from the man's mouth or windpipe, which could be a sign of poisoning. However, if he was shot, run over, stabbed, or murdered in any other way that doesn't involve the head, I would have no way of knowing without examining the rest of the body. What are the chances the body will turn up?" Jason asked.

"Practically nonexistent," Daniel replied morosely. "It could be anywhere by now, since the killer clearly did not want us to find the rest of Hobart quickly or easily or he would have left his remains in some conspicuous place."

"Yes, I agree with you there. The body is probably well hidden for that very reason. It might give too much away."

"I wonder if Mrs. Hobart realizes anything is amiss," Daniel said as he folded the paper and pushed it into his pocket. It seemed they had arrived.

Chapter 3

The Hobarts resided in Budge Row, just down the street from St Antholin Church. At just past ten in the morning, the street, which boasted a number of commercial establishments, was already crowded with shoppers and vehicles that ranged from fine carriages to dray wagons and hansom cabs. The Hobarts did not dwell above a storefront but lived in a three-story redbrick townhome, and Daniel couldn't help but wonder if they occupied the entire building or the space was divided into several smaller apartments.

Daniel used the brass knocker to announce their presence, and a sullen-looking maidservant of about fifteen opened the door, eyeing them with suspicion.

"The tradesman's entrance is round the back," she said haughtily.

Daniel held up his warrant card. "Inspector Haze of Scotland Yard to see Mrs. Hobart."

She seemed neither surprised nor impressed to find a policeman on the doorstep and shut the door in their faces while she went to inform her mistress that she had visitors.

The maidservant returned a few minutes later and held the door open. She did not offer to take their coats and hats, just made a vague gesture toward a door on the left.

"Mrs. Hobart will receive you in the parlor," she said, and walked away, presumably to the kitchen, since the entrance hall smelled of baking bread and soup.

Daniel and Jason removed their hats out of respect for the widow and entered the room the maid had directed them to. The parlor looked well used and, although not overly grand in either size or adornment, boasted several obvious luxuries. There were crisp lace curtains at the windows, a thick Turkey carpet that looked hardly worn covered the polished floor, and several ceramic knickknacks and picture frames that had the gleam of real silver were arranged on the mantel. Mrs. Hobart, when she stood to greet them, was not at all what Daniel had expected of a hangman's wife, although, in truth, he couldn't really put into words what he'd thought she would be like.

The woman before them was no older than twenty-two. Her eyes were the color of fine brandy, and her golden-brown hair was parted in the middle and coiled into a knot at her nape. She was very pale, possibly because the unrelieved black she wore looked harsh and unforgiving against her fair skin. Delicate, almost fragile wrists protruded from the lace-trimmed cuffs of her gown, and her slender neck reminded Daniel of a flower stem rising out of loamy earth.

He supposed it was possible that Mrs. Hobart had already been informed of her husband's death, but for some reason, he didn't think she was in mourning for him. She had the dead-eyed stare of someone who'd seen the lowest circle of hell yet still managed to cling to life, her demeanor that of a woman who never expected to feel a spark of hope or even the briefest moment of joy in the years left to her. Sadly, Daniel was all too familiar with that look. He'd encountered it for years in his own wife before unbearable grief had finally taken her from him.

"Mrs. Hobart, I'm Inspector Haze of Scotland Yard, and this is my associate, Dr. Redmond."

Jason always left the introductions to Daniel's discretion when they called on the individuals relevant to an investigation. At times Jason's rank was an asset, and at other times a detriment, since it could only intimidate and embarrass those who didn't move in such exalted circles and felt threatened by the presence of a member of the nobility in their humble home. Mrs. Hobart looked confused but was too polite to ask what they wanted outright. Instead, she invited them to sit, while she sank into an armchair covered with a lace-trimmed antimacassar and folded her pale hands in her lap. She looked from one man to the other, but the vacant look never left her eyes. Daniel thought she was just barely present.

"Mrs. Hobart, I'm deeply sorry to inform you that your husband, Philip Hobart, was found dead this morning. Please accept our deepest condolences on your loss," Daniel said politely.

Mrs. Hobart's eyes opened wider, and a faint blush stained her cheeks, and for a moment, Daniel thought he saw the woman she must have been before tragedy had eviscerated her spirit.

"Dead?" she exclaimed softly. "How?"

"I'm afraid he was beheaded," Daniel said with as much delicacy as he could convey.

Mrs. Hobart's hand flew to her mouth, and her eyes filled with tears. "I don't understand," she muttered. "Whatever do you mean, Inspector? Beheaded by whom?"

"That is what we're tasked with finding out."

"Mrs. Hobart, are you all right?" Jason asked when the woman's eyes turned glassy and her breathing came in short gasps, as if she were about to faint. "Shall I fetch some smelling salts? Or perhaps you'd like a drink?"

Mrs. Hobart shook her head. "Forgive me. It's just the shock," she muttered, but her voice quavered, and she seemed to hover at the edge of consciousness.

Jason walked over to the sideboard and poured a tot of brandy into one of two cut crystal glasses positioned next to the decanter, then pushed it into the widow's trembling hand. "Take a sip, Mrs. Hobart," he instructed.

She did. Then another.

"Now take deep breaths," Jason said softly. "And focus on me."

After a few moments, Mrs. Hobart seemed to recover her composure and handed the glass back to Jason, who set it aside. Daniel took out his pencil and notebook, but the look Jason gave him wasn't lost on him. Go gently, it said. Daniel nodded in acknowledgement.

"Mrs. Hobart, may I have your full name?" he asked.

If the widow was taken aback by the question, she didn't show it. "Lucy Jane Hobart."

"Thank you. And who lives here with you?"

"Just Philip," Lucy Hobart said. "And Hattie. She's a maid of all work."

"Is that the young woman we just met?" Daniel asked.

Lucy Hobart nodded.

"When was the last time you saw your husband, Mrs. Hobart?"

"Last night."

"And what time was that?" Jason asked softly, his gaze fixed on the widow should she become unwell again.

"We had supper together. We always dine at seven."

"Did your husband retire at his usual time?" Daniel asked.

Lucy Hobart shook her head. "I went up early. Just after eight. I had a dreadful headache, but Philip went out. He said he was going to have a drink at the Queen's Arms. It's just down the road," she explained.

"And did you hear him come in?"

"No," Lucy said, her voice barely audible. "Where was he killed, Inspector?" Her voice trembled, but she seemed determined to remain in control. "Did he suffer terribly before he died?"

"It would have been a quick death, Mrs. Hobart," Jason said. He seemed determined to cosset the widow and spare her unnecessary pain, which was just as well since Daniel could hardly question her if she were unable to answer. He felt terribly sorry for this fragile young woman, but at the moment, she was the only person who could offer him the information he needed, so he had to overcome his pity and press on.

"Where did you find him?" Lucy Hobart asked, her pleading gaze fixed on Daniel. "How long had he lain there?"

"His head was left on the steps of Newgate Prison," Daniel said.

"And his body?" Lucy whispered.

"We have yet to find it. I'm truly sorry, Mrs. Hobart. I know how very distressing this is for you."

"Distressing?" Lucy echoed. "I suppose that's one way of putting it."

"Mrs. Hobart, was your husband worried or upset last night?" Jason asked. "Or possibly even frightened?"

Lucy Hobart peered at Jason. She probably wondered what his role was, since Daniel hadn't explained why he'd brought a doctor along.

"No. Philip was his usual self last night. In fact, he was in fine spirits. Exalted, even," Lucy said slowly, as if trying to recall her husband's demeanor.

"Exalted?" Daniel asked. "By what?"

"He didn't say, but I assumed it had something to do with his work. He never discussed his vocation with me. He didn't like to upset me."

"Mrs. Hobart, how long were you married?" Jason asked.

"Nearly five years," Lucy replied, clearly thrown by the question.

"And do you have any children?" Daniel asked, and caught another warning look from Jason.

The naked pain in the widow's eyes told Daniel everything he needed to know. The Hobarts had recently lost a child. That explained the deep mourning Lucy Hobart was obviously in and the haunted look he'd noticed before he broke the news of Philip Hobart's death.

"I'm very sorry," Jason said.

Lucy Hobart inclined her head in acknowledgment but didn't reply.

"Does anyone else have a key to this house?" Daniel asked, swiftly moving away from the question of children, since that line of inquiry clearly wasn't relevant to the murder.

"No."

"Could someone have visited your husband last night, after he had returned from the Queen's Arms?"

"I didn't hear anyone," Lucy said. "I wasn't asleep. I don't sleep well these days," she added softly.

"Were you not worried when your husband didn't come to bed?" Jason asked.

Lucy Hobart's shoulders sank even lower. "I lay awake for hours, then took a sleeping draught. When I woke this morning, I assumed that Philip had already left for the prison."

"Did he not normally take breakfast?" Daniel asked.

The young woman shook her head. "Philip never ate before a job. He preferred to wait until luncheon on those days and went to a chophouse in Fleet Street."

"Was there to be a hanging this morning?"

Mr. Britteridge had mentioned that no executions were scheduled for today, but perhaps Philip Hobart had been meant to be someplace else. One of the outside jobs that the warden had spoken of.

"I don't know," Lucy Hobart said. "He never said. I just assumed—"

Daniel looked to Jason to see if he had any other questions, but Jason shook his head. He obviously didn't think Lucy Hobart knew anything that pertained to the murder.

"May we speak to Hattie?" Daniel asked.

"Of course. I'll get her."

She stood and immediately grabbed for the armrest to steady herself. Jason was on his feet in an instant, ready to offer support. He took her gently by the elbow.

"Mrs. Hobart, how much of the sleeping draught did you take?" he asked.

"Only a spoonful. Maybe two."

"Have you eaten today?" Jason persisted.

"I wasn't very hungry."

"You really must eat something. And then you need to lie down. You're in shock."

Lucy Hobart looked at him with gratitude. "Thank you for being so kind. I will do as you say."

"I'm glad to hear it." Jason let go of her elbow.

"I'll send Hattie in to speak to you."

Lucy Hobart left the room, and Jason resumed his seat. "I don't think she knows anything."

Daniel nodded. "She seemed sincere in her grief. And her husband clearly didn't discuss his cases with her."

"It would be highly inappropriate if he did," Jason replied. "No woman, especially one who's recently lost a child, should have to hear such things."

"You've been known to speak of murder with your wife," Daniel pointed out.

Jason grinned. "Katie has a strong stomach, and she'd never forgive me if I treated her as if she were too fragile to hear the truth of my daily reality."

Their conversation was interrupted by the arrival of the maidservant, whose indifferent expression had been replaced by a worried frown.